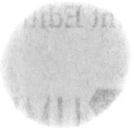
# BLIND SPOT

By Adam Zorzi

BLIND SPOT

Limitless Publishing, LLC
Kailua, HI 96734
www.limitlesspublishing.com

Formatting: Limitless Publishing

ISBN-13: 978-1-68058-887-3
ISBN-10: 1-68058-887-7

# Dedication

*Ai fantasmi di Richmond*

# CHAPTER ONE

## July

"New details have emerged in the murder of a nurse at Commonwealth Psychiatric Hospital in Petersburg, Virginia. Monday afternoon, Nurse Richard Bonham, forty-three, of Dinwiddie County, was killed during a session with a patient. The suspect's name has not been released."

The serious young reporter obviously couldn't access the hospital grounds. He stood at the gated entrance with a 3D map projected on the TV screen.

"As you can see, the hospital is a sprawling campus. The forensic hospital, which is the only one in the state, is housed in a secure freestanding building. It's where defendants who are awaiting competency hearings reside as well as those persons found Not Guilty of crimes by Reason of Insanity or NGRI."

Mug shots of patients who had spent time there for competency evaluations scrolled across the screen. The most famous was Lorena Bobbitt, who

1

was acquitted of cutting off her cheating husband's penis while he slept.

"Although lead investigator, Lieutenant Douglas Winston of the Virginia Bureau of Criminal Investigation, has not spoken publicly about details of the crime, this station has obtained an exclusive interview with a hospital staff member who asked not to be identified.

"The staffer said the murder occurred when Nurse Bonham attempted to restrain a twenty-two-year-old female patient. The patient, who remains anonymous, was being put in restraints for multiple violations of hospital regulations when she allegedly strangled Nurse Bonham with a white cotton bra. The patient denies any involvement in the murder. She claims a ghostly young woman strangled Nurse Bonham.

"According to the patient, the ghost said she had died from extreme cruelty at Commonwealth Psychiatric. Her doctor prohibited her restraint because she had epilepsy. Use of restraint during a seizure could be fatal. Nevertheless, the ghost said she'd been secured to a bed in five-point restraints and left unattended in a locked seclusion room for forty-eight hours. She died of asphyxiation during a seizure. Her motive in killing Nurse Bonham is believed to be protection of this patient from a similar fate.

"Sources who were on the scene immediately following Nurse Bonham's death say the patient was the only occupant of the treatment room. No one reported seeing a ghostly woman.

"I spoke with our own medical correspondent,

Dr. Charlene Branch, who said hallucinations and delusions are not unusual for patients in the forensic unit. Such patients suffer psychotic episodes in which they may violently act out. Dr. Branch is not involved in this case, so she cannot comment as to whether the patient suffered such an episode and killed Nurse Bonham."

An array of fuzzy images of purported ghost sightings of female residents at the hospital were shown.

"As most of our viewers know, Commonwealth Psychiatric Hospital, formerly known as Commonwealth Lunatic Asylum, was established in 1869 as an institution for African-Americans of unsound mind. It was opened to all races in 1967. The hospital has a long history of suspected hauntings and paranormal sightings. The chapel, which is the oldest section of the hospital, is on the National Register of Historic Places.

Back to you…"

\*\*\*

Dan turned off the TV on the kitchen counter where he was helping his wife load the dishwasher.

"I hate when he does that revisionist history. He made it sound like Virginia was at the cutting edge of mental health care, devoting an entire hospital to African-American psychiatric care. The place was built after the Civil War for freed slaves who had TB, epilepsy, and nowhere else to go. It was called Commonwealth Lunatic Asylum for Colored Insane and segregated until the Civil Rights Act forced it to integrate."

"Whatever it's called, I feel sorry for that poor man," said Jill. "I read that he had a wife and twin boys. What an awful way to die."

"What about that poor patient? Can you imagine being in five-point restraints? For forty-eight hours? If you weren't insane, you would be after treatment like that."

Jill shivered. "I think it's tragic for all of them. I don't want to hear anymore news reports about it."

Dan softened. "I don't either. I'll make sure to turn it off if they keep up intense coverage. I'm glad Katie is at camp and not here, where she could see it on TV. The whole episode is gruesome."

"She might not think so. She loves those vampire romance books. I think we have the only kid in the universe who isn't taken with Harry Potter. I don't want to discourage her from reading, but I wish she'd try something else."

"She's fine. She knows vampires aren't real."

"I think they're awfully gory for a nine-year-old." Jill frowned.

"Hey, I grew up with Friday night horror on TV—*The Twilight Zone*, *The Outer Limits*, and *Alfred Hitchcock Presents*. Rob, of course, tried to scare me even more by saying most parts were true or making me jump at just the right moment. I could barely sleep on Friday nights." Dan moved to stand directly behind Jill, put his hands around her waist, and swept her shoulder length brown black hair aside to nuzzle her neck. "It's Friday night. Know any reason why I might not be able to get to sleep immediately?"

4

"Too much exercise right before sleep?" She turned around and kissed him in a way that let him know she was interested in exercise.

"I'm in," said Dan.

# CHAPTER TWO

## November

"Hey, Norm. Norman Rockwell," shouted the driver of a silver Porsche Boxter that glided to a stop on the quiet, residential street. He stuck his tanned arm out and motioned for Dan to come over. His expensive gold watch caught the glint of the morning sun.

Dan jogged across the lawn to the car. "What's up?" said Dan to his former neighbor.

"Man, I just had to stop and say how sick you are."

"Why?" Dan rested his hands on the driver's side door of the idling convertible. It was an elegant machine. He got a blast of heavy sandalwood cologne he could have done without.

"It's Thanksgiving Day morning. I just dropped my kids off to spend the weekend with their mother and her latest boyfriend, going to the gym because I've got nowhere else to go, and boom! I round the traffic circle and see you jumping in piles of leaves in your front yard with your hot wife, your kid, and even your dog. Your life is friggin' perfect."

Dan laughed. "Thanks, I guess." He looked over his shoulder at his house and family. Picture perfect. They lived in an older neighborhood of spacious lots and mature trees in Henrico County just outside Richmond, Virginia. Pumpkins lined the brick steps to their front door where husks of Indian corn hung instead of a wreath. One side of the lawn had been cleared of fallen leaves. The other was filled with leaves where his wife and daughter were screeching with laugher as they fell back into the hollow, crunchy piles. Abbie, their black Schnauzer mix, barked and ran around the circle of leaves. Yes. It did look perfect.

"Don't screw it up," he said before he lowered his sunglasses, put the car in gear, and *vroom*ed out of the neighborhood.

Jill walked to the curb and took Dan's hand. "How does he fit three kids into that two-seater?"

"I don't think he intended it to be a family car."

Jill looked disgusted. "What did he want?"

"Just to wish us a Happy Thanksgiving," he said before he slung his arm around her shoulder and walked toward the house.

# CHAPTER THREE

That afternoon, Dan sat on his bed. Despite the happy "Normal Rockwell" morning, he was stalling. Thanksgiving was his favorite holiday, but this year he dreaded the family dinner. Even the peaceful surroundings of the pale peach bed, white furniture, and large, sunlit windows in the master bedroom didn't comfort him.

He seemed to be the only one in the family who minded that this would be the last gathering in his childhood home where his parents had lived for more than fifty years. His older brother might remember his parents' starter house, but he didn't.

Dan's parents planned to move to a two-bedroom villa in Boynton Beach in January. They talked a lot about getting rid of baggage—he cringed at that word—and enjoying good weather year round. Dan's dad said he didn't want to climb stairs anymore. He wanted to play golf and live in a low maintenance house. His mom loved the idea of a smaller place with a pool and a clubhouse.

"Dan," said Jill as she came into the bedroom

putting in her earring. "You're not ready. We don't want to be late."

She walked around the bed to where he sat staring at nothing. She sat next to him. "What's wrong, Dan? It's not like you to be down on Thanksgiving Day. Is Mørk coming?" she asked using the nickname for the depressive episodes he suffered. It was a shortened version of the Norwegian *Mørketid* or Dark Night.

He nodded and took her hand. "I keep hoping they'll change their minds and not move to Florida. I love having Thanksgiving with my parents. I like the intimacy of a small family. Mom and Dad, Rob and Suzanne, and us. All safe. All healthy. All under one roof."

"It's pretty great and not at all like stuffy formal dinners with my parents." She reached to stop a tear falling on his cheek. "Dan, your parents want to move. They don't need to maintain a big house. They want a small place in the sun near their friends. You can't object to that."

"I do. Why can't they continue to rent during the winter months? They've been snow birds for the past few years."

She squeezed his hand. "They've made a decision. The house they've rented all these years became available for sale and they bought it. We can't interfere. In some ways, they're doing you and Rob a great favor."

Favor. What was she talking about? How did moving nine hundred miles from their granddaughter become a favor?

"Your dad is pragmatic. He wants the house

9

sold, the furniture gone, and their personal keepsakes chosen. He doesn't want you and Rob to have to act in a rush if something should change in their health."

She was pissing him off. Dan stood. "There's nothing wrong with my parents. They're healthy," he insisted. "They're not going to die or need assisted living anytime soon."

Jill stood, too, but she didn't touch him. "They might need assisted living one day." She handed him his socks and shoes. "Your dad's thinking ahead. He's a planner just like you. He prepares for the worst and hopes for the best. In the meantime, he wants to play some kick-ass golf with his buddies. Be happy for them."

He managed a smile. "I'll try. At least Katie has what I did. Memories of Thanksgiving with her parents and at least one set of grandparents."

"And she's going to have another one today."

"Thank you for reminding me. I don't want to spoil her day." Dan kissed Jill lightly. "You're my sunny day."

"I love you, too. Let's go."

# CHAPTER FOUR

Dan savored the meal of comfort food and smell of a burning fire drifting from the living room. Conversation swirled around him, but he didn't participate. He was content to sit back and enjoy snippets of familiar topics—Rob's analysis of the University of Virginia Cavaliers' bowl game prospects and grousing about his Homeowners Association, his sister-in-law Suzanne's upcoming holiday concert schedule as a cellist with the Richmond Symphony Orchestra as well as her string quartet and solo gigs, Dad's redirection of any topic headed toward politics or controversy, and Mom's delight in her granddaughter. Jill went with the flow and added a dash of cheer as needed.

He dreaded any mention of his parents' upcoming move. They'd made that decision without consulting their sons. Rob didn't seemed bothered by it. Of course, Rob and Suzanne's sons each had eighteen years of gatherings in this house. Katie only had ten. The decision weighed heavily on Dan. It mystified and infuriated him.

"No holiday performances for me this year until the first week of December," Suzanne was saying. "Last year, the RSO wanted to start *Messiah* concerts the day after Thanksgiving and play three concerts that weekend. Even though we're not unionized, the orchestra members unanimously refused. Thanksgiving is ruined if we want to be with our families or travel. I don't believe people want to hear Christmas music on the heels of Thanksgiving."

"I don't either, Suzanne," said Jill. "I love Christmas, but I like fall best of all. I want to make it last as long as it can. No Christmas decorations until after December fifteenth." She smiled at Dan, who would postpone them until Christmas Eve if he could. "Suzanne, the table decorations are beautiful. I can't believe you can make all these things grow at home. I'm happy we have grass." Jill eyed the centerpiece with orange lilies, dahlias, and greenery as well as other freshly cut autumnal flowers in small vases around the living and dining rooms.

"And she makes beeswax candles," added Rob with a nod to his wife. Fat yellow candles on wooden pillars cast soft golden light across the ecru linen table cloth.

"I have a high bar. The table decorations have to live up to Selma's cooking." She smiled at her mother-in-law. "There were some new dishes this year, I noticed."

"Great food, as always, Mom." Rob snuck another roll from the linen covered bread basket.

Selma laughed. "I can't take credit for the new additions. Jill made them."

"I certainly did. With a little help from Kaitlyn and, thankfully, none from Dan," laughed Jill. "Our specialties are the spinach soufflé, baked whole yams with marshmallows, and cranberry relish. Thanks for the compliment, Rob."

Selma sighed. "Both of my daughters-in-law are so talented. Suzanne, you're a gifted cellist working all kinds of hours and wonderful gardener. Jill, you work, cycle like a demon, and make beautiful quilts. I can't believe someone so athletic can sit still long enough to quilt."

"It's soothing, gives me a creative outlet, and lets my mind wander. Cycling requires concentration."

"How did you learn to quilt?" asked Suzanne.

"My sisters and I learned from our grandmother. My mother thinks quilting and sewing can be done by seamstresses. Needlepoint, on the other hand, is an art and the mark of a real southern lady."

"Mom, am I a real southern lady?" asked Katie.

"No, I think you're a modern woman."

"What does that mean?"

"That means," said Jill, "you do a lot of things. You don't have to conform to what other people say you should do."

"To doing the unexpected," toasted Selma.

The three women raised their glasses. "Hear, hear," chorused Suzanne and Jill.

Predictably, their father spoke before the conversation skittered into the politics of modern women. "What's everyone doing for Christmas?"

Rob jumped in. "Suzanne and I are going to Houston for a few days and then on to Cozumel for five days." Both of their sons had moved out of state after college. "Given the choice of a son in Chicago and one in Houston in December, we picked Houston."

Dan let Jill answer. Mørk made him irritable. Couldn't they enjoy Thanksgiving before jumping to the next holiday?

"Dan, Kaitlyn, and I are going to Charleston for Christmas with my parents. Then it's up to Vermont for snowboarding for Kaitlyn and me, skiing for Dan, and ice skating and sledding for all of us. What about you?"

"Selma and I are staying here and making the rounds of parties of our Richmond friends. Of course, we'll see half of them the next week in Florida. I like the old traditions and beauty of a Virginia Christmas, but not enough to maintain a big house for another icy winter. Checking heating oil levels, worrying about burst pipes, and shoveling snow."

Rob burst out laughing. "Dad, you've never shoveled snow. Dan and I did until college and then you hired a maintenance service."

"Rob's right, Dad. Can't blame your move on snow removal." Dan spoke for the first time.

Suzanne turned to Dan. "So you are paying attention. You've been awfully quiet. Is your room empty yet?" she teased.

His parents had bought the Florida villa furnished and were having an estate sale the first week of December. Rob and Dan had been asked to clear out their childhood rooms in September.

"It most certainly is," answered his mother. "I've cleaned it, had it painted, and closed the door on both boys' bedrooms."

"Dan, did you throw anything away?" asked Rob.

"Yes, clothes." He'd hated dismantling the room filled with his childhood memories, video games from middle school, and all of his high school paraphernalia. Textbooks, Varsity Lacrosse jacket, and prom pictures.

"Clothes that were made for a thirteen-year-old boy?" Rob was trying to get a rise out of him.

"Pretty much." Dan speared an asparagus. "Plus a threadbare Metallica tee shirt that belonged to you."

"Not Metallica," Rob clutched his chest in mock horror. "Jill, what's in your garage?"

She laughed. "Not too much. Dan's bed, dresser, and bookcase along with some framed prints from the upstairs hallway. I've been assured I'll be pleased he saved things someday. In case you're wondering, we still have room to put at least one car plus my cycling gear in the garage." Her eyes twinkled at Dan as she spoke.

Rob shook his head. "Dan's such a pack-rat."

"And you, Rob, are obsessively compulsively neat," she smiled. "Isn't there a medical term for that? OCD?"

"Maybe, but I'll bet you have a box of photographs in your garage, too, Jill." Rob helped himself to more turkey. "Dan stole my camera when he was four and hasn't stopped taking pictures since. I only use my phone to snap something these days."

"Dad stole something?" Katie's eyes were wide. "Did you give it back?"

15

Dan gave Rob a sharp look. "No, Katie, Uncle Rob is exaggerating. He let me borrow his camera and I haven't given it back yet. I still have it."

"See," Rob pointed his fork at Dan," one hundred percent pack-rat."

"Big deal, Rob," said Jill. "Dan likes photo memories and he'll put them on a drive eventually. I love the book he made me from pictures in the pre-cell phone era of renovating the house while I was pregnant. Before and after are fun to look at. Dan did so much work himself. I didn't realize how much until I looked through the memory book. I do remember he insisted on hand-stenciling the kitchen ceiling border himself because he didn't want me on a ladder. I'd forgotten how loopy it was. Kaitlyn was in pre-K before I had the heart to redo it. The imperfection made it ours. We did a great job of making the smallish house work for the three of us. We wanted to be in an older neighborhood with no Homeowners Association."

"Don't get me started on our Homeowner's Association," pleaded Rob.

In an attempt to change the topic, Dan said, "Guess who I ran into Monday when I was downtown at a training session?"

"Our esteemed mayor," guessed Rob who had gone to high school with the nerd who currently held that position.

Dan shook his head. "Bigger."

"Tony Bennett," said Selma.

"Couldn't be." Suzanne shook her head. "He's not coming until December."

"Tell us, Dan. We don't know who's bigger than

16

the mayor and in town," said Rob.

"Can I have more yams, please, Gran?" asked Kaitlyn.

"Why of course you *may*," she responded emphasizing the word "may," and served her beloved grandchild.

"Bella," Dan said with a flourish.

Silence fell around the table except for Kaitlyn identifying the marshmallows she wanted on her yams.

"Bella Davis?" Rob asked. "The one with the fine ass?"

"That girl you went out with in college?" their dad demanded.

"The one who broke your heart until Jill came along?" asked their mom as she smiled in Jill's direction.

Dan nodded. "She was at the Omni, too, having given a speech to the Virginia Bar Association. She's a big time securities lawyer in New York."

"What's securities, Dad?" asked Katie.

"Financial stuff like the stock market, banks, and the Securities and Exchange Commission. Anything to do with regulations about how Wall Street works. Lots of technical rules."

"She must know a lot about math," concluded Katie.

"How did she look?" jabbed Rob. "Old and fat, no doubt." Rob passed the mashed potatoes around for seconds.

"She looked pretty much the same, except she was wearing a black suit and sky high heels. Carried a leather briefcase."

"Married?" asked their father who sent Dan a disapproving look.

"Widowed."

"Is that so?" mused Rob. "How long?"

"A while, I think."

"Widows are hot," said Rob. "Men don't have to deal with an ex."

"Kids?" asked Suzanne.

Dan shook his head.

"Sounds like you two had a pretty cozy chat," Suzanne noted.

Dan glared at his sister-in-law. "Hardly. Said hello, surprised to see you, what've you been doing for the last twenty-five years. She had a plane to catch."

"You told her you were married with an adorable daughter, I'm sure," said his mother graciously.

"Oh, don't tease him," said Jill. "He was shocked to see her. Never mind right where his training session was being held. Dan wouldn't be interested in an old bag like her when he's got a fun wife in her thirties." She winked at Dan.

"I don't know; she was really beauti..." started Rob before their father sent him a withering look.

"My son would never do anything as foolish as consider another woman when he's married to you, Jill. He's a good man," their dad said firmly.

Dan started to feel uneasy. He recalled three Thanksgivings when Bella joined them right at this table. Everyone had seemed enchanted with her. Bella had mesmerized a not-yet-married Rob with her beauty and hot bod. Their father had alternated playing chess with her and discussing world affairs that bored the rest of the family. He had been impressed that she was fluent in three languages. Even though Bella didn't cook, she had set an elegant table and relieved Mom of all kitchen clean-up duties.

Bella glowed. When she entered a room, she hypnotized everyone into being happy and comfortable and garrulous. Most importantly, this beautiful, brilliant, and sensuous woman had loved him. Him. From the day they'd met at seventeen, neither had questioned living separate lives. His parents had expected her to be their daughter-in-law.

Katie's voice drew Dan back to the present. "What's for dessert, Gran? Are we going to have pumpkin pie and oatmeal raisin cookies and ice cream?"

"Why, Kaitlyn, I hadn't planned to serve all three at once, but I can." Selma pushed her chair back and stood. "Help me clear the plates and we'll go look at desserts."

"May Abbie come?" Katie asked as she slid out of her chair and took her grandmother's hand.

"I don't think we can keep her away."

Abbie, who had been asleep by Dan's feet, trotted behind them. Jill and Suzanne cleared the table and took orders for coffee and tea.

With the rest of his family occupied, Dan felt a whoosh of relief.

***

After dinner, Katie slept on her grandparents'

four poster bed with Abbie curled at her feet. The Ramsay women took one last look around upstairs to see if there was anything they wanted as a keepsake. The three Ramsay men sat in the living room and drank what was left of the last bottle of cognac from the liquor cabinet.

Rob inhaled his snifter and was about to launch into the traditional post-Thanksgiving dinner analysis of the UVA Cavaliers bowl game possibilities when their father looked hard at Dan.

"You didn't do anything foolish over that Bella girl, did you? Drive her to the airport, exchange phone numbers, talk about when she'd be in town again?"

Dan was taken aback. He hadn't discussed his dating life with either of his parents since Bella had dumped him. "Dad," he scoffed. It was as though his father had read his mind. Dan had offered to drive Bella to the airport, but she'd already called a taxi. He'd gotten her cell number and asked when she'd be back in Richmond. She'd laughed and said probably never.

Secretly, he'd called her the next day, Tuesday, to ask if she'd gotten home safely as if travel between Richmond and New York was riddled with danger. He'd called again yesterday to wish her a happy holiday.

"That girl took every piece of your heart and held it for five years." Their father was fired up. "When she ripped it up and handed it back, you tried to kill yourself, Dan. Damn near succeeded. Took ten years off your mother's life. You saw a psychiatrist and took pills for depression for what—

thirty months afterwards? You couldn't live on your own; you didn't have a job. It was three years before you felt anywhere near normal. Your mother and I thought she'd ruined you for any other girl until Jill came along. You were forty years old by then."

Rob didn't say a word, but he kept looking at Dan for a response. He swiveled his head between the two as though he were at a tennis match.

"Enough, Dad," Dan said tightly. "She lives in New York City and has dozens of men around her. She had no idea I was still in Richmond. She thought I lived in Los Angeles. She's not interested in a yokel like me."

"So you did ask where she lived and if she was dating anyone seriously." Their father swallowed the last of his Courvoisier and looked like he might pound his fist on the coffee table.

"Dad, you heard Jill. Why would I want anyone else when I have her?"

"Because it's Bella. She's in your blood, under your skin, and in your mind. You can't think when she's around."

He'd had enough. Their dad was like a bloodhound. Dan stood. "Jill," he called from the bottom of the stairs. "Jill, we need to get going. I want to walk Abbie before it gets too late."

He had to get out of that house.

# CHAPTER FIVE

**November, One Year Later**

"I'm glad you and Mom could visit. I'm sorry we won't celebrate Thanksgiving together. With this new system being installed, I have to work the Friday after Thanksgiving for the first time in ages and be on call throughout the weekend. Jill and Katie are going to visit the Carters in Charleston."

Dan and his father were taking Abbie for a walk around the neighborhood Sunday afternoon before his parents flew back to Florida that evening. Indian summer had lingered through the weekend. Green leaves had turned red, but sun covered the neighborhood in warmth and gold light. The smells of fall were subtle but noticeable.

"No, son, we just came up for the wedding last night. Not many of my contemporaries live to see their friend's granddaughter get married. Beautiful wedding. Beautiful couple. More than a few wet eyes during the ceremony."

"Glad you enjoyed it." They stopped for Abbie

to sniff something slimy under a pile of wet red leaves that smelled disgusting. "Katie loved seeing you both. She misses you."

His father took time before responding. "Dan, you've got to stop this nonsense with Bella. It's bad enough you've broken your marriage vows, but you've got a fine wife and a daughter to raise together. Kaitlyn is a bright girl. She'd be devastated to learn that her father is a liar and a cheat. Her life would be ruined if Jill found out about you carrying on with Bella and divorced you. That little girl needs her parents to stay together."

Abbie moved on and so did they.

"Dad, nothing is going on with Bella." He felt blindsided. Why would his father bring this up? Dan felt panicky even though he was an adult and what his father thought didn't matter.

"Don't lie to me, Dan. You're my son. I've lived in your house for the past three days and observed. You're on another planet. You seem giddy for no reason. You can't wait to get to work where no doubt you call Bella or see Bella. You're distracted around Jill. You're not yourself."

"I can't believe this, Dad. You think I'm having an affair because I'm happy and like my job?" He could bluff this out.

"Don't insult me. You're having an affair with that woman, and it's written all over your face. I know what your Bella face looks like. It's not like any other expression. You can't control yourself around her. You're reckless. Sooner or later, Jill's going to notice, too."

Dan stopped and turned to face his father. He

didn't need to lie. He could do what he wanted without his father's approval.

"This is none of your business, Dad. I've loved Bella since the day I met her when I was seventeen years old. I never stopped. I can't stop. I don't want to stop."

"Oh, bull. You sound like you're a love-sick seventeen-year-old now. You're a fifty-year-old man with a wife and child. You can't turn your back on them just because that woman has shown up and bewitched you.

"How do you know she's not going to tire of you and leave you just like she did before? I'm not unaware of her charms. She's beautiful and smart and sexy. She's a sophisticated woman in the shiniest city in the world. She lives a high life. There are plenty of billionaires and celebrities for her to date. How long do you think she's going to trifle with a small time guy like you? She got bored before; she'll get bored again."

Dan's face flushed with anger. His father was uncanny. He went right to the crux of the sore spot with Bella. She was surprised and disappointed that he'd never followed the dreams he'd shared when they were young lovers. He'd never become an entrepreneur with offices around the world. He was stuck in a cubicle farm working at a civil service job not ten miles from where he grew up. Wasting his intellect, his education, his life. The man she'd known had big dreams. He'd never have settled for a paycheck and mediocrity. He'd explained that when she left, all his ambition and drive and confidence went with her. Bella said she understood, but he wondered if she'd forgiven him for being weak. He thought so. He hoped so.

"Well?" demanded his father. Abbie pulled at her leash so they moved faster.

"Dad, it's my life. I've tried to put Bella out of my mind. I spend more time than ever with Jill. She's great. We had a terrific time on our vacation without Katie in Banff this summer. I was scared to death when Jill had that emergency hysterectomy in August. I was crazy with worry about her until she was well enough to go back to work. I still think she tries to do too much. I'm not wild about her training for the one hundred mile cycling event. I know it's something she wants to do, but I wish she'd wait until next year. Jill says her doctor gave her the green light and she's going to train. Even Katie thinks I'm over-protective of her.

"I don't want to hurt Jill. She's the mother of my child, but she's not Bella. I'll take care of Jill. I'll always take care of Katie. I just can't live my life without Bella."

Dan's father made a noise that sounded like disgust. They turned around and headed back to the house.

"Dan, I'm asking as your father to break it off with that woman before it's too late. Before you lose everything that matters. You've already lost my respect. And your mother's. Think with that good mind of yours about what you're doing. Promise me you'll stop this nonsense. Be a man. A husband. A father. A good son."

His mother knew, too. His parents had obviously discussed it, but he couldn't live according to what his parents wanted. He wanted Bella for the rest of his life.

"Sorry you feel that way, Dad. I'm going to ask Jill for a divorce. Frankly, she deserves someone who can love her better than I can. Katie will be all right."

"I'm sorry, too, son. I didn't think I'd raised a cheat and a liar."

His dad picked up the pace. "Your mother's asked Rob to take us to the airport. Even she can't bear to be around you right now. You're childish and selfish and you reek of lust for that woman. You're a great disappointment. I'm embarrassed you're my son."

# CHAPTER SIX

"Did he really?" laughed Bella when Dan told her about his father's heart-to-heart before he'd left the previous night "After all we've been through to be together, did he think a stern talk from him would pry us apart?"

Dan arrived early Monday for the shortened work week. He sat in his office with the door closed. The staff were used to him spending at least two hours behind closed doors every day. He'd confided in the woman in the office next to his. She'd worked in the department as long as he had and didn't know Bella or Jill. She was a safe sounding board for his mixed feelings about divorcing Jill to marry Bella. Divorced herself, she didn't offer any advice. She seemed puzzled by his description of Bella as his soul mate, the other part of him that made him whole. She confessed she'd never had such a thing. She'd never known anyone who'd had that kind of love.

"He missed the part about my being way over twenty-one with a mind of my own. He talked to me like I was about twelve and had been caught with stolen hubcaps."

"Are you comparing me to hubcaps?" purred Bella.

"No. That's the tone he used with me. It was insulting." He was pissed that his father had spoken to him as though he'd been a naughty child. Growing up, Dan and his father had rarely clashed. Rob was the daring one who occasionally got into trouble. Having his father voice objections about his life now was infantilizing. He'd taken a long run after his parents left. Ever since Mørk came into his life, Dan ran to lessen anxiety and irritability—two hallmarks of his illness.

"Oh, Daniel, just put it behind you. He shouldn't have interfered. He's the one who should be ashamed, not you."

Dan tightened his grip on the phone. "I told him I was going to get a divorce." There was silence on the other end. "Did you hear what I said?" he asked.

"Daniel, you don't have to do that," she said softly. "I don't need to be married to you to love you."

"Bella, I want to be with you every day and every night. I ache for you. I hate that we live apart. I want to marry you. It's been almost a year. It's time." He sighed in frustration. Deep breathing or one long exhale was another technique he'd learn to battle Mørk.

"We'll be together for Thanksgiving. That will be lovely, won't it? Long walks in the woods, lighted fires, and lots of red wine."

He leaned back in his chair, closed his eyes, and

pictured the two of them. He desperately wanted to be with her for four full days. Forever.

"It sounds perfect. I can't wait for my wife and Katie to leave tomorrow for her parents' house. I'll have one night alone and then an entire weekend with you."

"Heaven," she whispered.

He rushed to tell her his plan. "I'm going to tell her about the divorce tomorrow afternoon before she and Katie leave for Charleston. She'll have the weekend to adjust and I'll have a clear conscience. No more hiding."

He heard a sharp intake of breath.

"Bella?"

"Daniel, is that a good idea?" Her voice stirred his heart. Bella trained as a classical pianist and singer. Her voice had colors and nuance that could make him weep. She didn't speak when they were intimate. She sang.

"Don't you want me to tell her?" He was hurt that she wasn't enthusiastic.

"I mean the timing, Daniel. Do you think she might cancel the trip to her parents to stay and talk things out with you?"

That thought had never crossed his mind. He stood and paced the office.

"No. The plane tickets are non-refundable. She has to go." He was adamant.

"You know best." The question in her voice hung between them.

"What do you mean?"

"Daniel, if I were in that position I wouldn't let a couple of air fares stand between me and my marriage. In fact, I'd put Katie on the plane to see her grandparents and stay to save my marriage."

*Huh.* He sat and massaged his temples. He'd never considered that.

"My wife wouldn't do that. She doesn't think like you. She'll stick to the plan."

Surely, she would. She wouldn't let her parents down and she'd probably think Katie was too young to fly alone, even if it was just a short hop to Charleston. His stomach lurched. What if Jill wouldn't go?

"How did we get on this depressing topic, Daniel? Tell me what you're wearing. Piece by piece by piece...."

# CHAPTER SEVEN

Jill had to go to Charleston. The tickets were non-refundable. At ten, Katie was still too young to fly alone according to Jill. Katie would think it was weird to go alone, especially at the last minute. The Carters, particularly Jill's mother, will badger Katie about why the plans changed. What would he and Jill do other than argue for the weekend? Where would they eat Thanksgiving dinner? Rob and Suzanne were visiting their son and his fiancée in Chicago. Would they eat at a restaurant? Would they even eat together?

A sharp bark from Abbie brought Dan's attention back to the present. He was running too fast for Abbie to keep up. He realized they'd reached the halfway point of his usual route in the park near his home.

"Sorry, Abbie." Dan bent to pet her head. He checked for labored breathing, but found none. She wasn't even panting. She looked at him with those big brown eyes as if to say what's the rush. She'd probably seen a squirrel she might have chased if

31

ADAM ZORZI

Dan hadn't been running so fast and oblivious to everything outside his head.

"I'll get you a drink, sweetheart." He pulled Abbie's portable water dish out of his pack, put it down just off the dirt path, and filled it with bottled water. Abbie, wagging her knob of a tail, slurped the water. Dan gulped the rest of the bottle. He jogged in place while Abbie drank. He didn't want to get a leg cramp. He already had a brain cramp.

Abbie finished drinking and pawed his leg. He packed her bowl and set off again at a slower pace. He nodded to a speed walker coming toward them. Dan hadn't noticed if there'd been other runners or walkers during the first length of his run. His mind was totally concentrated on what Bella had said.

Could Bella be right about the timing for raising the topic of divorce? Bella was smarter than anyone he'd ever met, but she wasn't like other women. Bella could be wrong about what Jill might do. Hell, Bella didn't know anything about Jill. Not even her name.

When their affair began, they'd agreed to make it completely their own. They didn't talk about anyone beyond the two of them. He was secretly pleased that Bella was a widow. He didn't have to think about her marriage to a nameless man described only as someone who worshipped her but also didn't back down when Bella challenged him. Knowing someone else loved Bella almost as much as he did chafed enough. He didn't need to know the man's name, profession, or nationality. He didn't exist. Dead of a vague cancer.

Bella showed no interest in Jill. Given Katie's

32

age, Bella observed once that Dan had married a much younger woman. Beyond that, she didn't seem curious about Jill in the least. It was her suggestion that they not even exchange the names of their spouses.

Dan thought it would be easier to just say Jill's name. The topic of Bella's husband never arose, but in the course of making plans Dan sometimes had to refer to his wife. Yesterday's conversation was typical. Discussing Jill's trip with Bella was awkward when he considered Bella to be his soul mate. Wife sounded insignificant compared to what he felt for Bella.

Maybe he should postpone mentioning divorce to Jill. That would eliminate any risk of a change in plans. He'd chosen tomorrow in order to have a clear conscience to enjoy his weekend with Bella. Jill would know the marriage was over. Even if she found out he'd spent the weekend with Bella, it wouldn't matter. They were was on track to divorce.

"Heads up," called a passing jogger. Dan and Abbie had drifted to the middle of the path. He still wasn't thinking clearly. He saw the end of his trail. Abbie raced ahead on her leash extension and automatically stopped at the end. Dan did some stretches. He didn't feel like going home yet so he walked to a more sedate section of the park with benches. He sat on a bench in the waning sun while Abbie lay across his feet.

Jill had to go to Charleston. There would be too many complications if she didn't. He and Bella had rented a small home in a wooded area he'd found online at one of those pet-friendly vacation home rental sites. Bella refused to stay with him in the house he shared with his wife and daughter. A rental with fireplace, sky lit bedroom, and Jacuzzi tub wouldn't hold any memories or distractions for either of them and give them the privacy a hotel couldn't. He'd lose the entire fee if he canceled this late.

He stood, spoke to Abbie, and started walking home. He'd stick with the plan. He and Jill would both go to work in the morning. Jill would work until noon. He'd come home at lunch and tell her. Then, they'd pick up Katie at school and he'd drop them off at the airport. He'd go back to work if for no reason other than to keep the excitement of seeing Bella to a simmer.

"Heard you're going to be a bachelor this weekend," called a rail thin blonde just as he and Abbie turned into the neighborhood. How did she know that? Did Jill already know?

"Hi, Monika." Dan did his best to sound casual when she caught up to him. He'd met this long legged woman who was slightly taller than he was a few times. She was Jill's biggest competition in the cycling club.

"Aren't you?" she persisted.

"What?" Abbie tugged at her leash. Home was in sight.

"Going to be a bachelor for the weekend with Jill and Kaitlyn out of town?"

Dan kept walking. "More like a workaholic. Installations are never as easy as they sound and the staff expects smooth going when they start work Monday morning."

Monika stayed hot on his heels. "Where are you eating Thanksgiving dinner?" Nosy troublemaker. Surely, she wasn't going to invite him to join her.

"One of my colleagues has invited me to eat with her family."

"A female colleague. How thoughtful." She glanced sideways at Dan.

"It was. Jill and I sometimes play tennis with her and her husband. He's got a killer serve." He picked up his pace, turned his back on the insinuating gossip, and called over his shoulder. "Happy Thanksgiving, Monika."

# CHAPTER EIGHT

Dan dressed quickly Tuesday morning and went downstairs to feed Abbie, let her dash outside and back, and make himself breakfast to go before Jill and Katie got up. He didn't want to have *bon voyage* sex with Jill that morning.

They'd had sex last night as he expected. It was their last night together before she returned late Sunday. He enjoyed sex with Jill. It just wasn't like what he had with Bella. Jill was a petite hard-bodied athlete who preferred quick, vigorous action. Their code name for sex was exercise. Last night, that's exactly how it felt—a short satisfying workout.

Making love with Bella was tantric. They'd explored each other's bodies for five years as teenagers and young adults. Everything was slow, languorous, and sensuous. Bella herself had toned womanly curves. He'd never seen a more beautiful woman's body. She looked barely older than when he'd last seen her at twenty-two. She still had the ability to make him climax without touching by merely sitting or standing naked in front of him. He couldn't blame Jill for not being Bella. He just didn't want to have a repeat of last night, especially when it would be the last.

He was about to leave when he heard Katie pouring granola into a bowl. "Good morning," he kissed the top of her head. In her school uniform of navy blazer and plaid skirt, she looked like a mini-Jill.

"Dad, why do teachers assign tests two days before Thanksgiving? I have an American Studies test and a biology quiz." She sat at the table and started to eat. Dan reflexively handed her a banana and poured a glass of the fresh-squeezed orange juice he'd made for himself.

"Katie, it's precisely because it's a holiday that you're having tests. They want to make sure most of you show. You'll be absent tomorrow and so will a lot of other girls. I think American Studies sounds appropriate given that Thanksgiving is the first American holiday. You'll ace the biology quiz. You did study, right?"

She rolled her eyes. "Dad, it's like second grade biology. How am I going to get into vet school if they teach us baby biology until middle school? I'm in fifth grade and still getting quizzed on photosynthesis."

She was certainly his daughter given her predilection for planning and preparation. She wanted to be a companion animal veterinarian and charted her academic path accordingly.

"Why are you leaving early?"

"This is a busy week for me. I'll come home at noon to make sure Abbie has some time outside before your mom and I will pick you up at school at exactly one forty-five, okay?"

She nodded. "Mom…"

"Has told her a dozen times to be ready," said Jill as she walked into the kitchen. She took Dan's free hand. "Our plans are to meet here around noon for lunch, let Abbie out for a bit, and make sure the luggage is in the car so we won't be late to pick up Kaitlyn at…."

"One forty-five," the three of them said in unison. Dan kissed Jill and fled to the office.

\*\*\*

Dan couldn't concentrate on work after his regular morning conversation with Bella. He'd found a solution as to how to tell Jill about the divorce without risking her staying in Richmond. He'd written a letter to slip into the bag he'd check for her at the airport. She'd be in Charleston by the time she read it.

Bella's silence when he told her his idea meant she didn't like it. When pressed, she said she didn't have an opinion. It was his wife. His marriage. His divorce. He'd dropped the topic.

"I can't wait to be with you this weekend, Bella, but I do have to work tomorrow until noon. After that, I'm all yours."

"I thought you already were," she teased.

"Always and forever."

"Don't forget I'm renting a car, Daniel. I'll wait for you at the house whenever you're free from work."

"I'd like to be free right now, but knowing I'll see you tomorrow means everything. How will I recognize you?"

She laughed her Bella laugh. "I'll be the naked woman lying on a plush throw in front of the fire with a bottle of Cabernet and two glasses."

He closed his eyes and envisioned ecstasy, but stopped himself. He had to work. "We'll talk tomorrow morning before you leave. Your flight's at nine, right?"

"Details, Daniel, details."

Dan sighed and headed to a meeting that focused his attention on the system installation. By the time he looked at his watch, it was almost noon. He dashed out. "See you later this afternoon, guys. I've got to drive my family to the airport."

When he pulled into his driveway, he saw Jill's car in the garage and Rob's car parked at an angle on the lawn. Something was terribly wrong.

"Hello," he called as he entered through the kitchen.

"In here." Jill was in the den. Impatient that some screw-up by Rob was going to ruin his plan to get Jill and Katie out of town on time, Dan strode into the room. Rob was slumped in a chair, his shirt unbuttoned and his tie loosened around his neck. He was sweating and making terrible noises. He looked like he'd had a seizure. Jill sat on the ottoman in front of him holding a glass of water and a bottle of aspirin. Her free hand was on Rob's knee.

Dan didn't know what to do. "Do I need to call 911? What's going on? Is he having a heart attack?" Why would Rob drive to his house to have a heart attack?

"Pour something stronger. Scotch, maybe?" said Jill.

Rob swallowed the aspirin with water. "Golf," he croaked.

Jill looked un-nerved. "He just showed up about fifteen minutes ago and collapsed in the front yard. I helped him into the house. I don't know what's wrong. I called 911 and Suzanne. They should be here soon."

Dan instinctively put his arms around Jill's small shoulders. He knelt on the floor next to Rob. "Do you have chest pain?"

Rob violently shook his head.

"Nausea? Do you need to throw up?"

The front doorbell rang and two burly EMS techs clomped through the house to the den off the kitchen. They maneuvered themselves between Jill and Dan to reach Rob. Jill left the room while they assessed Rob. Dan heard her on the phone in the kitchen speaking in calm precise tones.

A third EMS tech appeared in the doorway and asked to speak to Dan in the kitchen. "You're the brother?"

"Yes, younger."

"Did he say anything?"

"Not to me. My wife was here first."

"He said golf." Jill went to Dan and wrapped herself in his arms. "I just got home from work and locked the car in the garage when Rob pulled up behind me. He sort of fell out of the car and waved his arms at me. He started walking toward me and collapsed on the lawn. He was conscious, so he was able to walk up the steps with my help.

"I'm certified in wilderness first response training. The two things I thought of were shock and cardiac infarction. He doesn't have epilepsy or diabetes or allergies. I called you right away and gave him an aspirin. That's as far as we got."

Dan had the feeling the tech was containing them in the kitchen. "What's wrong? Are you going to take him to the hospital?"

"I'm just here to get information. My colleagues are examining him. Does he have other family?"

"I called his wife and got voice mail. They had a one o'clock flight to Chicago to see their son and his fiancée for the holiday. Rob's a dentist, but he didn't have on his lab coat or suit jacket. He may have gone into the office for a few hours this morning. Something may have happened there."

Suzanne came rushing through the back door. Jill had apparently opened the house for anyone to enter during the emergency. "What's going on? What's wrong with Rob?"

"Ma'am?"

Suzanne turned to the tech. "I'm Dr. Ramsay's wife, Suzanne. I got a text from Jill to come here ASAP. What's wrong with Rob? He felt fine this morning. Has there been an accident? I want to see him."

One of the two techs who had examined Rob stepped into the kitchen. He looked serious and directed his comments to Suzanne. "He's in shock. We're giving him oxygen and IV fluids."

"He's not having a heart attack? Are you taking him to the hospital?"

41

"No, ma'am, he's just in shock. We've made him comfortable. The three of you can speak to him, now. We'll stick around for a few in case you need us."

Dan looked at the two women. Jill knew. Whatever medical training she had led her to a conclusion. Suzanne looked like Dan felt—clueless and helpless. Suzanne led them into the den.

Rob was lying on the sofa wrapped in a warming blanket. Tubing ran from his hand to an IV bag attached to a pole next to the sofa. Suzanne immediately perched on the sofa next to him and stroked his cheek. "Rob, you're going to be all right. You don't have to go to the hospital."

Rob closed his eyes and shook his head.

Suzanne opened her mouth, but Jill rested her hand on her shoulder. "Let him speak, Suzanne."

"Dad's dead. Heart attack."

"NOOOOOOOOOOOOO."

Jill, who stood between Dan and the sofa, threw herself into Dan's arms to prevent him from tackling Rob. "Dan, your father's dead. Rob wouldn't lie about this."

He could be wrong. Maybe he wasn't lying, but he was wrong. Dad wasn't dead. He'd just seen him Sunday afternoon. Less than forty-eight hours ago.

Dan sat in the chair Rob had vacated. Tears flowed down his face onto his shirt. Between fits and starts with prompting from Jill, Rob managed to say that one of their dad's golf buddies had called him.

"Dad played nine holes of golf. They'd had an eight o'clock tee time. When they'd finished, the foursome went to the clubhouse for iced tea. It was too late for breakfast and too early for lunch. Dad was talking and then he wasn't. He fell headfirst onto the table and then his chair tipped over. Someone performed CPR, but it was too late. No warning. No fix. No time."

"That can't be right. He has acid reflux. Didn't he go to the hospital? He probably has a bad case of indigestion. Or heat exhaustion. It must be in the eighties there."

"No, Dan. He's dead."

Dan stood. "Look," he held out the picture he'd taken of his parents before they left for the wedding Saturday night and framed last night. His dad wore a custom tuxedo tailored twenty years ago that still fit. His mother wore a pretty lace dress that accented her silver hair against a light tan. Diamonds twinkled in her ears. They were holding hands. They'd been married almost sixty years and still looked happy. "That was three nights ago. He's not dead."

Jill sat on the ottoman in front of Dan offering the scotch he'd poured. "I'm sorry, Dan." He sipped and tried to make his mind work. He couldn't. He kept bumping against a barrier that said his father was dead.

When Rob drifted into sleep. Suzanne left to speak to the EMS technicians. Jill sat holding Dan's hand. "I'm so sorry, Dan. It's terrible news. Kaitlyn's going home with Sofia after school. She can stay there this afternoon."

Katie. She'd be waiting at school exactly at one forty-five. He put his face in his hands and sobbed.

How would he tell Katie? She was closer to his father than Jill's because she saw him at least once a week. Aside from living in Charleston, George Carter was a reserved man. Sometimes, George acted like he hadn't raised three daughters. He seemed more at ease with his grandsons.

Dan's mind finally lit on his mother. She must be devastated. She needed her sons. Maybe he and Rob should fly to Florida so she wouldn't have to fly to Richmond alone. He started choking. Jill handed him water. He greedily drank it and asked for a refill.

He could hear Suzanne and Jill talking in the kitchen, but Jill returned quickly with a glass of water.

"What about Mom?"

"She hasn't spoken to anyone except the wife of the friend who called Rob. I think her name is Barbara. They're both with her so she's not alone. Once you feel up to it, one of you should call her."

He couldn't. He couldn't talk to his mother if everyone thought his father was dead. Rob would have to do that. Rob was the one who made up this story. He'd have to be the one to fix it. Dan had enough to deal with. Mørk had arrived.

# CHAPTER NINE

"Disappointment. Great disappointment. You're a great disappointment. I'm embarrassed you're my son." Those words—the last his dad spoke to him—whirred in Dan's head like a bat banging against the walls of an attic.

Dan cried silently as he sat at the far end of the row of folding chairs with green canvas slipcovers to identify family next to the open grave at the cemetery. The green canvas awning provided shelter from the sun, but Dan sweltered in his navy tropical wool suit in the Florida heat. The smell of dirt, freshly mowed grass, and sweat combined with side effects of two new antidepressants nauseated him. Jill, who sat to his right, held his hand. She, in turn, had her arm wrapped around a sobbing Kaitlyn.

"Don't put Granddad in the ground," Katie had begged in the white limo as they were driven to the cemetery. "He likes to be outdoors. He can't be in the dark."

Dan's mother had given Katie a wan smile.

"Kaitlyn, that's just Granddad's body. His spirit is free and soaring and living right inside you and me and your dad and uncle. This is just an earthly show of respect."

How could his mother be so wise and kind when he felt like screaming his lungs out. Goddammit, the last time he'd seen his father they'd fought about Bella. Five days later—Thanksgiving Day—he was front row at his father's burial. His dad hadn't taken those words back and now, he never would.

The officiant stopped speaking. Dan wasn't sure what to do next. His mother closed her eyes and rested her head on Rob's shoulder after the officiant clasped his hands over hers. The man made his way up and down the row offering his hand to each of them. Dan stared at it dumbly. He didn't want to shake hands with this man he didn't know who had just said words that allowed his father to be lowered into the ground. Jill shook her head at the officiant and he went away.

A crying Katie stood with a pink rose in her hand, walked to the casket, kissed the petals and placed it on top. She ran back to her seat and buried her face in her mother's shoulder.

The ushers signaled the family to stand and proceed to the waiting limos. They did. His mother left first, leaning heavily on Rob. Suzanne followed between her two sons. Jill and Katie were next. Dan stood motionless in front of his chair. He couldn't force himself to move. Jill leaned down to speak to Katie, who ran ahead and grabbed Suzanne's hand. Jill walked back and grabbed Dan's hand in both of hers. "Come, Dan. He's not here. Come back to the family."

He'd never loved her as much as he did in that moment.

***

Dan didn't know the details of how he found himself at the funeral in Florida. Jill made it happen. She handled logistics and took care of him. Although she didn't seem frazzled, she must have rushed that Tuesday to change flights during the busiest travel period of the year, pack for him and repack for Katie and herself, and find a place for Abbie to stay. She must have made dozens of phone calls with tough ones to his department head at work and her parents. She found a suites hotel near his parents' villa and rented a car.

"Are the meds helping?" She sat on the bed where he lay in their freezing hotel room after the funeral. She'd picked up the suit he'd flung on the carpet and hung it properly on a hanger behind the door to the sitting room. He'd yanked it off and put on running shorts and a tee shirt before lying on the pink and green duvet covering the bed. Jill held the tie he'd dropped on the floor on her lap and smoothed it flat.

She took his right hand in hers. His skin was especially sensitive during the early days of Mørk's nastiest appearances. Dan felt comforted by having his hand held, but couldn't stand to be touched anywhere else. He felt like he was being shot through with electricity until medication calmed his nervous system. Mostly, he felt leaden. Talking tired him.

"Not really. I'm still in the side effects stage."

"Headache, nausea, and fatigue?"

"All three." He closed his eyes. "Light hurts my eyes."

"Dr. Spellman said the meds were the most powerful he could prescribe without hospitalizing you. He said you might have short-term memory loss. You definitely sleep a lot."

He knew exactly what to expect. The worst episode he'd had took three years of his life before he recovered. Bella. That was when Bella left him twenty-five years ago. The short episodes since then usually took only two or three weeks before he fully recovered.

"It's Thanksgiving Day. Tell me again why Mom had the funeral today. It's a holiday."

"That's why she chose it. She didn't want to wait another day just because it was a holiday. After a morning funeral, their friends could spend the day as planned. She didn't want to endure a funeral reception with lots of people."

Dan nodded. He hated the idea of funerals. Bella considered them barbaric. Why torture the family? There was no reason to force those most bereaved to follow a schedule. Bury the useless body and take comfort where it could be found.

"Why Florida? I don't remember."

"Everything was set by the time we arrived with Rob and Suzanne late Tuesday night. Your parents pre-arranged their funerals, including buying burial plots, in both Florida and Richmond. Your dad was pragmatic. Statistically, he expected to die first and didn't want your mom to have to travel no matter where it happened. They had close friends in both places and the rest of us could come to Florida. She felt the same about him."

"They didn't tell us?"

"No. Rob said he didn't know, either." She kicked off her shoes. "Dan, your parents were independent. Once they had the two of you out of the nest, they didn't feel obliged to put anyone ahead of the other. They didn't feel the need to consult you and Rob about their life. It's healthy. Selma's in a place where she shared happy times with your dad and is surrounded by friends."

*Huh.* This sounded a lot like the conversation he and Jill had last Thanksgiving when he thought the worst that could happen was his parents moving away. Jill said then his father was a good planner. Streamlining at their own pace made things easier for his parents and ultimately for Rob and himself. He still didn't agree. If they'd stayed in Richmond, his mother would be in the family house with her children and granddaughter nearby. What he wanted hadn't mattered. Mørk had paid a short visit then, too.

"Are you going to nap for a while?" Jill asked.

"Probably."

"Will you be okay if I go to the pool? I'd like to get some exercise. I'll take my phone and leave the number right next to the bed. Call me on the hotel landline, and I'll be back pronto."

"Why? Why am I calling you on the hotel landline?"

"You couldn't find your cell Tuesday before we

49

left. It doesn't matter. I'm told people managed without having a phone attached to them twenty-four seven for centuries."

"Okay. I'll use the landline. Got it." Tears started flowing.

Jill was an athlete. Sitting as much as she had for the past few days probably had her craving activity, but she'd deprive herself of something as simple as going to the pool if he needed her.

Dan squeezed her hand. "I'm fine. Go do laps."

She slipped her hand out of his. "I promise to wear my Speedo training suit and not flirt with any cabana boys."

He managed a smile. "I don't think this place is snazzy enough for cabana boys."

She winked at him. "Call me. I mean it, Dan."

Dan deliberately closed his eyes so he wouldn't have to look at this woman who trusted him and took care of him. Liar. Cheat. Liar Cheat.

# CHAPTER TEN

Dan knew attending a buffet lunch for family and his parents' close friends at the villa Saturday was a bad idea. He didn't know just how bad.

"It's a good thing they got rid of that albatross in Richmond. It's a relief to Selma not to have to handle selling it alone."

"What?" Dan must have misheard one of his parents' neighbors. He'd lost his ability to be polite. His social veneer was not highly polished during one of Mørk's visits. He didn't say niceties like "I beg your pardon."

"Selma won't have to rattle around in it alone or deal with an estate sale and putting the house on the market. Last year's real estate market was much better for sellers. Your dad had a great sense of timing." The man made a toast with his bottle of cola to his father's business acumen.

"I can't believe you're saying that to me. My father just died and you're talking about real estate prices in Richmond?"

The man's eyes widened against his tan leathered

face. "Sorry for your loss," he mumbled and walked away.

Rob grabbed his arm. Dan flinched and jerked it away. Too late. His nerves were shocked raw He was wearing a short-sleeved polo shirt that left his forearms bare. Jill had suggested wearing a cotton long sleeved shirt, but he was too hot. He'd been sweating since he arrived in Florida.

"What's wrong with you? He was only making conversation. You're embarrassing yourself. And Mom."

"Like you're one to talk." He started to turn away when Rob grabbed his arm again. "Stop it, asshole. That hurts."

Suzanne was beside them in seconds. She handed car keys to Rob and ordered them to go for a drive or to the beach or a bar until they could behave themselves.

Scuffing his feet along the glistening cement/mineral mix driveway and kicking at stray gravel, Dan reluctantly followed Rob and got in the passenger seat of a white rented SUV. Apparently, no one drove a car in a color other than white in South Florida. White wasn't even a color. Neither said a word until they had parked along A1A, fed the meter with whatever loose change they found in their pockets, and entered Atlantic Dunes Park on the ocean. The park was small and used mostly by locals. The picnic tables they passed on their way to the sandy stretch were all taken by families.

"No chairs," remarked Dan. He had on a baseball hat and his darkest sunglasses to protect his eyes against the bright sunlight. The air smelled salty. At least there wasn't much of a breeze. He'd feel like he was being burned alive if sand blew on his bare face and arms.

"I've got beach towels, bottled water, and a Thermos of cucumber water. Sports drink for you." Rob kicked off his shoes and socks, rolled up his khaki pants to reveal pale ankles and feet, spread out a five foot beach towel with a giant pink flamingo against a palm tree background and sat. He tossed the other towel to Dan who sat on it without unrolling it.

"What's with you? You're sitting at a beautiful beach on a rolled towel like you're at a yoga class with your tennis shoes on looking like you're in prison."

Dan so wanted to wring Rob's neck. This was all his fault. He started the rumor that Dad had died and now everyone believed it. If they'd stayed at the villa a few more minutes, Dad would've walked in with a smile and a pleasant greeting for everyone. He'd sit in one of the wicker chairs on the lanai and apologize for the confusion.

"What's wrong?" Rob repeated.

"Where do I start? Aside from this whole business with Dad, Mørk is here. You, more than anyone, know what that means. Every time you touch me I feel like I'm being electrocuted. I'm irritable and have a killer headache."

Rob unbuttoned his shirt. "That's no excuse for being rude to Mom's friends. Jill said you're on meds."

"That I started barely four days ago. I'm still in the side effects stage. I've got ten more days before

ADAM ZORZI

I might—just might—feel some therapeutic benefits. In the meantime, I want to kill myself, you, and anyone who gets in my way. Like that jerk who was talking about what a great deal Dad got on the house in Richmond."

"You've got a fixation on that house. You need to let that go." Keeping his eyes straight ahead staring at the smooth ocean, Rob drank from a litre-size bottle of water. "Both of us are hurting, you know, not just you. Mom's lost the man she loved since she was sixteen so suddenly she didn't get a chance to say good bye. With an early tee time, Dad left without waking her. He let her sleep in. She never got that last kiss. Mom's heartbroken, but she has innate good manners that prevent her from alienating everyone around her."

"I wouldn't know." Dan looked around for something to throw, but saw nothing. Not even an abandoned Kadima ball. "You're the one who's staying with her. You're the one she talks to. You're the one she physically leans on. I might as well be invisible."

"You're depressed and heavily medicated. She knows that. She's not going to add to your health problems. Give her a break. Give Jill a break, too."

"What's that supposed to mean?" Rob couldn't possibly be more of an asshole if he tried.

"It means," said Rob digging his toes deep into the sand at the end of his towel, "that you've done nothing but complain since you got here. Hell, you were even rude to the clergyman who conducted the funeral service."

Dan stood and immediately regretted it. Dizzy.

54

He sat back down on the rolled towel. "We're in frigging Florida. Why couldn't Dad be buried at home? Why did we all have to travel here? The funeral was on Thanksgiving Day. That makes no sense. It's my favorite holiday. Why we had to have a funeral with all those strangers is beyond me. Bella said they were barbaric. She was right."

Rob turned to stare at him. "Bella? Bella Davis? What does she have to do with this?"

"Nothing." Dan looked down at the sand in front on him. A tiny sand crab crawled away from him.

"Drink this, Dan."

He took the Thermos from Rob and drank what tasted like some sort of blueberry flavored electrolyte drink. He spit it out. "Give me the bottled water." Rob quietly handed him the cold bottle. Dan reached in his pocket, took out a blue tablet and put it under his tongue. He closed his eyes.

"What on earth does Bella Davis have to do with anything?"

"Nothing, Rob. We got into a discussion of funerals one day in college—somebody's grandmother died and had to go home for the funeral—and Bella said they were barbaric. I think all of her grandparents died before she graduated high school. She said funerals tortured the family rather than comforted them. That popped into my mind Thursday. She was right. I feel like I'm being tortured on top of Dad dying."

Rob looked relieved. He probably thought Dan was hallucinating or time travelling or couldn't tell Bella and Jill apart and wondering if he was going to have to find the nearest psych hospital. The explanation seemed to satisfy him.

"Rob, I've got to get out of the heat and sun. Take me anywhere that's dark and air-conditioned." He stood, snatched the car keys off Rob's towel, and strode to the car.

Rob was sweating by the time he jumped into the driver's seat. "This is what I mean. You make demands and expect everyone to accommodate you. I'm lugging towels, drinks, and my shoes and socks walking across deep sand and the hot highway while you sit in air-conditioned comfort like a prince. You can't do that."

"I can't do anything else, Rob. I can't. That's what Mørk does to me before the meds get to a therapeutic level. I'm in a twilight period. If I didn't take them at all, I'd have killed myself by now." Tears flowed and he turned his head to the window so Rob wouldn't see.

"Sorry," said Rob. "I remember those years you lived at home after college. Not well, because Suzanne and I were newlyweds and you weren't high on our list of priorities, but I remember. Mom and Dad thought you might never get better. They even set up a special needs trust for you."

Dan turned his head back to Rob. "They did? You mean like the kind to take care of disabled children should the parents die?"

Rob looked chagrined when he nodded. "Dan, you were disabled. You couldn't function. Hell, you couldn't even leave your room to go downstairs for a meal."

Dan had never thought about Mørk from his

parents' perspective. They'd gone through a lot to get him sane. Maybe that's why his father was so opposed to his reunion with Bella. He probably believed she'd drop him again and he'd be back where he was all those years ago except he now had a wife and daughter to consider. Dad couldn't have known Bella would never do that now.

"You know, Dan, it was easier then. Mørk made you vacillate between being comatose and suicidal. Now, you're enraged all the time. It's not good. Jill handles it well, but nothing fazes her. She's unflappable. Kaitlyn's afraid of you."

Hatred rose from his core. "Take that back."

"C'mon, Dan. We're not ten and six. Kaitlyn is afraid when you bark and snap and can't be touched. She's hurting because her grandfather died and her dad is acting like he hates her. She avoids you by spending as much time at Mom's as Jill allows. Jill is around, but she's focused on you. She knows Suzanne and I can take care of Kaitlyn while we're here. Mom is going to grieve for a long time, I think, and there's nothing any of us can do. You, I hope, can pull yourself together."

Dan let himself cry. He didn't care that Rob saw. He couldn't believe he was so sick he scared Katie. Why hadn't Jill told him? He, of course, knew the answer. She didn't want to make him feel worse than he already did. Mørk made him miserable.

"I'm going to take you back to your hotel, but I've got to ask. I know you and Dad had an argument before he left Richmond last weekend. Did you get that worked out?"

"No. He died having said terrible things to me."

"That must be rough. Guilt on top of grief."

What? He didn't feel guilty. Dad had been wrong. He didn't have any right to interfere with Dan's decision to divorce Jill and marry Bella.

"I don't feel guilty. Dad was wrong."

Rob remained silent for a long time before he spoke. "I think you might want to reconsider that." He turned the key in the ignition and started the car.

# CHAPTER ELEVEN

Jill declared Saturday to be family night after the fiasco of the lunch buffet. She'd picked up food from a local Japanese restaurant and handed Katie the plastic-wrapped silverware, napkins, and sauces. "You set the table and I'll unpack the bags. I think they gave us paper plates, too."

Jill moved easily and deftly as she unpacked. "Tonight's menu includes avocado, cucumber, and California rolls, seaweed salad, and Hibachi shrimp. Looks like they included six tangerines. Dan, do you feel like eating?"

"Sounds good." He didn't have much of an appetite, but he took a seat at the small round table. "Thanks for picking it up."

"Not a problem. It was a just a few blocks away. The parking lot was full. That's always a good sign that everything will be fresh and good quality if it's popular among the locals."

Katie didn't sit until Jill did. Rob was right. She was afraid of him or at least avoiding him. She passed bottled water to everyone without saying anything.

"We can make tea after we eat if anyone wants it. There's a nice assortment of tea bags in the pantry. Kaitlyn, try not to have too much soda while we're here. That's all anyone offers."

"Mom, I can't resist Dr. Brown's cream soda. I've never seen it at home."

"I'd forgotten about that, Kaitlyn. I like it, too. Where did you see that?"

"At Gran's." She lowered her eyes. "Granddad kept a six-pack in the refrigerator, but he limited himself to two a week. It was his favorite drink. Gran said it had too many calories to drink more often."

"Maybe we can find a store in Richmond that carries it," Dan said. "I'd like to have one once in a while. Can we add that to the shopping list, Jill?"

"Of course." She put her hand in his and squeezed lightly. "I'm going to impose the same restriction as Gran. Soda is not a healthy drink. Too much sugar. It's only a treat."

"Whatever you say as long as I can have one occasionally." Dan took a few bites of his California roll. He left the cucumber and avocado ones for Jill and Katie. "What's the movie tonight, Katie?"

"*Apollo 13*," she said into her plate. "Granddad and I liked to watch it. Gran said I could borrow it tonight. I wish there were more movies about space travel. *Star Trek* is lame. *Apollo 13* is really scary because it's true.

"Granddad said he remembered when it happened. The whole country held its breath.

Everyone stopped what they were doing to watch the splashdown on TV. He said seeing those three parachutes come into view was one of the scariest and happiest things he'd ever seen." Katie finished an avocado roll and took a bite of shrimp. "How far is Cape Canaveral from here?"

Jill looked to Dan to answer. "About two and a half hours, I think. Is that something you want to visit?" Katie nodded. "Maybe on our next visit. Christmas?"

"Negative on that, Delta Dan."

They both looked at Jill. "Sorry, I promised two weeks at Christmas to my parents when I cancelled the Thanksgiving trip."

Katie looked like she was going to burst into tears. "But Granddad died, Mom. It's not like we're on vacation. We didn't mean to miss Thanksgiving. Two weeks with Grandmother and Grandfather Carter? Mom, we can't stay two weeks."

Two weeks with Jill's parents? No way. Dan pushed his plate away. Nausea had returned.

***

Dan didn't make it to the end of the movie. Between the tension at his mother's lunch, his afternoon with Rob, and the effects of his meds, Dan fell asleep within the first fifteen minutes. Jill sent him to bed. She and Katie stayed up to watch.

He woke around two in the morning and got up to take a scheduled dose of three different pills. Looking at the tiny sleeping form of Jill, Dan marveled that he'd been given such a gift. She'd slipped into bed without a sound and slept as far from him as she could so as not to irritate his skin. The notepad on her nightstand contained a schedule of his medications, telephone numbers for his doctors and department head at work, and directions to the local hospital. His health was her priority.

Everything she'd done since they'd received news of his father's death had been to make his life bearable. She was accustomed to Mørk making a short appearance in the fall. Compounded with his father's death, Dan doubted he'd survive without Jill's care.

Although Jill kept an eye on his mother and Katie, she focused her attention on him. She made his excuses when he needed to rest at the hotel and avoid receiving condolence calls. She let him cry unabashedly. She anticipated his needs and guarded him fiercely.

He could hear his father's voice as he watched her sleep. *Liar. Cheat. Liar. Cheat.*

By the time they left Florida Monday afternoon, Dan was still sick with Mørk. The side effects of the medications had abated, but he didn't feel better. At least Katie didn't seem as skittish around him. When he looked at his mother, all he saw was disapproval. Just before he left, his mother patted his hand and whispered, "Do the right thing."

She was his father's spokesperson on earth. Offering no comfort for his loss, his mother echoed his father's words of shame and disappointment.

# CHAPTER TWELVE

Dan burrowed himself deep into the house. Although Katie went back to school Tuesday, he took the entire week off. Travelling back to Richmond Monday exhausted him. Jostling crowds, voices and shouts, and bright lights of the airport terminals overwhelmed him.

He knew he needed another full week before his medication would allow him to function. He might be able to tolerate one-minute conversations, focus on topics in thirty minute increments, and maybe answer emails in small batches next week. His experience as a project manager was by the time he received a third email on the same topic, the problem had been solved or no longer mattered.

His narrow attention span and slow reflexes prohibited him from driving. He'd have to rely on Jill to drive him anywhere just as Katie did. He trusted Jill to make arrangements so he wouldn't be stuck in a car with a trio of ten-year-old girls going to and from St. Margaret's.

He'd start work for half days the first week and

return to full time the following week. What he thought or guessed or planned didn't matter. Mørk would decide; Mørk dictated his life.

He now sat in Dr. Spellman's office discussing Mørk. Dan tried to concentrate on the young doctor's questions. Yes, he understood he was here because Dr. Spellman didn't like to prescribe such strong medication without seeing the patient immediately upon return to town. He recited his symptoms and described the lingering side effects No, he didn't have any questions.

Wait. He did. It would break through his consciousness any minute now. Katie. Yes, something to do with Katie. "Dr. Spellman, my daughter is afraid of me when Mørk appears."

"You've never mentioned this during past episodes," was the placid response.

"I never noticed it. My brother told me when we were in Florida. After he mentioned it, I watched for signs. He was right. She's afraid."

He got the look psychiatrists perfect to mean he should continue even though every word was a chore to find in the cotton that was his brain and then force it out of his mouth between aching jaws and over his dry tongue.

"My brother said I was irritable, demanding, and rude. I shouted and snapped. My daughter responded by avoiding me. She wouldn't sit with me alone. She waited for her mother to initiate conversation between the three of us. She sat on the aisle seat with her mother between us on flights."

"All normal reactions for someone close to a man who acted as you described. Your daughter was grieving, too."

"Yes. I hadn't realized how intensely she feels things. I knew she had some of my moodiness, but mostly she's very much like her mother—extroverted, fun to be around, and sweet. I'm worried she's inherited depression from me."

Dr. Spellman refocused his eyes to the painting to the left of Dan's head. "Depression runs in families. We haven't discovered a specific genetic marker to track. At ten, her brain is immature. Even if I were to examine her, I wouldn't be able to give you a definitive diagnosis.

"It sounds like you were bad-tempered, focused on your own grief, and unaware of anything around you. All normal for a grieving person. Textbook for someone whose depression is as bad as yours. Had she ever witnessed you with such a severe episode?"

Dan shook his head.

"Her response was normal and healthy. You, along with your wife, need to explain the nature of your illness. Make sure she understands that you have an illness that disturbs your thoughts and actions and lasts about two to three weeks with medication.

"Your wife is quite attuned to your symptoms and my suggestions when we've spoken. She seems to have a firm grasp of your condition. She's never expressed fear for her safety or that of your daughter. She's unusually accepting. Realistic with some optimism."

"Unflappable is the word my brother used."

He nodded. "I agree with your brother."

Great. Everyone agrees Jill is perfect. Next question.

"Why do you refuse to discuss your father's death?"

He didn't have the energy to lie. "The last time we spoke, we argued. Intensely. He said he was ashamed I was his son."

"That's quite strong."

"He'd been saying it for more than a year. He was angry he couldn't control me."

"Why would your elderly father believe he could control you?"

He wasn't going to argue that his father wasn't elderly. He didn't have the strength.

"Dad and I never had any real conflicts. Growing up, I wasn't a kid who got into trouble. My parents were my caretakers during my first experience with depression. My brother told me this weekend my parents were so worried about my ability to recover, they established a special needs trust. They're relieved I live a normal life. They like my wife. They love Katie."

"Why would your father believe he could control you?" Spellman repeated.

"We disagreed on one issue. He thought his opinion was morally superior. He thought I should defer to that."

"This thing is?"

Why didn't Spellman just bring out the rack? This was torture. He'd spell it out, but he spoke as if by rote.

"My first long depression was triggered by the break-up with my girlfriend, my soul mate, in graduate school. We'd been together five years. We had an accidental encounter last year and have been having an affair for a year. My father knew it and asked me to stop. The last time I saw him, I told him I planned to divorce my wife to marry this woman. She's a widow. He disapproved from a moral perspective and a practical one. He considered me a liar and a cheat. He also believed this affair wouldn't last, the woman would drop me just like she had when we were young, and I'd have ruined my family for no reason."

"You disagreed that it wouldn't last?"

"Yes. I've loved her since I was seventeen. Not many people get a second chance. We have. I don't want to lose her again."

"And now?"

"Now, I realize I underestimated the effect a divorce would have on Katie. She was devastated by the death of her grandfather. She's sensitive and emotional like me. I thought she was as sunny and optimistic as her mother. I can't imagine how she'd cope if her parents divorced."

"What about the woman?"

"I haven't spoken to her."

"About what? Since when?"

Wasn't it time for the session to be over? This was agony.

"She and I planned to spend the long Thanksgiving weekend together and had rented a vacation house. My wife and daughter were flying to visit her family in Charleston the Tuesday before Thanksgiving. I'd written a letter to my wife asking for a divorce that I planned to put in her checked baggage at the airport. She wouldn't read it until she arrived in Charleston. My girlfriend, for lack of a better word, was coming Wednesday morning. I'd have told my wife about the divorce and have a guilt-free weekend with her."

Spellman looked at his notes.

"Your father died Tuesday."

Dan nodded.

"How did your girlfriend take that news?"

"I didn't tell her."

"How did you explain the change in plans?"

"I didn't."

Spellman looked at him directly. "You haven't spoken to this woman you profess to be your soul mate since your father died? You didn't tell her there'd been a change in plans? Did she come to Richmond from wherever she lives?"

"New York."

"You've gone into radio silence with this woman?"

Dan looked down at his hands. This was like talking to his father except Spellman was taking Bella's side.

"Has she tried to contact you?"

"I don't know."

"Dan, you suffer from depression not stupidity. Your judgment is clouded and medication causes sleepiness, but you're able to understand facts. Has this woman contacted you?"

"If she has, she would have called my office. We used burner phones. I keep mine at the office. I left it there when I went home for lunch Tuesday and learned my father was dead. I haven't been to my office since then."

"And out of the sheer courtesy you would have shown any houseguest, you didn't inform her there'd been a change of plans? You didn't share what was one of the most emotional events of your life—the death of a parent—with someone you call a soul mate? In particular, the father who knew about the affair?"

Dan kept his eyes on his hands and shook his head.

"Your boss was informed, I presume. He knew not to expect you at work. Correct?"

"Jill called him."

"At your request."

Enough. "I couldn't very well ask Jill to call her and cancel, could I?"

"I suppose Jill made arrangements regarding the dog, newspaper and mail deliveries, and your home security company. "

"Yes."

"Yet, you didn't make this one phone call."

Dan gave up. He had nothing to say.

Spellman swiveled in his chair to his computer. "I'm adding another medication to take first thing every morning with food." He tapped on his keyboard. "Still using Raintree Pharmacy? They deliver?"

"Yes," squeaked Dan. His voice was shot with this much conversation. Two mouse clicks. Spellman stood. "Dan, I suggest you think about that behavior before I see you next week. The same time. Call me if you have any problems with your meds."

Spellman held the door open for Dan to leave.

# CHAPTER THIRTEEN

After the exhausting appointment with Dr. Spellman, Dan slept the remainder of Tuesday. Jill and Katie ate dinner alone. He slept most of the week, but he was always awake for dinner with his wife and daughter and at least an hour afterward. He encouraged Katie to talk about school, sports, and her friends in an effort to ease their relationship back to normalcy.

Jill took the entire week off, too. Abbie slept in the master bedroom with Dan during the day. Jill didn't hover. She left for short periods to run errands and car pool for Katie. He could hear her as she kept busy with fall cleaning, de-cluttering, and packing boxes for charity pick-up. She maintained her exercise regimen. Maybe she did some work from home. Most importantly, she was available if he needed her.

What he needed most was to be left alone by everyone except Jill. She protected him. She made excuses to condolence callers as she had in Florida, re-routed flower deliveries to senior citizen centers, and kept a condolence call journal. He was in no condition to write thank-you notes and didn't want Jill to do it on his behalf. His plan was to pretend nothing had happened.

By the end of the week, he and Jill took brisk mid-morning walks with Abbie. They chose a time between the pre-work runners and lunch-time runners when the park was quiet. They travelled along his usual running route. The weather wasn't wintry, yet. Both of them wore light running jackets, but the walks felt good. Dan knew he was recovering when the slight breezes didn't sting his face and legs. He no longer felt like target practice for lightning bolts.

Mostly, they walked in silence holding hands. Abbie danced along seemingly thrilled to have not one but two humans accompanying her. They completed half of the six -mile circuit by Friday. Dan expected to jog during the weekend and run by Monday. He'd go back to work Monday.

Surprisingly, there hadn't been any phone calls from work about the installation. He'd told Jill he'd take those calls, but so far his team seemed to be managing without its leader. He dreaded returning to the office not because of work, but because of Bella. He simply couldn't face a conversation with her.

He thought about what Dr. Spellman had said about his inability to call her even as a courtesy to let her know there'd been a change in plans never mind his life. He doubted he would have been coherent if he'd attempted such a call. Rob had required treatment by an EMS team before he'd been able to convey the news. Dan knew it would have been impossible for him to say his father was dead aloud.

They went to dinner at Rob and Suzanne's house Saturday night. Dan enjoyed being out of the house with people he considered safe. Suzanne had prepared a simple meal, but presented it beautifully. She was preparing for holiday concerts with the RSO, her quartet, and solo gigs. She always had stories about mishaps both in front of and behind the stage. At a special performance Thursday night, the stage lights had gone out and the orchestra, along with the vocal soloists, continued in darkness. The audience had raved about the experience and suggested that more concerts be performed with lighting effects.

"How did you know what to play if you couldn't see the score, Aunt Suzanne?"

"There's a small LED light attached to each music stand. Even if there hadn't been, I've been playing that particular piece for thirty years. I have it memorized. Most of my colleagues do, too. All the vocalists sing from memory. The challenging part was seeing the conductor. I enjoyed it. The audience was completely silent. There wasn't any coughing, flipping program pages, or rattling of cough drop wrappers. The artistic director is thinking of doing something similar for Halloween next year. It was a novelty and successful."

"Sounds like you had the most exciting week of any of us." Dan spoke for the first time. "Anything else going on? Rob?"

"Work was busy, having shuffled patients last

week. I'm really glad I added two colleagues last year. Makes things much easier to schedule now that there are five of us in the practice."

"I completed fall house-cleaning and sent a lot to charity," said Jill. "I don't know how three people and a dog can collect so much stuff."

"Because, Jill, one of them is Dan the hoarder."

"Stop, Rob." Jill shook her head. "I mostly got rid of my stuff—CDs, worn training gear, and business suits and pumps I'll never wear. I'd been hanging onto clothes thinking at some point I might have to make a presentation to a straight laced client, but if it hasn't happened in five years, I think I can let it go. I also got rid of some of Abbie's worn toys, collars, and leashes. Kaitlyn and I picked out two new collars and leashes one day after school. She deserves to look snazzy. She's black and looks good with red and bright blue. She needs a new winter sweater, too."

They'd bought stuff for Abbie—his dog— without consulting him? Dan didn't like that, but he kept quiet.

"Gran's lonely."

They all looked at Katie. "She misses Granddad so much. She's sick of people coming over any time they feel like it. She sent an email to all her friends to ask them to call before visiting and that if the phone goes to voice mail, it means she's resting not that she's lying on the floor in need of 911. She told three people that she didn't want one of those Medic-Alert necklaces for old people who fall and need help getting up. People make really stupid suggestions just because Granddad died. She's not sick. She's sad."

Tears flowed down Dan's cheeks. He couldn't help himself. His mother sounded like she was in terrible pain and there was nothing anyone could really do to help.

"How do you know this, Kaitlyn?" asked Rob.

"I email her every day after school, Uncle Rob. Sometimes, she doesn't write back until bedtime. She takes afternoon naps like Dad." Katie shot a furtive glance at Jill. "I told her I was working on not having to go to Charleston for two whole weeks at Christmas. She said she'd be fine and that Grandmother and Grandfather Carter missed seeing me at Thanksgiving. I didn't tell her Grandmother Carter just missed a chance to show me off and tell everyone I went to St. Margaret's, too, like she did plus Mom and her sisters."

Jill gave Katie a stern look that Dan knew meant they'd talk later. He was rooting for Katie's persuasive abilities.

"That's very thoughtful of you to keep in touch with Gran. I called her once, but she didn't want to talk. She said for your dad and me to wait for her to call us."

"That's what she told me, too, Uncle Rob. She needs privacy."

Before they left, Rob took Dan aside and asked how he felt. Dan told him the truth. Still grief-stricken, still on heavy meds for Mørk, and seeing Dr. Spellman once a week. "I'm going back to work half-days starting Monday. I hope to be back full-time by the following week. Dr. Spellman added a new prescription that helps me focus in the mornings."

"Good. I'm sorry if I pissed you off in Florida."

"No, Rob, it helped. Katie was afraid of me. She'd never seen me have a visit from Mørk. That, combined with being upset herself, must have been awful for her. Dr. Spellman said it's too soon to know if she inherited this awful depression. Symptoms don't show up until about age seventeen. Rob, you're one lucky man that you and your sons didn't inherit it. I wouldn't wish this on anyone."

"Do you think Dad had it?"

"He must have had some mild form. I remember he could be moody, but I now see that he lived exactly the structured kind of life that keeps episodes to a minimum. He never worked long hours, was always home for dinner with the family, and had a standing card game with other couples on Friday nights. He golfed every Saturday morning, went out with Mom and friends Saturday nights, and did something with us as a family on Sundays.

"I once considered that boring, but we grew up feeling loved and secure. I think that's why he was such a careful planner. He wanted to limit surprises. I understand now why he wanted to downsize and sell the house. He didn't want Mom to have to do things alone when they could make decisions together and then enjoy their lives. I forgive him that."

"And the other problem?"

"I can't forgive him, Rob. I can't."

# CHAPTER FOURTEEN

Dan spent the first two hours of his first day back at work with the team. They offered condolences, expressed their willingness to help him ease back into work, and moved on to debrief him. It had gone extremely well with only a few hiccups. Each team member congratulated Dan for being so precise and detail-oriented with the vendor. His anticipation of problems in key areas and making design adjustments had prevented downtime. The training he supervised was precise and brief. As a result, the help line hadn't been flooded with questions. Staff hadn't been overburdened with information. As Dan had insisted, they'd been given instruction not tech-speak. Feedback from department heads was positive—staff saw a sleek user-friendly design and experienced a faster, more efficient system. Productivity in the first quarter after installation was projected to rise.

After a quick coffee with some of the key team members, Dan steeled himself to go into his office. He closed his door and approached his desk cautiously. He dreaded what he'd see—the message light on his landline was on. He ignored it. He sat and reached into his locked bottom desk drawer and removed the burner phone he used for calls to Bella. He scrolled through the caller ID list. Bella had called every work day morning between 8:30 and 9:15 as usual, including this morning. He didn't check for messages.

His landline voice mailbox was full. He put his head in his hands and wept. He couldn't bear to listen. Very few would be work-related. The staff would have been informed he was out of the office. Most formal requests were made via email rather than phone calls.

Bella refused to email him or provide her email address. Another one of her rules to keep their affair private. She had a nothing-in-writing, no gifts, no evidence policy. When his burner phone was close to expiration, he bought a new one and gave her the number.

He couldn't bring himself to tell Bella his father was dead. He couldn't say no one could have taken better care of the sick, grieving man he'd been than his wife. He couldn't say his eyes had been opened to the fragility of his child.

Almost every voice mail would be Bella. She was the only person on earth who called him Daniel instead of Dan. Hearing her mellifluous voice say his name would break his heart. It was the most beautiful sound on earth. It really didn't matter what she said. She had the ability to evoke fiery declarations, exquisite pain, and the purest of pleasures. Whatever tone she used or role she chose would break down every defense he had. He'd shatter. He'd never be able to function. He'd be of no use to anyone.

He simply couldn't listen to her recorded voice. He wouldn't make himself press call and hear her live voice. She'd pull him back into the deepest darkness in which he lived without her if he told her how much his father's death had changed him. He'd disappoint her again. For the first time since learning that his father had died, he considered ending it all. Life without Bella wasn't living.

# CHAPTER FIFTEEN

Dan paced in Dr. Spellman's outer office. It had been three weeks since his father died and his medication had worked until now. The receptionist had told him he'd have to wait five to seven minutes given that he'd been worked in on the last weekday before the Christmas holidays. He felt like five to seven hours had passed. Dr. Spellman's office would be open every day except Christmas and New Year's Days. Why did everyone have to see him today?

He was next. Dan endured a quick vital signs assessment by a nurse before the great man walked in. By that time, he was hyperventilating.

"Dan, sit still, take deep breaths." He handed Dan a chilled bottled water from a small refrigerator beneath his desk. "Drink this. Take your time. There's plenty of time for you to tell me what's bothering you. You're safe. I'm your doctor. I'm not going to let anything happen to you."

Dan did as he was told and slumped in the comfortable upholstered chair like the deflated person he felt. He continued to take deep breaths until he felt able to speak coherently.

Dr Spellman sat on a swivel stool in front of his desk. Dan's chart was visible on the computer monitor. Spellman ran through the usual checklist of symptoms, medication efficacy, and need for prescription refills and made notes in the chart before allowing Dan to speak without interruption.

"That bitch ruined my marriage and my life," he finally spat.

In that infuriating way doctors have of playing stupid or uninformed, Spellman questioned him. "What bitch?"

"Bella."

"The 'girlfriend, for lack of a better term'?"

"Yes," he said through gritted teeth. He'd already been put through interrogations twice in two days. He couldn't bear a third by a condescending jerk with an MD after his name.

"My notes indicate that you've responded to medication, returned to work, and plan to leave tomorrow for a two-week holiday trip. What's changed?"

"Everything. Everything's changed. I'm not going to Charleston although I'd hardly call it a holiday trip. It's more like penance for my father having the bad timing to die at Thanksgiving and having to do double duty with my in-laws at Christmas to compensate."

"Not going sounds like a relief."

"Jill disinvited me."

"Even better. That sounds quite thoughtful."

Dan struggled to stand so he could walk out in a

huff, thought better of it, and settled himself deeper in the chair. Spellman was going to play Devil's Advocate indefinitely unless Dan told him the story from the beginning.

"Don't shrink me. Just listen."

"I'm listening. Please continue." Spellman sat with his hands relaxed on his lap and the heels of his shoes hitched on the lowest bar of the stool.

"Work is going okay except that my voice mailbox is filled with messages from Bella since the Wednesday before Thanksgiving. She calls every work day on the burner phone during our regularly scheduled time. I don't answer. I can't answer. I don't want to hear her voice."

Spellman didn't respond so Dan plowed ahead.

"Two days ago, I was looking for a computer file at work so I could get a jump on the year-end activity report. I couldn't find it. I don't know if it was deleted or misfiled or what, but I couldn't find it. I was annoyed that I wasted an hour and still couldn't find it.

"I didn't want to go through hard copies in the filing cabinet, but I did and still couldn't find it. I yanked hard on the top file drawer and spilled coffee into it, ruining not just pertinent files, but all my files for the year. I first went to the men's room to get paper towers. None there. I went to the break room, grabbed a roll to take to my office to mop up, and argued with some prissy type who didn't want me to take it. By the time, I got back to my office, I was pissed. The aroma of coffee coming from the file cabinet was nauseating, and the burner phone was ringing.

"I was sick of Bella harassing me so I picked up. She said she was so relieved to hear my voice. She thought something terrible had happened to me. She'd called hospitals. She'd checked online obituaries looking for my name. She sounded frantic and relieved.

"I blew her off. I told her she should have known if she hadn't heard from me that I wasn't interested in talking to her. She pressed me. I finally told her that my dad died the day before she was to have visited at Thanksgiving. She was Bella at her most compassionate. It made me sick.

"She sweetly insinuated that I must have been in a coma if I hadn't had the presence of mind to give her the courtesy of a call to tell her there'd been a change of plans. She'd come to Richmond. When I never showed at our rental house, she became seriously worried. She made calls to the police, hospitals, and even the morgue. She thought I'd had an accident or heart attack."

He paused, gulped down the remaining water in the bottle, and took a deep breath.

"I basically said it was over and she was harassing me. Bella is brilliant. *Phi Beta Kappa*, *Summa*, Order of the Coif. Even before she became a lawyer, she could best just about anyone in an argument by calmly pointing out things that were obviously unreasonable and mistakes in logic. Kind of like what you do, Dr. Spellman."

Spellman didn't react. Of course not. Prick.

"I was angry. I took all the feelings I had—anger, guilt, grief—out on her. I screamed and shouted. She kept asking questions in that infuriating reasonable tone of hers that I didn't want to answer. I finally told Bella I needed my wife and couldn't see her anymore. I told her I'd kept a log of her daily calls and if she didn't stop calling me, I'd get a lawyer to get a restraining order or sue her for harassment or whatever legal thing I needed to get her to leave me alone.

"She hung up. I felt relieved. I could focus on my marriage and not feel guilty about Bella. That night, I slept well for the first time since Dad died.

"Yesterday, my wife got an email at her job from Bella that basically told her to get me in line because I was about to humiliate her and our daughter for no reason. Court proceedings are public and I had zero chance of getting a restraining order. I'd be lucky to keep my job when my employer found out I'd had phone sex at least once a day at work for a year." Dan rolled his hand in the air to indicate on and on and on. "You get the idea.

"Jill was furious. She told me I was no longer invited to spend Christmas with her family in Charleston. She and Katie would go without me. Katie didn't want to go to Charleston. She can't stand the thought of spending that much time with Jill's pretentious mother. I told Jill Katie could go with her for a week and I'd come get her and go on to visit my mother in Florida for the second week. Jill said no. She refused to negotiate time with her child.

"That's when I told her everything—the year-long affair and my plan to divorce her and marry Bella, thwarted by my father's death. I told her that's not what I wanted anymore. I wanted to keep our family together. If she needed time to adjust, she'd have the week at Christmas with Katie and another with just her parents and sisters. She told me not to say anything to or plan anything for Katie. She called me a raging time bomb she wouldn't allow near her child. Katie had finally overcome her fear of me and Jill wasn't going to allow any setbacks. She left to pick up Katie from school.

"I pretended to have a headache and went to bed so I wouldn't see either Jill or Katie last night. I took a taxi here first thing this morning."

Dr. Spellman hadn't taken a single note. He took a few minutes before speaking in his neutral voice.

"I'm sorry you've experienced such upheaval in addition to your father's death and a major depressive episode. I'm going to re-evaluate your needs, but there are some gaps of information for which I need explanations."

Dan shrugged. Ask away.

"Were you evasive about your father's death when you spoke to Bella?"

"She had no right to the details of my father's death. She stressed me when I was consumed with work while I was grieving. She pushed too much."

"In what way? You stonewalled her for weeks. You exaggerated your importance at work…."

"No, I didn't. I was the project manager," he interrupted.

"They managed to complete the installation without you. You received a commendation for doing a stellar job and leaving a clear blueprint for your team to follow. As to Bella, you withheld simple information about your father's death that you freely shared with neighbors, co-workers, and possibly passing strangers. We've discussed your poor decision not to notify her of the change of plans for Thanksgiving weekend. Were you deliberately provoking her?"

"I don't know. I just couldn't talk to her. I wanted to be alone with my family."

"Yet you threatened her. Bella knows you well and recognized your habit of digging in your heels even when you're wrong. Arguing with you would be futile so she protected herself. The best way to force you to see reason was to tell your wife the consequences of your temper tantrum."

Everyone was so hard on him. Yes, he was wrong to threaten Bella. It was stupid, but he'd been angry. He didn't intend to actually sue her.

"I don't understand a key point. Bella sounds like a woman who wouldn't bother with a man who wasn't interested in her and would quickly shift her attention to someone who did. If you made it clear you didn't want a relationship, Bella wouldn't pursue it. Why the email?"

Dan felt like he was the loser in a boxing match that the referee refused to stop. He was going to be pounded into a knock-out. He surrendered. He exhaled and spoke quietly.

"I described contact as anything from or about her during my rant. The affair started when I ran into Bella at the Omni hotel after she'd made a speech to the Virginia Bar Association. She's an expert securities lawyer who literally wrote the standard textbook on securities law. She's represented by a speaker's bureau. I subscribed to her mailing list. Bella said an unsubscribe request might not be processed before the next update was disseminated. I told her I considered that to be contact and she'd better get me off that list."

Spellman looked skeptical. "Even though you, as a computer specialist, know that a client's control of a third party's database is nonexistent." It was a statement not a question.

Dan nodded.

"Bella, being a savvy woman with a reputation to protect, sent the email to Jill in order to keep you in line should you do something rash if the brochure or email or whatever arrived, correct?"

"Yes." He sighed deeply. It was all out. Every last bit of it.

Spellman eyed him carefully. He swiveled to consult something on the computer monitor and back to face Dan.

"Dan, do you have any support who will be in town over the holidays?"

"My brother and sister-in-law will be in town. They're not going away until mid-January."

"Good." He closed Dan's file, swiveled away from the computer, and spoke without humor.

"I have no treatment for stupidity. You're functioning at a level where your judgment shouldn't be clouded by depression. You have a quick temper. What you described isn't depression-related irritability. It's cowardice, selfishness, and anger.

"My prescription is that you stay in Richmond and take your scheduled vacation from work. That's a bad environment for you right now. Your wife sounds determined to keep her plans with your daughter and her family in Charleston. She's behaving rationally and protecting your daughter from adult subjects. Don't object. Encourage your daughter to enjoy herself.

"I'm diagnosing you with a serious case of mumps for which you must stay inside, stop running, and lay low for the weekend. There's a three-hour daily anger management program at Richmond Memorial Hospital in which I'll enroll you starting Monday. You don't need a change in medication. You need an attitude adjustment. The anger management facilitator is an expert. Take advantage of that."

Dan was screwed.

# CHAPTER SIXTEEN

## March

Ruh.        RRRRRRRRRRuh.        Ruh.Ruh.
RRRRRRRRRRRRRRRRRuh.

Long howls of pure doggie joy from the black Schnauzer mix started before the car stopped. She sensed home. When the car door opened, she jumped out and raced across the grass to the front door of a white brick rambler, leaving her leash and the woman attached to it at the curb.

The young redhead who opened the front door welcomed the dog with open arms. The dog licked her face while her thumb of a tail ticked back and forth. The woman wrapped her arms around the dog and cried unabashedly.

The blonde woman who had arrived with the dog reached the front door. "She's happy to be home."

"Oh yes," gushed the redhead. "We didn't think we'd ever see Maggie again, and here she is. I can't thank you enough." She buried her face in the dog's soft curly black coat. She looked up at the slender woman in front of her. "Forgive me. I'm overcome. Won't you please come inside?"

"No, thank you," she said. "It's best to do this quickly. We'd no idea Abbie, that is, Maggie, belonged to someone. My husband got her after she'd been picked up by animal control. She had no identification."

The redhead didn't bother to wipe her tears. "We were just sick. Our house sitter had impeccable references, but he let Maggie out rather than walking her on a leash and she got away. Of course, we didn't pay him, but that didn't replace Maggie." She started to cry again. "My children will be ecstatic. They were three and five when Maggie went missing. They've never wanted to go on vacation again. I can't say I blame them. They didn't want another dog because they expected Maggie to come home. And here she is." She sniffed. "When you called this morning, I couldn't believe she'd been found. Thank you. Thank you. Thank you."

"Your happiness says it all." She nodded and took a step back. "We had an ID chip put in her ear. It's been updated so she'll be returned to you should she ever become lost again." With her car keys at the ready, she started towards the car. "She's up to date on all her shots," she called over her shoulder.

"I can't think you enough." The woman waved.

She was almost in the car when the redhead called, "I'm sorry. What was your name again?"

"Mrs. Ramsay. Jill Ramsay."

# CHAPTER SEVENTEEN

Rain. More than a mist. Less than a spray. There hadn't been a grey cloud in the sky when he pulled into the driveway. Home from work.

Dan pulled his damp hand back inside the bedroom window. The weather was wet, but felt warm enough to run. His daily six miles through the nearby park had kept his sanity for the past three months. He closed the window and turned away.

Sitting on the heirloom quilt spread over one of the twin beds, Dan tied his old navy running shoes. The ones with thick tread but worn uppers he wore in bad weather. Jill would be pissed. He was supposed to leave his running gear in the mud room and not track it through the house and upstairs into the guest room. He'd forgotten. It wouldn't matter. Everything he did was wrong these days. She was pleasant to him but no more unless Katie was around.

He exhaled deeply. He ran to forget what was

going on in his marriage. Running could be mindless. He went through the motions of warming up. Circled his arms eight repetitions forward, eight reps back. Stretched upward as high as he could reach, at the waist, and touched his toes. He jogged in place.

Dan grabbed his keys and bounded down the stairs, calling "Abbie, here girl. Time to run." No response. Usually, the black Schnauzer-mix sweetheart who loved him no matter what met him before he reached the first floor. He called again. No answer.

"Damn," he said. She'd vomited two nights ago, which was unusual for her. He hoped she wasn't sick. She was six. She wasn't old.

He walked into the den where her plush forest green bed lay empty. He circled the kitchen, dining room, and stood at the door of the living room while his eyes swept the room. He didn't dare step inside wearing these old shoes. Nothing should disturb the house museum. Jill had inherited her grandmother's dark Victorian style furniture bursting with rose velvet, pale green silks, and a fine Ourshak rug. He'd always hated the decor, but the furniture had been important to Jill when they married.

Dan trotted up the stairs and looked in every room, including the off-limits master bedroom. The rest of the house looked like something out of *Country Living* magazine. Leather, pastel plaids, and cherry wood. Hooked rugs, rocking chairs, and quilts Jill had either made or inherited. No sign of Abbie. Maybe she was in the back yard or maybe she'd dug her way under the foundation again. He went outside and called. No answer.

He was sure there was an explanation. Abbie couldn't have gotten out of the fenced back yard. Katie was still at school and Jill at work. They wouldn't have let her out before leaving the house. Maybe Abbie just wasn't up for a run in the drizzle. She didn't have marital problems to escape for an hour.

He sighed, lifted his shoulders, and jogged down the blossoming crabapple tree-lined street, turned left at the gated entrance of the neighborhood, and ran a half mile along the sidewalk and into the park. He started off slow, then upped his pace until he reached optimum heart rate. He didn't wear a heart monitor. He knew his body. Soon he was in his zone. His head was clear, eyes blind to blooming pink and white azaleas along the path, ears deaf to birdsong. Steady, steady, steady. He ran the three mile path once. Twice. Six miles.

He stopped, bent his head to his knees, and exhaled deeply three times. He pulled a bottle of water with electrolytes from the pocket of his running shorts and drank. A mix of sweat and rain poured down his face. No one else was around. He noticed the rain was coming down harder. He started the jog/walk cool down towards his house. Surely, Abbie had come out of hiding.

\*\*\*

"Dad, where's Abbie?" cried Katie as soon as he walked in the door of the mudroom. She must've been watching for him and the dog.

Dan sat on the bench and pulled off his socks and shoes, careful to put the socks in the hamper and the shoes in the copper boot tray. He smelled teriyaki and guessed Jill was just off the mudroom in the kitchen making salmon for dinner.

He kissed the top of his daughter's head. She squirmed away.

"Where's Abbie, Dad? Why didn't she come in with you?"

Trying to hide his concern, Dan spoke evenly. "She didn't go for a run with me. I think she hid because of the weather."

"But her leash is gone," she insisted. "She had to have gone with you."

Dan stood. "No, Katie, she didn't. Let's take a look around the house."

"Her name is Kaitlyn. She's not a baby." Jill shouted from the kitchen.

Dan took his daughter's hand in his and walked into the kitchen. He felt small and vulnerable in bare feet and damp running clothes around Jill. He almost felt naked.

Jill was standing in front of the microwave setting the timer for fish. Even though he knew she'd lost weight since Christmas, she still looked great and toned in slim jeans, a red sweater, and her beloved short Ugg boots. He couldn't get used to the short hair. She'd shorn her shoulder-length brown black hair on New Year's Day and looked almost like Demi Moore in *GI Jane*. It wasn't becoming. She looked like a boy. It made her face look gaunt. Even she knew it was bad because she'd bought a pageboy wig with bangs to wear to work until it grew. At least it had grown enough that she no longer wore the wig.

"So, where's Abbie?" she asked without turning to look at him.

"Hiding, I think."

"No," howled Katie. "She wouldn't hide from us now. It's dinner time. She's hungry."

Dan squatted to be eye level with Katie.

"She's hiding somewhere, but she couldn't have gotten out of the back yard because of the fence. Only the three of us know the combination so no one could have let her out."

Katie cried harder.

"Kaitlyn," Jill turned to her daughter. "We are the only three who know the combination, aren't we? You didn't tell anyone, did you?"

Katie hugged herself and choked out sobs.

"Kaitlyn Carter Ramsay, who did you tell? Josie? Sophia? Not Jada, did you?"

"Jill, don't," he started and stopped when she gave him a look that said "don't mess with me." The look he'd never seen before December.

She took Kaitlyn gently by the shoulders and said, "Who did you tell?"

Katie looked down at her tennis shoes, laces one untied. "Sophia," she whispered.

"Why?"

"So she could get in and come on the deck if I didn't hear her ring the bell."

"We'll have to change the combination," she exhaled. "After dinner, your father will call Sophia's family and go get Abbie. Go wash your hands. Dinner is in three minutes."

"I'm not hungry," said Katie in a voice barely above a whisper. "I can't eat until Abbie comes home."

Dan chose to go upstairs, take a one-minute shower, change, and come back. He couldn't bear to watch Jill and Katie going at it and he dare not step in. Abbie was his dog. He'd chosen her from animal control three years ago probably hours before she would have been put down. He'd always had dogs and missed not having one. He thought Katie, as an only child, should have an animal companion. He wanted to burst into tears himself and didn't want to eat, but this wasn't a battle he could fight right now.

When he returned and took his place at the table, Katie was sitting with tears running down her cheeks looking at her plate. Jill was serving with a determined look on her face.

The three of them ate silently. Rather, Katie moved her food around her plate, Dan choked down some food, and Jill seemed content with the quiet. She ate her meal and drank an extra glass of Chablis.

The missing leash bothered Dan. Sophia would have had to have let herself into the house—at least the mud room—to get it. The house was always locked and alarmed. Surely, Katie hadn't had a key made for Sophia and told her the alarm code. Why Sophia would take Abbie home with her without telling Katie puzzled him, too. Dan excused himself without dessert saying he wanted to call Sophia's family and get Abbie before it got too late. He promised to do the dishes after he returned with Abbie.

In less than five minutes, he returned to the kitchen where Jill was eating a compote of peaches with almonds and raspberries and Katie was twirling her spoon, her fruit untouched.

"Can I go with you, Dad?" Katie said when he walked in the room.

He felt like sobbing.

"No, Katie. Abbie's not at Sophia's. Today was Sophia's piano lesson so she didn't come this way after school. She went straight to the studio."

"You mean Abbie's gone?" cried Katie, her brown eyes wide with hurt and fear.

Katie ran from the table, up the stairs, and into her room faster than Jill could say, "Now look what you've done."

# CHAPTER EIGHTEEN

Wide awake.

Dan knew sleep wasn't going to come tonight. At least he was lying down. His body would get some rest even if his mind couldn't.

Rain sluiced down the gutters. Occasionally, a thick gust splashed rain onto the windows above his head. It was a normal spring rain.

Nothing else in his life was normal. Not for the past fifteen months. Now his dog was gone. He'd cried. Deep, heaving sobs. Tears soaked his pillow, but he'd merely gotten a towel from the hall linen closet and put it under his head.

He'd held himself together during the evening and tried to soothe Katie. He'd selected two pictures of Abbie and uploaded them, typed in her description, and printed out a LOST DOG flyer. He printed out twenty and gave ten to Katie to tack up around the neighborhood. He'd post some on his way to work tomorrow, make more copies at the office, and do a long search beyond their gated community. He'd also posted a plea on the community website reserved for lost pets, tag sales, and swapping concert and sports tickets. He'd e-mailed Abbie's veterinarian a poster to print and hang at her clinic. He'd call animal control tomorrow to be on the lookout for Abbie. He couldn't think of anything else to do. She had a chip, so if anyone found her, she'd be identified. Unless. Unless that person wanted to keep her. He couldn't think about that. His mind hummed that there was more he could do. He just couldn't see it.

He'd left Katie to Jill after printing the flyers. Katie was inconsolable. Part of her blamed him for Abbie's disappearance. She'd asked him if Abbie had gotten off her leash while he was running. That hurt. How could she think he'd not only let his beloved Abbie get away, but that he'd come home and pretend she was lost? He wouldn't lie to her. She must know that.

"Liar. Cheat," his father had said.

"Liar," Jill had screamed at him when she'd found out about his affair. "Liar. Liar. Lying bastard."

He protested he wasn't. He considered himself to be an honest man. He wanted to explain Bella was different. He wasn't really cheating. Bella was the first and only woman to hold his heart. She'd come back. He felt he was cheating Bella by being with Jill. He couldn't say any of that to Jill, but he still didn't think of himself as a liar or a cheater.

Jill wasn't a curser. She didn't have the foul vocabulary to call him all the terrible things she'd like so she stuck with liar. Alternating with traitor. A traitor to the family. And now, his daughter thought he was so treacherous that he'd lost the family dog and was lying to cover himself. He wanted desperately to be out of this nightmare.

# CHAPTER NINETEEN

By mid-morning Saturday, the sun returned. Abbie had not. They hadn't received any responses to the flyers other than neighbors who had called or e-mailed to say they'd stay on the lookout. Katie grilled him constantly. *Are you sure she didn't get off the leash when you ran with her? Could she have gotten in someone's car and been driven hundreds of miles from home? Could someone have stolen her? What would she be worth to an animal testing lab?*

That's when he'd lost his temper. "Shut up, Kaitlyn! Shut up!" he'd shouted when they'd been watching *Dancing With The Stars* after dinner two nights ago. Abbie's empty bed was in plain view as a silent reminder of loss. He didn't need Katie on his back, too.

Katie had looked shocked. He rarely raised his voice to her.

He'd stood and looked down at her. "I mean it, Kaitlyn. I know terrible things can happen. I don't need you to list them for me every minute I'm

101

home. Try thinking positive. Maybe a family took her in and didn't know about identification chips. Maybe she chased a squirrel over the fence and is exploring the woods. Maybe someone's found her and hasn't seen our flyers yet."

He knew he'd sounded hysterical. His suggestions were ludicrous. Even his ten-year-old knew that, but he hadn't want to hear it. He'd put on his running clothes and had run eight miles in the rain that night. Katie hadn't said much to him since then.

Jill seemed curiously disinterested in the whole problem. When he'd raised the subject the day before, Jill had responded calmly. "What's the point of both of us being upset around Kaitlyn? She's hurting. One of us," she'd looked at him with disappointment, "needs to check his feelings at the door and act like a parent." They hadn't discussed it since.

Dan had continued to go to the county's animal control center after work every day to ensure that Abbie hadn't slipped through any bureaucratic cracks. The pleasant young assistant manager kept reassuring him they'd call the minute Abbie showed up. Nevertheless, Dan felt the pull to check for himself each time, even if it meant walking between the walls of cages and seeing those other dogs whose families, if they had one, weren't looking quite so hard.

At least the sun had come out. Maybe it was a sign for optimism.

\*\*\*

Saturday afternoon, Dan watched a college basketball game on TV. He heard Jill come in the back door and slam her keys and purse on the breakfast bar. She'd been out to lunch with some of her girlfriends, which usually put her in a good mood. He'd stayed home to be with Katie. Not that much was required. She was in her room with the door closed and had refused the egg salad sandwich, apple, and iced tea he'd prepared for lunch.

He tensed at the sound of Jill's footsteps coming quickly toward the den.

"Haven't you humiliated me enough?" she cried at the doorway. Other than the fact that she was crying, she looked terrific. A pretty spring dress. Even her hair had been styled so she didn't look quite so haunted.

She walked over, snatched the remote from the sofa beside him, and turned off the TV.

He didn't know what he'd done. Not the faintest idea. "Jill, what are you talking about?"

"Humiliation. By you. Towards me." She was still standing near the TV.

"Could you be more specific?" he asked. "Maybe you should sit down."

"Yes, I'll be specific. Three of my friends and I were having a good time at the new Stony Point bistro. The sun was shining and we had a table outside. It was the first time I'd enjoyed myself in months. Everyone loved my haircut. I got compliments. I felt great.

"It was my turn to pay. We were finishing our coffee, enjoying the chocolate mints that came with the bill, and deciding whether to get our nails done

ADAM ZORZI

when the waiter asked me if I had another credit card because mine was no longer valid.

"The only other card I had with me was for Costco. We weren't lunching at Costco," she almost spat. "I didn't have enough cash so everyone paid for their own meal plus mine. I was the hostess and I couldn't pay for my lunch much less my guests. Humiliating.

"They all said it was nothing, but I saw the looks they gave each other. Pity. Poor, stupid Jill with the cheating husband who has now cut off her credit cards. Needless to say, we didn't go for manicures." She dissolved into more tears.

"What card?" he asked calmly.

She looked at him with swollen eyes.

"Don't pretend. Just tell me why you did it." She gulped.

Aside from the fact that Jill never got manicures, he didn't know what she was talking about. He ran through their credit cards in his head. American Express for big purchases and vacations. Visa for household purchases. Costco for bulk shopping and gas. She had a business credit card. Each had a debit card for their joint checking account. That was it. None of them had been closed.

"I haven't done anything. I haven't even looked at our balances since Abbie went missing."

She moved towards him. "Why not? You told me you had to check our finances daily. Sometimes more."

He shook his head. "Not really. I was being overly cautious."

What he couldn't say was that Bella had mocked

his day trading. He'd insisted he wasn't a day trader. He was a serious investor who analyzed everything. Bella had laughed. "Don't you realize Wall Street is one big casino and the house always wins? Do you really think you, all alone in your office, can outwit all the financial institutions all over the world with their twenty-four seven research staffs of thousands? Keeping in mind that a lot of corporations and institutions want to lose money for tax purposes. It's legal gambling."

His oversight sounded stupid phrased that way.

"I read *The Wall Street Journal*, *Forbes*, and watch MSNBC every day," he'd said defensively.

"Oh, Daniel, *The Wall Street Journal* is a gossip rag. Anything printed there was known weeks ago by the real players. Same for TV news and magazines. They're outdated before they're aired or printed. Who do you think feeds them?"

"They have investigative reporters," he'd answered in a huff.

"They have public relations firms feeding them carefully crafted press releases and leaked misinformation. Do you really think that little brunette with the skunk stripe in her hair could read a financial report much less analyze it? She's on-air eye candy." When Bella had seemed to realize she'd wounded him, she'd softened her position. "Daniel, I don't care if you have ten cents or ten million dollars. I don't want your family's nest egg to get broadsided because you're out of your depth. You're too smart for that. Too responsible."

"Dad always…"

Bella had stopped him. "Dan, your dad starting

saving and investing in a different era. Automated trades, global investments, and institutional cartels didn't exist. Following his example of being prudent with household finances is admirable, but you can't follow his exact practices. They're outdated."

He'd thought about what she'd said for a long time. She was a well-regarded securities lawyer in New York. She knew what she was talking about. He'd stopped day trading and immediately, felt less stressed about money.

"Dan? Why did you need to humiliate me even more?" cried Jill.

"What card?" he repeated.

She didn't answer, but went in the kitchen and pulled the offending card out of her wallet. He trailed her. "This one," she said as she handed it to him.

He looked down at their Visa card. It was valid. It was current. He always paid the balance before it was due so as not to incur interest. Their credit limit was $7,500. Had the card been stolen?

"Jill, I swear, nothing's wrong with this card unless someone has stolen the numbers and pushed it past the limit. I'll check right now."

He hustled upstairs into the small room they called the office. There was a desk in front of the window overlooking the front yard, bookshelves, and a computer with scanner and printer. He logged in and looked at the account.

Zero balance. Closed at cardholder's request. Two weeks ago.

That wasn't right. He hadn't closed it. Jill obviously hadn't. They'd been hacked.

He called the toll free customer service number, punched in numbers four times, and then heard himself shouting "representative" into the phone as he pounded his fist on the desk.

\*\*\*

Dinner didn't improve the atmosphere in the household.

"How long is Dad going to sleep in the guest room?" Katie asked as she picked out a warm jalapeno muffin and passed the basket to Dan. He didn't respond and kept his eyes on his fajita and black beans.

"Until his condition is better," said Jill as she dished out corn *insalata*.

"What condition?" Katie wasn't going to let this go.

"We've told you, Kaitlyn. He has a condition called sleep apnea, so he sleeps alone in a room with a machine if he needs it. The equipment is too noisy for me to sleep through."

"Josie said her dad slept in the guest room for three weeks and then moved out. He and her mom got a divorce and now he has a new wife."

"Kaitlyn, you shouldn't listen to gossip or repeat it." Jill sat and served herself.

"Are you and Dad going to get a divorce?" Katie pressed.

Jill didn't look at Dan. "I've never heard of sleep apnea causing divorce. Eat, before your food gets cold."

Katie rolled her eyes. "That's what you always

say when you don't want to talk about something."

"That's right. I want to eat dinner without gossipping." She took a bite of her fajita and turned to Dan. "Were you able to straighten things out with the credit card company?"

How could she ask that? The customer service representative who told him Jill Carter Ramsay had closed the account gave him the exact date and time it had been closed. Jill had staged that whole scene. He couldn't believe it. He'd thought Jill was completely guileless. She couldn't be that cunning and vindictive.

He'd vastly underestimated how much his affair with Bella hurt her. He believed Jill deserved someone younger, less serious, and more fun than he was. She deserved someone who loved her with his whole heart without any portion eternally reserved for another woman. He thought if he'd divorced her to marry Bella she'd recognize that and move forward. Now, he was the one who desperately wanted to keep things together for Katie. She was trying to hurt him somehow. One of her friends must have dreamed this scheme up. Jill simply didn't think that way, and she had no financial acumen. She entrusted him with all their financial and insurance matters. "Dan," Jill said again. "Is the credit card problem fixed?"

"Yes," he said playing along in front of Katie. "We'll get new cards next week. Apparently, it happened to customers whose accounts are serviced in Phoenix. They apologized."

"We were hacked?" asked Katie.

Dan sensed her excitement. "Not really. More

like a giant mistake."

"And you got them to apologize?" Katie seemed awestruck.

"I made a phone call."

"That's so cool, Dad. We got hacked and one phone call from you made them apologize. You're awesome." Maybe she was thawing a little after days of believing he'd lost Abbie and lied about it.

"I'd like to give them the telephone numbers of my friends so they can apologize to them, too," said Jill.

Dan smiled. "I didn't think of it. I should have. I'd love to see the looks on their faces."

"Me, too." Jill smiled.

# CHAPTER TWENTY

She didn't have to wait long in the classic southern gentleman's law firm reception area. Silence reigned. Thick antique carpets and heavy velvet drapes muffled sound. A tastefully dressed receptionist spoke in muted tones to callers.

After being offered coffee, tea, and cucumber water, she'd been left in privacy. Appointments seemed to be scheduled so clients didn't meet. From where she was seated, she had a view of the James River as it wound around and defined the city.

"Please, come this way. Mr. Bowles will see you now," said a conservatively-dressed young woman who escorted her to what must be a coveted corner office.

He rose to welcome her from behind his highly polished mahogany desk. He clasped her hand. "It's a pleasure to meet you, Mrs. Ramsay. Your father-in-law and my father were longtime friends. I'm sorry for your loss."

"Thank you," she said. "It was a terrible shock." He offered her the same beverages and she declined. He showed her to one of two Chippendale chairs in front of his desk and returned to his seat across from her.

William J. Bowles, III was identical to any number of affluent white men native to Richmond. He was neither tall nor short, had brown hair and blue eyes, and wore a navy suit from Beecroft and Bull with a rep tie. No doubt his shoes were black wing-tips from Church's. He was perfectly bland.

"I wasn't sure what you needed, so I pulled all the trust documents for your family. How would you like to proceed?" he asked smoothly.

"Mr. Bowles, my husband and I are having…marital difficulties." She closed her eyes and let her long lashes linger on her cheeks before looking up again. "He's admitted a long affair with another woman." She paused again, as if she were still bewildered by what her husband had done.

"I'm sorry to hear that, Mrs. Ramsay."

She nodded. "Naturally, I'm considering some form of separation, but my understanding is that everything we have, except for a small brokerage account and our home, is tied up in multiple trusts. Your father, of course, was my husband's family lawyer. He created trusts when my husband and I got married, and I believe more were created when our daughter was born. I'd like to know how complicated it would be to unwind—if that is the correct term—the trusts without damaging our daughter in any way.

"I also believe our daughter and I were named in one or two of my late father-in-law's trusts. I'm not sure of my position with regard to them now that he has died."

She took a deep breath as if mustering the courage to pose her questions.

"Could you explain them to me, Mr. Bowles? That's not breaking any confidence, is it?" She dabbed at her eyes. "I'm ashamed to admit I know nothing about investments. I don't know the difference between a trust and a will." She gave a small shrug. "I work in marketing. My husband handles our finances."

The lawyer's face remained unchanged. "I'm sorry to hear that you and your husband are considering ending your marriage. It's my obligation as your attorney to urge you to reconsider. Divorce is costly and difficult even in the best circumstances."

"Are there best circumstances for divorce?" she asked softly.

"There are some that are more amicable than others," he rephrased and smiled slightly.

"My husband has been abusive, Mr. Bowles," she whispered. "I don't want our daughter to grow up thinking that's acceptable." She folded her beautifully manicured hands in her lap and sat very still.

"I'm sorry." His manner softened towards her. "That changes things, of course."

"Am I allowed to know about the trusts?"

"There's no confidentiality problem with your trusts nor those of your father-in-law in which you or your daughter, Kaitlyn Carter Ramsay, are beneficiaries."

She made a little noise that she hoped sounded

like gratitude.

"Mrs. Ramsay, estate planning usually involves three types of instruments—a will, a trust, and some form of insurance. Wills are documents in which a person specifies who should inherit whatever he owns at the time of his death. That sometimes causes a beneficiary—a person who inherits something—to pay taxes he didn't anticipate.

"Trusts eliminate that problem. A trust instead of a person is created to own something Assets owned by a trust may be bought and sold and donated at any time instead of being linked to a life event like death. Trusts aren't considered part of an estate and don't pay estate taxes. Your family estate planning doesn't include insurance."

She nodded. "Thank you. I understand about the will, but I'm still not sure about trusts. Do different trusts own different things?"

"Yes, for example, a person could establish a trust for his artwork. There are some advantages in making the owner of the art a trust instead of a person. The disadvantage is that the person gives up control over the artwork. A trustee, not the original owner, makes decisions about when it's a good time to sell a painting or buy a piece of sculpture or donate a piece to a museum."

"I understand. Thank you, Mr. Bowles." She brightened a bit as she spoke. "What a good example."

He beamed at her praise.

"Your original question is a good one. When a trust instead of a person owns something, it usually can't be considered property in certain legal actions such as divorce or bankruptcy."

"Oh, I see." She looked crestfallen.

"Let's start with the educational trust your father-in-law established for Miss Ramsay. Funds from that trust can only be applied to an educational institution such as an elementary or secondary school, college or university, or professional or vocational institute. Whatever assets remain after Miss Ramsay completes her education will be distributed to her when she turns thirty-one. Your father-in-law's death doesn't affect the trust at all. Trust assets will continue to pay for Miss Ramsay's education."

She looked confused. "I'm sorry to sound foolish, but what do you mean by trust assets?" A flash of pity crossed his face.

"Assets are what the trusts owns. Like the example of an artwork trust. Artwork is the asset of that trust. The assets of Miss Ramsay's trust are a mix of cash, stocks, and bonds. Without assets assigned to it, a trust is empty."

She tried to appear surprised. "You mean we could have trusts with no money in them?"

He nodded. "It's possible, although unlikely."

Her hands started to shake. She must have paled because the young woman who had escorted her into the office now entered with a glass of water as if by magic. Mr. Bowles must have silently signaled her.

"May I get you something, Mrs. Ramsay? Do you feel all right?" she asked. She probably had smelling salts in her pocket for faint-hearted female clients.

"I just need a few moments, please. This is all so…unsettling."

"Of course." Bowles rose. "My secretary and I will step outside for a bit. Feel free to rest on the sofa."

Bowles returned in about fifteen minutes and walked to where she was now seated on the sofa.

"Better?"

"Yes, thank you. The water helped and I did lie down until the spell passed."

"Good." He pulled up the knees of his trousers to prevent creasing before he sat on the sofa. "This is a distressing time for you. Why don't we table our discussion. I'll examine the documents, summarize the contents, and itemize the assets associated with each trust. I'll note if any of them refer specifically to dissolution of the marriage."

"That would be so helpful," she said softly.

"We can meet again after you've had a chance to review them."

"You're so thoughtful. Thank you."

"It shouldn't take more than two days to prepare the summary. I'll call you when it's ready."

A look of horror crossed her face. "No, Mr. Bowles, please don't do that." She dabbed at her eyes again. Tissues sat on the end table next to the sofa. She took a handful. Her voice quivered. "I can't risk my husband seeing any of this. May I call your secretary in two days to ask if it's ready and make arrangements to pick it up?"

He nodded. "I understand. I'm sure Mr. Ramsay is aware of the terms and assets of the trusts, but I understand your need for discretion. You don't want

Mr. Ramsay to know you've made inquiries."

"You don't have to tell him about my...inquiry?"

"No, Mrs. Ramsay. I'm not obligated to inform Mr. Ramsay of your request. The two of you are equal beneficiaries." He was so helpful, yet he failed to mention he'd tell Daniel in a heartbeat if asked directly about her questions.

Bowles extended his hand to help her to her feet and asked his secretary to escort her to the elevator and down to the lobby. She would have considered this a gentlemanly gesture had she not guessed the real purpose was to limit any liability should she hurt herself on her way out.

# CHAPTER
# TWENTY-ONE

## April

Damn. Could his life get any worse? Dan ran through the park without pacing himself. His father had died. He'd lost his dog, he was still sleeping in the guest room, and now, he'd lost his job. Reduction in Force.

It had always been a possibility. The governor had built his campaign on eliminating government waste. Dan couldn't argue with the logic. He had the most seniority in the department and made the most money. Having overseen the installation of a new system, he could be replaced with a less experienced person for half his salary. The system itself eliminated the need for three jobs.

He couldn't get full pension benefits for another fifteen years. He wasn't worried about the long term. He'd been single until he was forty and lived frugally. He and Jill were comfortable and had retirement savings. He'd just inherited a sizeable amount from his father. In the meantime, he needed to find a job. Like employers were eager to hire men over age fifty.

He ran out of energy and plopped himself under a young magnolia tree beside the running path. A petal fell on him. He reflexively picked it up and smelled it. Bella. Bella loved magnolias.

Dan put his head between his knees and sobbed. He held his knees with his arms and rocked himself back and forth. He didn't know how long he did that, but rain started to drip and then fall on him.

He got up and walked home.

\*\*\*

"Dan, what's wrong?"

He showered after his run, put on sweats, and lay down on his single bed. He thought he might nap before Jill and Katie got home. Sleep was his answer to everything. Problems didn't go away and situations didn't change, but he was blissfully unaware of them while he slept.

Jill walked into the room, sat on the bed, and felt his forehead. It was the first time she'd touched him voluntarily in a long time. "You're warm and a little clammy. How do you feel?"

There was no positive spin. "I got fired."

"Dan. Why?" Worry creased Jill's forehead.

"Nothing personal. Part of the division's plan to streamline."

"You said when the launch of a new system was announced two years ago that this could happen."

"And it did."

"Anyone else?" Just like Jill. Worried that other people were hurting tonight, too.

"Three analysts. Two of them saw it coming and had just been waiting to take new jobs. The third wants to try staying at home. She's got three kids."

"Janice?" Amazing. She remembered everyone's name.

He nodded.

"Her husband has a good job, though, doesn't he? They'll be okay."

"Yes, they will. So will we."

He wanted so badly to reach up and stroke her face in reassurance, but didn't think it would have the intended effect.

"Are you sure?" Jill had a terrible poker face. She was scared.

"Absolutely. We can go over things later, but we have plenty of savings, the house and cars are free and clear, and Katie, sorry, Kaitlyn's school is paid by her trust. We'll be fine. We just have to be careful."

"You're not saying this just to keep me from worrying?"

"No. I'm confident we'll be fine. You have a job. You still like it, don't you?"

"Very much. I got a new client. Pop-up stores. It's going to be such fun coming up with a marketing plan to build the brand."

"Congratulations. Are you the lead?"

She made a face. "Co-lead with Chloe. She's a pain, but I can finesse her. Dinner's almost ready. Red beans and rice. Do you feel like eating?"

"I don't think my stomach can take that. I ran faster than I should have. I'm light-headed."

She moved her hand from his forehead to his wrist to check his pulse. If he didn't know better, he'd have said she was a champion girl scout. She was superior. She'd taken wilderness survival courses and could treat anything from snakebites, frostbite, to cardiac problems. Or at least recognize them. She'd been invaluable that awful day Rob came to tell them of his father's death.

"A little fast. I'll get you an aspirin. Sleep for a bit, and I'll bring you something to eat later. Are you warm enough?"

He hesitated.

She pulled the quilt up to his neck and took a blanket from the closet and folded it so he could easily reach it if he needed it.

When she was back with the aspirin and a glass of water, he asked how Katie was. "Still missing Abbie. I can't imagine what happened to her. I hope she comes home soon."

"Me, too."

She turned out the light and left the room.

# CHAPTER
# TWENTY-TWO

Dan sat in bed with pillows behind his back eating dinner on a tray. "Perfect," he said.

"There's nothing better than scrambled eggs, whole wheat toast, and orange juice to cure just about anything," smiled Jill. "You can have ginger ale for dessert."

She'd turned on a low light in the room. It was enough but not too much. Her features were softened by the light.

"What happened on your run?" she asked in a solemn tone.

"I ran too fast and then hit the wall. This job thing is just the cherry on top of everything else. I sat under a magnolia tree and had a good cry."

"Oh, Dan," she look small and young.

"Then the rain came and you know the rest."

"Did you sleep?"

"Yes, it felt good. I think my temperature's down and I don't feel light-headed."

"Do you think Mørk is coming?"

"Mørk has taken up residence. I've been on meds since Dad died. I see Dr. Spellman Tuesday. I don't think I need any adjustments before then."

"Okay. That's means a stricter schedule, too."

"It'll be harder now without a job to occupy me for most of a day."

"You're not going back at all? Not even for two weeks?"

"No. Someone in Human Resources called each one of us in for a meeting and had us sign a release that we understood the circumstances of our terminations. We were asked to leave. My salary for the final two weeks will be automatically deposited in our bank account."

"We'll really be all right?"

"Yes, Jill. I have a packet of termination papers to go through. You and I can go through our accounts and see if we need to make any changes, but we're okay. I promise."

A shadow flitted across her face.

No, his promises weren't worth much these days. "There's no need to panic. Dr. Spellman will encourage me to take a break before job-hunting. I'm going to have to re-brand myself. I've worked for the state my entire career. I don't know how to break into the private sector.

"Maybe it's time to do something new. I hear rap DJs make good money." She laughed.

"Okay, where do I go to rap DJ school?"

"Your daughter's room, I think." She smiled.

"It's not the rap I mind; it's the background. I can't understand the words."

"Dan, you can't hear the words," she teased.

He was hesitant to make a suggestion, but decided he had nothing to lose. "Jill, what I'd really like is to take a vacation. I want to get away. I want to hike, climb rocks, ski, anything to keep my mind quiet."

She didn't say anything immediately.

"I'd have to look at Kaitlyn's calendar."

"No, I want to be spontaneous. Around your job, of course, but Kaitlyn can stay with Suzanne and Rob or Sophia's parents or Josie's. Hell, your mother could come up for a week."

"You're either desperate for a vacation or delirious."

"Hey, you're the one with the problem with her. She doesn't bother me."

"Dan, I don't know if I'm ready."

"I'm not going to push. I'm not asking to be back in your bed. I just want to go away and I want to be with you. No strings."

"You're right. I need a break, too. Let's do it."

"Yes," he pumped his fist in the air. "We can do travel searches tomorrow."

She stood and took his tray. "I'll bring you ginger ale, and then it's lights out for you."

He hadn't felt so hopeful in a long time.

# CHAPTER

# TWENTY-THREE

She waited quietly in the Wealth Management reception area of Virginia's largest bank in downtown Richmond. Daniel's father had loved the feeling of having money in the main office of a bank. He'd said it seemed solid and secure and thought customers received better attention. At least, the staff dressed better. He'd hated to go into a branch to find women in cheap, brightly-colored pantsuits and men in shirtsleeves rather than a suit.

"Mrs. Ramsay, I'm sorry to have kept you waiting." A well-dressed, polished middle-aged woman introduced herself. "Please come this way."

She stood and followed the banker into a large elevator and down one floor to the safe deposit area.

"Do you have your key?" The woman admonished herself. "Of course you do. That's why you're here." The banker opened the vault door, and together, the two women unlocked the Ramsay locker. The banker pulled out the long box and carried it into one of the four nearby private rooms. She placed the box on the counter and pulled out a Chippendale chair upholstered in Williamsburg blue damask.

"I hope you'll be comfortable here. Would you like coffee or tea, Mrs. Ramsay?"

"Thank you, no."

"Then, I'll leave you. Just press the green button on the side of the counter when you're ready. I'll come get you. Feel free to press the white button if you need assistance."

"Thank you. You've been very helpful."

The banker backed out of the room.

After examining the room for security cameras and finding none, she proceeded with her mission. She opened the box and slowly examined its contents. The senior Ramsay's birth and marriage certificates. No other documents. Rob probably had everything else.

Gold coins. She counted seventy-five. In today's market that would be just under $100,000. Daniel probably considered it rainy day money.

Daniel's great-grandmother's jewelry included a gold wedding ring, several gold bracelets, and what must have been an engagement ring. She took out a jeweler's loupe and examined the delicate filigree ring with what appeared to be a one carat Ideal cut diamond. Nice.

The earrings were breath-taking—diamond open cut drops, ruby and diamond double cluster drops, and sapphire cabochon clips surrounded by diamonds. A heavy diamond and pearl brooch was the last piece. The cut and clarity of the stones from each piece were very good.

No girl would ever wear these. Even if the stones were reset, a twenty-first century woman wouldn't want anything here. Why was Daniel keeping them? Especially now that he'd lost his job. Daniel was sentimental, but this was too much. Keeping tens of thousands of dollars of heavy, ornate Russian jewelry in a box when the family was on a tight budget seemed too sentimental. Surely, there was a market for them with wealthy collectors.

She made a startled noise when she found a picture of the baby taken in the hospital. Of course. Daniel was superstitious and a bit anxious. He probably thought if a tornado tore through their neighborhood and leveled their house, they wouldn't be crying over a lost baby picture.

Daniel had mentioned keeping his childhood toys before his parents' estate sale. There were Batman action figures—Batman, Robin, The Joker, The Penguin, Catwoman, and the Batmobile along with The Beatles trading cards and a 45 rpm record of "Proud Mary" by Creedence Clearwater Revival. She'd always preferred Tina Turner's version. She could never remember who wrote it. There was also a ticket stub from a Washington Redskins game dated 1975. Daniel must have gone with his father and Rob.

There was nothing else here. No love notes. No greeting cards. No letters.

She breathed a sigh of relief and pressed the green buzzer.

# CHAPTER
# TWENTY-FOUR

"Are you sure we can afford for me to go?" Jill asked again.

"Yes," he responded impatiently. "You're just driving sixty miles to a meet. Your bike is tuned up. You've got gear. You packed food. The only cost is gas. It's nothing. Besides, Kaitlyn's at a sleepover, so there's no need to rush back. You said someone in the club lives in Fredericksburg and offered a place to crash if any of you are too tired to drive home, right?"

He'd loaded her bike onto the car yesterday afternoon because he knew it would be still be dark this morning if she left at the proper time. Standing in the kitchen, now dressed in her thin warm-up clothes, Jill looked small and helpless. "Dan, I'm afraid we're going to lose everything. That Kaitlyn will have to leave St. Margaret's. We can't get a refund on her summer camp. We can't live on my salary." Her voice quivered.

"Stop it, Jill." His patience was shot. It was too early for him to be up. He seemed to unable to soothe Jill's irrational concerns. "We went through our finances together. The house and cars are paid for. Our expenses are low. Kaitlyn's trust pays for her education through veterinary school or a PhD if she wants it. We just inherited money from my father. I'll get another job. It might take longer because I'm over fifty, but I'll find one." He stopped short of asking her to trust him. "Why are you thinking about this now? Do you not feel well? You know I think you're pushing yourself. You had major surgery in August and have been hitting the gym hard for the past few months."

"I feel okay. "

"Then what? Are you nervous?"

She nodded.

"Jill, go. Concentrate on something other than what's going on here. You'll be with your team. You've been planning to do this one hundred mile race for two years. You've already lost months of training. I'd prefer you not do it this year, but if you're determined to compete you've got to be prepared. Go. Just go."

He could see traces of tears welling in her yes. She'd cried so much he'd become immune to her tears. He sometimes thought of them as manipulative not sadness, but he knew that wasn't the case with Jill. God, he hated that haircut. It emphasized her soft brown eyes that seemed sunken and defeated.

He didn't have the energy to go through another round of reassurance and plans. In the past three days, Jill had changed her plans as often as she questioned whether she should go. She wanted to make the trip in one day, but she wasn't in peak shape. She might not be able to make the roundtrip drive and train. Maybe she should spend the night with another cycler. Maybe she should attempt the roundtrip. Maybe she shouldn't go at all. He couldn't discuss it any further. She should go, train, and see how she felt about making the return trip. Done.

"Good luck," he said and walked towards the stairs. He needed to work on his résumé. A beautiful spring Saturday and he'd be at the computer researching jobs. He intended to sleep for a few hours first.

"I'll call if I'm going to be later than ten." She left through the back door.

Later, sitting alone in front of the computer overlooking the magnolia trees in the front yard, Dan grew restless. The sun was out and the weather was warm. There was life outside. Here, in this house, there was nothing but silence and his dark thoughts. Mørk bayed.

*Shut up, Mørk.* He wasn't going to squander this beautiful day inside. He was going for a long run. Outside this neighborhood, this city, this county.

Dan changed into his running clothes, grabbed his keys, and fled.

\*\*\*

Dan returned about seven. He felt less stressed and had a clearer mind. He'd needed to get away

129

and just run until he couldn't. He still hadn't gotten used to coming home to a house without Abbie. He missed her greeting of frenzied barks. No one had ever been so enthusiastic to see him so consistently.

On the way to the stairs and a shower, he stepped into the den and removed Abbie's bed. He put it in the utility closet where it could be stored until she came back. In the meantime, he didn't have to look at the constant reminder that Abbie wasn't home.

He showered, put on his oldest sweats, grilled a steak, steamed broccoli, and poured a new red wine. He ate in front of the TV. Some British game show, but it was just mindless enough to be entertaining. When he finished eating, he loaded and ran the dishwasher. He did a load of laundry, too, including the clothes he had worn that day. His muscles were fatigued from the long run and his book wasn't holding his interest. He went to bed in the guest room about eleven-thirty.

The sound of rain against the windows woke him about three o'clock the next morning. He swung out of bed and padded into the office to make sure the windows were closed. He hadn't turned on the alarm because Jill would be home late. When he looked out the side window, he didn't see Jill's car.

Down the hall, he quietly opened the door to the master bedroom. No Jill. The bed had been made and not slept in. He was unsettled. Jill usually called if she was going to be late. Of course, anything was possible with her now. She could have stayed overnight in Fredericksburg, not wanting to make the drive back to Richmond. Or hell, she could have left him and wasn't ever coming back. He went back

130

to his single bed and fell into a deep sleep.

# CHAPTER
# TWENTY-FIVE

Dan slept until almost noon Sunday. He went downstairs and made coffee. While he waited for it to brew, he sat at the breakfast bar, drank orange juice, and opened the laptop to read the paper. Continued good weather. Cavaliers were doing squat in baseball. Grass seed was on sale at Costco.

He drank black coffee and ate a bowl of cereal. He wondered if he should call Sophia's parents to see if Katie was okay. No, she'd think he was treating her like a baby.

He'd run hard and long yesterday. His calves ached. Maybe he should call the club and see if he could get a half hour massage. That, and some steam, would ease his muscles.

The landline rang three times, but he didn't answer it. He'd stopped answering it months ago. Jill's friends had no problem telling him just what they thought of his cheating if he picked up. There wasn't anyone he wanted to talk to. Katie would call on his cell if she needed him. He wasn't sure what time he was supposed to pick her up if Jill didn't get home in time. Jill had probably told him, but he'd expected her to be home.

At the club, his masseur Orlo noted how tight his legs were. "Did you run a marathon yesterday?"

"No, just harder than I should have in sand. It was gorgeous outside, and I just kept going."

"Time got away from you, huh? Don't run for a couple of days. Sit in the Jacuzzi. Take some steam. You'll be okay."

Dan got off the table.

"You've got some big bruises on your right thigh."

"Yeah, spring cleaning." He didn't want to admit to Orlo that he'd fallen out of his single bed one night and banged his thigh on the night table. Damn, he missed that king sized bed.

In the locker room, after he'd showered and dressed, he met Henry, his neighbor, who asked if he wanted to play some video games.

"Man, it's too nice to be inside. What else you got?"

"Shuffleboard," laughed Henry.

"Okay."

"You're kidding, right?"

"No. I'm on the DL for a couple of days. That works for me. You?"

Henry, who wasn't even forty, and Dan played outside for about an hour. Dan won easily. When they finished, Dan declined Henry's offer of going for a beer.

Dan looked at his watch. "I think I've got to pick

up my kid. She's at a sleepover."

"Where?"

"At the Cruz's. Sophia's birthday, I think."

"Viv went to that, but she had to be picked up by noon. I think Sophia's grandparents were coming for a family party."

"Wow. I'd better call. Jill made the arrangements, but she's off on a cycling trial this weekend."

He hated the look Henry had in his eyes. Henry didn't say anything, but Dan felt his demeanor change to look at him as a bumbling, neglectful parent.

"Later," said Dan and he walked to his car.

# CHAPTER
# TWENTY-SIX

Dan's stomach fell through the floorboard of his car when he turned into the neighborhood and saw two police cars parked further down the lane in front of his house. An officer was standing in the driveway to prevent entry. A few neighbors had gathered to see what was going on from a respectful distance.

*Please, let Katie be okay.* He didn't think not picking her up on time would be a problem. He hoped she hadn't walked home by herself. Images of abducted, raped, and murdered children from TV crime shows whirred in his head.

He stopped the car, jumped out, and ran to the first uniformed person he saw.

"Katie. Is Katie all right?" he shouted.

"Mr. Ramsay?" asked the officer in the driveway.

"Yes, yes. Daniel Ramsay. My daughter is Katie, Kaitlyn with a K Ramsay. Is she hurt? Where is she?"

A more senior officer offered his hand and introduced himself as Lieutenant Winston. He had a partner—a detective—who was also introduced.

"Mr. Ramsay, let's go inside."

"Tell me, please tell me, is Katie okay?" he begged.

The two investigators herded him towards the house and up the front steps. The officer who'd been standing in the driveway took the steps two at a time and handed Lieutenant Winston Dan's keys. Dan had been so crazed with fear he'd stopped the car and hadn't turned it off before he leapt out.

"We're not here about Kaitlyn," said one of them.

Dan went limp with relief. They grabbed him under his arms, unlocked the door, and led him into the house.

"Is there an alarm code? Mr. Ramsay?"

Dan shook his head. He hadn't turned on the alarm just to go to the health club.

"Is this about Abbie?" he asked longingly.

The two investigators looked at each other. "Abbie? Who is Abbie, Mr. Ramsay?"

"My dog. Our dog. She went missing a while ago."

"No. We don't know anything about Abbie. Why don't you sit down." They steered him to a velvet wing chair in the living room. He sat. Velvet bristles brushed his thighs and the back of his knees. He hated this chair.

Winston stayed with Dan while the other got a glass of water from the kitchen. Dan dutifully drank it when offered. He was utterly confused. His stomach muscles were contracting every few seconds. The investigators re-introduced themselves. "Mr. Ramsay, I'm Detective Elba from the Henrico County Police and this is Lieutenant Winston from the Virginia Bureau of Criminal Investigation." They didn't introduce a uniformed young woman stationed in the foyer by the front door.

Winston looked familiar. Like he'd seen him on TV. What did they want?

"Mr. Ramsay, a vehicle was found parked overnight in Lake Anna State Park off Route 208 in Spotsylvania. It's registered in your name. A blue Kia Sorento. Model Year 2012. Is that your car?"

"Yes," said Dan. He still wasn't connecting anything. "Detectives, I've got to find my daughter. If you don't have her, where is she?"

"Where is she supposed to be?" asked Detective Elba.

"At a sleepover. I thought I had to pick her up at four o'clock, but a friend at the health club said the kids had to be picked up by noon. I haven't heard from her all day."

"Where is this sleepover?"

"In Heritage Hills. Sophia's birthday. Sophia Cruz. Her parents are Anthony and Samantha. I've got to call them." He started to lunge for the landline in the foyer. Winston put out his arm to stop him. "Just a minute." Winston walked over to the small table where the red light was flashing on the landline. "I'll dial the number. What is it?"

"I don't know. Just press the directory and Cruz

will come up. It'll dial automatically if you press Call."

Winston looked over the phone, made a few motions, and spoke into the phone. He identified himself, confirmed that Samantha Cruz was on the line, and handed the receiver to Dan.

"Samantha? Where's Katie?"

"Dan, what's going on? Why are the police at your house?"

"Goddammit Samantha, where's Katie?" He was approaching hysteria. Cold sweat trickled down his neck into his shirt collar. He struggled to breathe.

"She's right here. We expected her to be picked up at noon. We tried calling, but no one answered. We have family guests now." A hint of indignation colored her tone. Jill never would have gotten the time wrong.

"I don't care about your guests. Is my daughter all right?"

"Yes, Dan, of course she is. She's in the great room with Sophia and her cousins."

Winston took the phone out of Dan's hand.

"Ma'am. I'd like Kaitlyn to stay there for a while. Don't let her leave, and don't let anyone other than a trooper in a car clearly marked as a Virginia State Trooper vehicle collect her. Be sure to ask for identification. You can call me at this number if anything out of the ordinary happens."

Winston turned his back to give her his direct number and finish the call.

# CHAPTER
# TWENTY-SEVEN

"What's going on? Why can't I see Katie? Why does she have to stay at Sophia's?" Dan's questions tumbled out.

Detective Elba spoke. "Mr. Ramsay, about your car...."

"What about it?" Dan snapped.

"Why is your car there? Was it stolen?"

"No, no, nothing like that." Why were these guys hounding him about the car when clearly his child was more important?

"Mr. Ramsay, the car was parked overnight. Overnight parking is prohibited without a camping sticker. How did your car come to be there when you're here?"

Dan exhaled. Tension flowed out of him. He sat. "I'm sorry. I didn't understand. My wife drove that car to a cycling trial near Fredericksburg yesterday."

"One of those three-day events?"

"No, this was a practice not a sanctioned event. It was prep for the one hundred mile race."

"So, your wife. What's her name?"

"Jill. Jill Carter Ramsay."

"Mrs. Ramsay is a semi-professional cycler? Does that mean she's on a team? Travels a lot?"

Cycling was hard to explain. Most people only knew about the *Tour de France* and Lance Armstrong's doping scandal. "No, nothing like that. She's an avid cyclist and member of a local club. They have regional trials to prepare for larger events like the one hundred mile race. This was her first trial with her team since she had surgery just before Labor Day. She doesn't really travel."

"Just overnights?"

"Not even that. She said she'd be back last night, but I thought she overestimated her stamina to train and drive three or four hours roundtrip, depending on traffic. One of the club members lives in Fredericksburg and offered housing for out-of-towners."

Elba nodded. "What time do you expect her?"

"Soon. Katie's supposed to be home by now. Jill will want to make sure she's ready for school tomorrow. Jill has work tomorrow, too."

"She hasn't called to let you know when to expect her?"

"No. I haven't spoken to her since she left yesterday morning."

Winston moved to stand in front of Dan. "This seems like a rather loose arrangement. Mrs. Ramsay left yesterday, didn't come home last night, and hasn't called. You don't think that's odd?"

Dan probably looked as sheepish as he felt. "We've been having problems. I assumed she needed a night off when she could get one. Katie was at the sleepover. I'd be here if Abbie came home. Jill had an opportunity to relax with her teammates."

"She didn't tell you what time to pick up Kaitlyn today?"

"She did. I thought four o'clock, but obviously, I got it wrong. I forgot to check the family calendar in the kitchen." Dan stared at them. Still unsure why they were there. Winston stepped back. "Can Katie come home, now?"

"We have a few more questions. Mr. Ramsay, is it possible that she went elsewhere for the weekend? The cycling trip was a cover story? Maybe she met a friend and left her car at the park?" asked the one with a northern accent.

"That's a stretch. She wouldn't need a cover story to go away for the weekend. She worked out at the health club a lot to be in shape for this trial."

"If she did, do have any idea who this friend might be?" Elba. That was his name.

"Jill has dozens of friends. I don't know them all." Jill had friends from college, work, and the neighborhood. Her best friends were from her quilting group. Mostly, Jill was outgoing and fun to be with and lots of people considered her their friend.

"Mr. Ramsay, might she have met another man for the weekend?"

*Wham*. Maybe all that working out had been to get in shape for another man. "Detective Elba, it's possible. I hope not. I hope we're working things out."

Elba conferred with Winston. "Mr. Ramsay, is there anyone we can call for you? To come sit with you until she comes home?"

"Do you think that's important?"

Detective Elba nodded. "It's not a bad idea."

"My brother. Rob. Robert Ramsay. His number is on the landline, too. You make the call just like when you called Sophia's parents." Why did they drag in someone else? Maybe they needed someone to drive him to get the car.

Winston made the call to Rob. "Mr. Ramsay, the message light is blinking. Do you mind if we listen to the messages?

Dan shrugged again. "Go ahead." He was certain none of the calls were for him.

# CHAPTER
# TWENTY-EIGHT

Rob was admitted by Lieutenant Winston. Suzanne had come, too.

"Everybody all right?" Rob eyed the scene curiously. They sat on the uncomfortable rose colored velvet couch across from Dan.

"Thanks for coming. Hey, Suzanne. I don't know what's going on. I think they want me to pick up the car Jill left overnight. Parked illegally."

Suzanne pounced. "Why would they do that? Where's Jill? Where's Kaitlyn?"

He explained about the cycling trial, his failure to pick up Katie on time, and his uncertainty about when Jill would return.

"Why are two investigators here? State troopers could've just had the car towed." Suzanne sounded perplexed. "Why did they want us to come over?"

Rob interrupted. "Suzanne, could you round up something to drink, please? Ask the officers if they want anything, too. I'd like iced tea or club soda.

Dan?"

"Either one," Dan said. Suzanne made sense. Why were the cops here?

"Dan, something's not right," said Rob. He moved to sit on the footstool next to the wing chair. "Think about it. They must think she's done something."

"Like what? They've already asked if she might have gone somewhere else for the weekend."

"Did you fight before she left?" Rob's question seemed natural. He knew about Bella.

"Not really. She was fretting about whether we should spend money on gas and I told her to just go. She left and I went back upstairs."

"No shouting?"

Dan snorted. "We're way past the shouting stage. She cries or looks at me with those haunted eyes. I don't know how much more of this I can take."

"What do you mean? "

"I can't sleep in the guest room forever. Katie's eventually going to realize it's not because I have sleep apnea and need a noisy machine. If Jill's friends know and their husbands know, then their kids know, too. Kids talk. If she's going to hear that her parents' marriage is on the rocks, I'd rather it be from Jill and me than one of the Mean Girls."

Rob gave him a blank stare.

"The clique of cool girls at St. Margaret's who pick on younger girls. Jill needs to decide whether she wants to keep our family together or not."

"Give her a break, Dan. You were screwing Bella for more than a year. You planned to divorce Jill and marry Bella and you told Jill that was your plan. That's not something she's going to get over in what—two months, three months?"

"I know it's my fault, but I can't keep beating myself up or letting her beat me up. She ought to know by now if she wants to stay married or not."

"Have you been in touch with Bella?" asked Rob.

Dan vigorously shook his head. "No. Absolutely not. I promised Jill I'd never speak to her and I haven't."

"You've been tempted, though, right?"

"Of course, I have. I love her. She's in my skin, but I don't want to put Katie through a divorce. I don't want to have to unwind all our trusts. Jill and I don't have a dime in separate accounts. I thought Jill would forgive me. I didn't realize how devastated she was. She's so young, Rob. She's not even forty. She'd have men lined up for her."

"What about Bella? Has she been in touch?"

Dan shook his head again. "Not since she sent that email to Jill. I'd forgotten what a temper she has. I was blown away that she contacted Jill."

"Two club sodas," said Suzanne as she walked in with a tray, napkins, and two small bowls of nuts. She handed a glass to each of them and turned to offer cola to the officers. She put the bowls down and returned to the kitchen.

"Mr. Ramsay?" Detective Elba came back in the living room. "There's a long list of calls for Mrs. Ramsay, most of them asking where she is and if she's all right. We'd like to go through the list with you."

Rob spoke before Dan had a chance. "This seems

like an awful lot of questions for an illegally parked car. What's really going on?" Dan started to speak. "No, Dan, I don't think you should answer any more questions without a lawyer."

"Mr. Ramsay, can we go through this list?" persisted Detective Elba.

What was going on? Why was Rob suggesting a lawyer? Why hadn't the car just been towed? Without the structure of a work week, Dan's ability to focus had diminished. Dr. Spellman had increased the dosage of one med, but it hadn't become effective yet.

"Detective Elba," said Dan, "I'm trying to be helpful here, but I don't understand the problem. If you need me to get the car, I will. Otherwise, I want Katie to come home. Jill will be home later tonight."

Elba moved closer to Dan. "Mr. Ramsay, let me be clear. It's after seven o'clock. The parking lot is closed for another night. Your wife hasn't returned for the car. If she planned to drive it back tonight, she can't get it."

"Then her friends will drive her home," Dan said reasonably.

"Her friends are calling asking her whereabouts." Elba pushed back. "Mr. Ramsay, the car was found with a bicycle on a rack attached to it."

Dan's eyes widened. "Jill just left it there? In a public parking lot?"

Elba nodded.

Jill didn't like to leave her bike on the car rack overnight in their locked garage. Cyclers always worried that someone would tamper with their equipment. She'd never leave it in a public park unless she was sick or hurt. "That doesn't sound like Jill. She wouldn't leave it unprotected. She must have over-extended herself and been too tired to drive or injured herself and not have been able to drive."

Rumblings started in Dan's bowels.

"That's important if it's out of character. Mrs. Ramsay hasn't called. Her teammates haven't called to let you know she's with them."

Dan looked at Rob. Jill wouldn't have left her bike. If she'd been forced to, she or one of her teammates would have called. She might be in the hospital. "Dan, I think what the detective means is that Jill might be missing. Is that right, Detective?"

"I think there's cause for concern," Elba responded.

Dan suddenly feared the worst.

# CHAPTER
# TWENTY-NINE

"Missing?" Dan sat down hard in the wing chair. "You mean kidnapped? Foul play? You think something's happened to her?"

"We're concerned, Mr. Ramsay. There were eleven calls on voicemail before the box was filled. One was from Mrs. Cruz about picking up Kaitlyn. The rest were from people in the cycling club asking where she was and expressing concern that she hadn't made it to the trial."

"Didn't make it to the trial?" Dan was incredulous. She'd left the bike in a public space and hadn't met her teammates? Could merely driving to Fredericksburg have tired her?

"It would help if we could compare the names on the cycling club roster with the callers. Maybe a name would jog your memory about how seriously we should take the calls," said Detective Elba.

"The team roster may be in the kitchen. There's a drawer for things like that. Katie's school directory,

Jill's staff directory, maybe the cycling club. If not, there's one on the family computer."

"I know where it is," volunteered Suzanne who headed toward the kitchen. "I'll be right back."

"Mr. Ramsay, did Mrs. Ramsay take her cell phone with her?"

"Of course. She always wants a way to be in touch with Katie."

"You're sure?"

"I didn't see it when she left, but I wasn't looking for it. I assume she had it. She never goes anywhere without it."

"Have you tried calling her on her cell?" asked Elba.

"No. I didn't think she was missing. I didn't have any reason to call her." No reason to call his wife. The one he was presumably trying to keep. He hadn't called to see how training was going, whether she was too exhausted to drive home, or to say that he missed her. He'd screwed up. He didn't deserve Jill.

"Would you try now, Mr. Ramsay?"

"Sure. Let me get my cell." He stopped. "It's in my gym bag in the car. I didn't bring it in."

"We'll get your gym bag."

"Here's the list," Suzanne said and handed the light green sheet of paper with a stylized bicycle as a watermark to Detective Elba.

A trooper appeared with the bag and left. Dan stood, reached for the bag, and pulled out his cell. He didn't have any messages.

"I'll try now." He stood by the front window for best reception and touched the icon for Jill. Voice mail immediately. The phone was off or the mailbox was full.

"Voice mail," he said and handed the phone to Elba.

Elba motioned for him to sit and review the list of callers with him.

"Lily, three calls."

"Lily Taylor, she's a worrier. She calls if she sees her shadow."

"Monika, three calls."

"Monika Traymore, Jill's rival in the club. She hates me."

"Friendly rival?" Dan shrugged. Monika was nosy. Maybe Jill kept her at a distance.

"Ainsley, two calls, and Beth, two calls."

Dan shook his head. "I don't know them."

"Tom, one call."

"Tom. I forgot his last name. He's her team leader. He'd call if she didn't show."

"Tom Chaudri is on the list."

"That's him," said Dan.

The phone rang. The trooper answered.

It was Samantha Cruz wondering how long she was supposed to keep Kaitlyn. The trooper said he'd get back to her.

Lieutenant Winston and Detective Elba huddled in the foyer.

"Mr. Ramsay, we're going to let Kaitlyn come home. We'll have a female trooper pick her up. We'll have some questions for your daughter."

Dan stood. "You can't interrogate my child about her mother. You'll scare her. She's ten years old."

"I'm aware of her age, Mr. Ramsay. She may

have spoken with her mother between the time Mrs. Ramsay left and now. Mrs. Ramsay may have told her if plans had changed. That's all."

Dan was incapable of making a response. He wanted to wake up. He wanted this to be a nightmare. He wanted Jill to walk in the back door right now. With Abbie.

"Would it help if I went with the trooper?" offered Suzanne.

"Yes, thank you. We'll have her swing by here to pick you up and then go on to the Cruz house."

"I'll wait outside." Suzanne left.

Elba moved closer to Dan. "Mr. Ramsay, we're officially treating this as a Missing Person case. We'll need a picture and a description to issue a BOLO—Be On The Lookout—for Mrs. Ramsay. It will go to all state and local law enforcement, hospitals, and first responders."

"Oh my God. You really think something has happened to her, don't you?" whispered Dan.

"I wanted you to know before your daughter got here."

Dan pointed to a silver framed photograph on a side table next to the hideous sofa. His mother-in-law, Jill, and Katie taken last year at Christmas. When he'd been left behind. Winston picked it up and looked at it. "We'll make copies."

"There's one more thing," said Dan. "Jill shaved her head New Year's Day after an argument. Her hair hasn't grown completely. It's not close to shoulder length like in the picture."

"We'll make that correction."

Dan shifted uneasily. "Jill has a wig, too. She

wore it to work after she cut off all her hair because even she realized how awful it looked. She no longer wears it to work, but she may still have it." He sounded ridiculous.

"What did the wig look like?"

"It was sort of a page boy with straight bangs. Dark brown. Jill's hair is more brown black."

"Anything else? No new glasses? Contact lenses?"

"No. I just wanted you to know the picture wasn't one hundred percent accurate about the hair."

Winston nodded. The police seemed to think either Jill was in a disguise and on the run or missing. Neither made any sense.

# CHAPTER THIRTY

"Dad!" Katie yelled as she raced in the house and into Dan's arms. She dropped her Lily Pulitzer backpack at the door. "You forgot to pick me up. Then the police brought me home. Did you send them?"

"Yes, Katie. I knew you were with Sophia, and I had to talk to the police about something."

"What, Dad?" she asked. "What did you talk about?"

"In a minute," he said.

He just wanted to hold her. He kissed the top of her brown black hair. She had traces of makeup on her soft face. He ran his thumb over one cheek to wipe it off, but he merely made the smudge larger.

"We experimented with Josie's make-up. Her mom works for Lancôme and sent us each a bag of samples. I look terrible in blue eye shadow. I look best in gold shimmer."

Dan made an effort to smile. He hoped the police were wrong. He hoped he wasn't going to have to tell Katie anything bad. She'd had a terrible time when her grandfather died at Thanksgiving. She still cried for him. She missed Abbie and cried about her, too. He didn't know how she'd fare if anything happened to Jill.

She squirmed out of his arms.

"What's going on, Dad? Why are the police here? And Aunt Suzanne and Uncle Rob?"

"The police had some questions for me."

"Is Mom home, yet?"

"Not yet. She'll be home tonight. She has to work tomorrow. And you, Katie, have school."

"Kaitlyn," asked Suzanne, "have you had dinner?"

"Not really. I wasn't hungry before, but I guess I am now."

Dan hugged Katie again. "Go in the kitchen with Aunt Suzanne and she'll heat up some chili. The trooper will go, too." Katie hesitated. "It's okay." He must have sounded reassuring because she headed for the kitchen.

Both investigators went outside, leaving Dan and Rob alone in the living room.

Dan looked at Rob. "What do you think?"

"I don't know. Maybe Jill called Kaitlyn and told her something and this will all be a misunderstanding."

"Should I be with Katie while that woman questions her?"

"Probably, but she may just make it conversational over supper. Suzanne will keep an eye on things. It's not like she's going to threaten Kaitlyn."

Another missed cue by Dan—how rough the

questions would be for Katie. Damn Mørk. He couldn't think at all. Dan moved to be close to window where the curtains were still open and he felt he could breathe. This room made him claustrophobic. Rob joined him.

"Does Elba think Jill has a disguise? With the wig? And maybe glasses?"

"Sounded like he's considering it. I can't imagine why she'd need one, though."

"What do you think happened, Rob?"

Rob didn't speak immediately. Dan felt like he was looking for a nice way of saying something awful.

"Jill hasn't been herself, Dan. She used to be light-hearted and fun. Now, she seems guarded or feisty. Maybe she's playing a trick to scare you into missing her or not taking her for granted and it got out of hand."

"You mean she didn't expect the police to get involved."

"Right. Maybe she plans to waltz in late tonight or even tomorrow morning to see just how upset you are. She probably didn't expect her teammates to call you a million times, either."

"That doesn't sound like Jill. It sounds like something her girlfriends would put her up to." Dan relayed the story of Jill canceling the credit card and staging a scene about it to Rob.

"No way would Jill think of that," Rob said. "No offense, but Jill and finance aren't usually used in the same sentence. You're right. Sounds like her girlfriends are still trying to get Jill to punish you for Bella."

"I wish she hadn't told them. I know I've got Dr. Spellman and can vent to him, but I don't give details to anyone, Rob."

"Including me," he said. "I appreciate that. I don't want to know anymore than I already do about your marriage and what went on with Bella."

Dan needed time alone. Having all these cops around and being in this room confused him. "How long do you think the cops are going to be around?"

"Beats me. All I know about cops is what I see on TV. I do know they always suspect the spouse."

"Me? Of doing what? Not knowing where my wife is? I know I'm not winning any Husband of the Year awards, but being clueless isn't a crime."

"Dan…" Rob paused before he continued, "Do you think Jill could have been with another man for the weekend? I hate to ask."

"I couldn't fault her if she was. I don't know who it would be. I don't know any members of the cycling club or her colleagues at work or her clients. I know our next door neighbor thinks she's hot, but I don't think the feeling is mutual. He's a little too married and drinks a little too much.

"Of course, she never knew anything about Bella. She wouldn't even know I'd run into her that first time at the Omni if I hadn't been stupid enough to tell her. I thought it was a one-time sighting and such a coincidence I told her. I didn't realize I'd be sucked into an affair."

Rob looked skeptical.

"All right. I pursued Bella. I wanted her back. I basically lost my mind over her. If anything, Bella was reluctant. She said she didn't do married men."

"Well, she got over that," smirked Rob.

"Because it was me. We have that connection. If I was willing to risk my marriage, it wasn't her problem. She's the one who set all the rules. Burner phones, nothing in writing or gifts, and no talking on weekends. She refused to come to the house. She said she wasn't going to set foot in the home I shared with my wife and daughter."

"Sounds like she'd done it before."

"I don't think so. She's just more sophisticated than we are."

"Dad knew." It was a statement. "Bella was the cause of the rift between the two of you." Rob looked to Dan for confirmation. "That's why he was so angry with you."

Dan nodded. "I told him I planned to divorce Jill and marry Bella."

"No way. Dad would have been pissed on so many levels. Mom knows, too, doesn't she? That's why she's always said no to you visiting her in Florida."

"Yes. Satisfied?" Dan moved away from the window. "Let's deal with one situation at a time. I don't want to rehash Dad's disapproval of my marrying Bella."

Rob looked like he was about to speak when Kaitlyn came in. She grabbed Dan's hand. "Dad, "Come have cookies with us. You, too, Uncle Rob." Dan followed her into the kitchen.

# CHAPTER
# THIRTY-ONE

"Do you want anything to eat besides cookies?" asked Suzanne.

"Not for me," said Dan.

"I'll pass," said Rob who went over and kissed Suzanne's cheek. "What are you ladies up to in here?"

The four adults and Katie sat at the rectangular oak table. Oatmeal raisin cookies were on a platter in the center. Katie had milk. Suzanne and Trooper Sanders were drinking coffee. It smelled good, but Dan didn't think he could drink it.

"I told them about Sophia's party," chimed Katie. "Dad, this is Trooper Sanders. She's been with the Virginia State Police for two years. She had to go to a forensic academy after college. She works all over the state not just one city. I think she should come to school on career day."

"That's a good idea. Nice to meet you, Trooper Sanders."

"Mr. Ramsay," she nodded in his direction. "I'd enjoy going to career day. Law enforcement needs people with education in medicine, chemistry, and computer science. We always want more women on the force. Speaking at an all-girls' school might broaden their horizons beyond law and medicine."

Dan nodded politely He could just imagine how welcome a state trooper would be at St. Margaret's career day. His stomach roiled, but he took a cookie to make things seem normal for Katie. She knew he loved them and never passed one up.

"Dad, I forgot to tell you, Mom called me just before breakfast yesterday morning on her way to the cycling trial. She wanted to make sure I was having a good time. Like I wouldn't? I told her not to call me again at Sophia's. It's embarrassing. Nobody else's mom called."

"We miss you when you're away." There. Jill was all right. She hadn't called because Katie asked her not to.

"Dad," she said with an exasperated sigh. "At least you could get me a cell phone so when you call, you don't bother Sophia's parents."

"We've discussed this, Katie," responded Dan.

She shrugged as if to acknowledge it was worth a shot. "What did you do while I was gone?"

"Yesterday I went for a long run. Today, I went to the health club and played shuffleboard with Vivian's dad."

Katie frowned. "Shuffleboard's for old men."

"My calves hurt from running on Saturday so I took it easy today. I still beat Vivian's dad."

Suzanne intervened. "Kaitlyn, I think it's time for

you to go to bed. What time do you leave for school in the morning?"

"Seven-thirty. Dad takes me. He lost his job, you know."

Dan cringed. Yes, Suzanne and Rob and now Officer Sanders knew he was unemployed.

"Wait, Dad knows computer science. When we were hacked, all it took was one phone call from him and the company apologized. Maybe he could get a job with the State Police," she said to Officer Sanders who nodded non-committally.

Dan's tone was strict. "It's time for bed. No TV before you go to sleep. You probably didn't do a lot of sleeping at Sophia's."

Katie came to his side. "Goodnight, Dad."

"'Night, Katie." He kissed her cheek. "I love you even without gold shimmer."

# CHAPTER

# THIRTY-TWO

The three of them sat in the den. Dan had no intention of spending any more time in that museum of a living room. He wanted to be comfortable in his own house. It was bad enough he had police outside. He was going to be comfortable inside.

"Damn," said. Dan. "I forgot about Jill's parents."

Suzanne looked surprised. "You think she went to see them? In Charleston?"

"Maybe, but the media will pick up the BOLO. Her parents might hear about it."

"And you don't want them to find out from TV," said Rob.

"Or from friends in Richmond who've heard about it. I've got to call them. What time is it?"

Rob looked at his watch. "Almost ten."

"It's not too late. Damn, I thought Jill would be home by now."

\*\*\*

"That went about as well as I expected," said Dan when he came back into the den. "I told them the police were over-reacting because she'd parked the car illegally. I didn't get too far. The conversation turned into when was I going to find a job. "I'm tired." he flopped into his comfortable club chair with his arms hanging over the sides. Tired from his run Saturday, sore from Orlo's massage, and confused by Jill's actions and the police questions. "I don't know what's up with the cops outside. Who knows how long they'll be here. Maybe you two should go home. There's nothing to do here."

Rob and Suzanne exchanged a worried look. Rob looked reluctant to leave. "You'll be okay on your own?"

"Yeah, I'm surrounded by cops."

"If you're sure." Rob stood.

"I'm sure. Go."

"Call us as soon as Jill comes home no matter what time." Rob squeezed his brother's shoulder.

"Thanks for everything, Suzanne," said Dan. "You made things a lot easier for Katie." She kissed Dan on the cheek.

"Happy to help. I think Jill's trying to make a point. To make you a little uneasy. To miss her. She'll be back."

Detective Elba stepped inside before they made it to the front door. "Mr. Ramsay," he called from the foyer.

Dan hauled himself up and wearily walked to the

front of the house.

"Yes?"

"Mr. Ramsay, may we sit for a moment?" Suzanne, Rob, and Dan returned to the living room with Elba.

"Mr. Ramsay, Officer Sanders told us that Kaitlyn spoke to her mother and that she'd asked her not to call again. That may explain the lack of contact."

"I think so," said Dan. "Ten is a hard age. She wants to be more independent, but Jill is cautious."

"Mr. Ramsay, Kaitlyn mentioned something about your family being hacked. Is that correct?"

Ah, another humiliating moment from his marriage to be revealed.

"That's what we told Katie." Dan was so tired it was an effort to talk. His body ached from overdoing the run Saturday and his mind struggled without a regular dose of meds. He'd probably missed at least one dose of two different meds. "Jill came home from lunch with her friends one Saturday and said our credit card had been rejected when she paid for lunch. She was upset because her girlfriends assumed the worst—that I'd cut off her credit cards in addition to being a cheater. She said I'd humiliated her again.

"I'd no idea what she was talking about. I pay all our bills before they're due. When I called the credit card company, I was told the account had been closed by Jill two weeks earlier. The next time we discussed it was at dinner in front of Katie. I didn't want to accuse Jill of fabricating a scene, so I said we'd been hacked along with a lot of other customers."

"Jill wouldn't do that," said Suzanne.

Elba ignored her. "Did you discuss this with your wife?"

"No. I let it go. The card was re-issued."

"Mr. Ramsay, did you think this was unusual behavior for your wife?"

"Yes. Jill isn't a drama queen. She's not vindictive. I couldn't imagine her plotting to stage a scene, but the credit card representative said the caller was verified. She knew the account number, social security numbers, and my mother's maiden name. I don't think Jill did it, and if she did, it sounded like something her girlfriends talked her into and then played along."

"Why would they do that?" asked Elba.

"They hate me. The girlfriends would spread the story of how I'd humiliated Jill even more."

"That's ridiculous. Jill wouldn't do that," repeated Suzanne.

Detective Elba turned to Suzanne. "Mrs. Ramsay, you seem very certain that this would be out of character. Why is that?"

"Because I've known Jill for ten years. We're a close family despite Jill being fifteen years younger than Rob and me. She's bright, funny, and optimistic. She's not calculating at all. She doesn't plot revenge. She lets most things roll off her.

"No woman who loves her husband would let an affair roll off and Jill didn't. She was deeply hurt by Dan's affair, but the Jill I know is focused on moving forward and not on payback. Even if her girlfriends tried to talk her into it, she wouldn't do it." Suzanne sounded as tired of inane questions as he did. Her tone was uncharacteristically brisk.

"She wouldn't do it to Kaitlyn," added Rob.

"What do you mean, Mr. Ramsay?"

Dan felt like he was watching this conversation from behind a screen. Suzanne and Rob were defending Jill for him. He sat on the sidelines and couldn't get off the bench. He just couldn't.

"If the intention was to spread gossip about Dan, Jill would never agree. Her friends have children Kaitlyn's age. She wouldn't put Kaitlyn in a position to hear mean things about her father. Dan and Jill hadn't told Kaitlyn about the affair. They told her Dan had a medical condition that put him in the guest room. So far, none of Kaitlyn's friends passed gossip on to her. Kaitlyn would have mentioned it. She stands up to Mean Girls."

Yes. Yes. Suzanne and Rob both made good points. "When did this happen?" asked Elba looking at Dan.

"March. The Saturday after Abbie went missing."

"That would mean the card was canceled approximately two weeks earlier?"

"I have the exact date." He didn't have the strength to go upstairs and look for the information in the desk. He couldn't get his mind, legs, and muscles together enough to do it.

Rob was on his feet. "Dan, I'll get it. Where is it?"

"In my desk calendar. The notebook. Not the one on the computer."

With what seemed like amazing speed, Rob went

upstairs, got the calendar, and brought it down.

"May I?" asked Elba.

"Sure," said Dan.

Detective Elba paged through the dates in March and made a notation of the information provided by the credit card representative.

"Is this important?" asked Rob.

"Maybe. Someone might have a grudge against your brother or his wife or both of them. It's worth checking." He stood and looked at Rob and Suzanne. "I understand you were leaving…Please don't let me keep you."

With another round of urging Dan to get some sleep, Rob and Suzanne left.

Elba remained standing in the living room."Mr. Ramsay, there's nothing more for us to do here tonight, but I'm going to leave a patrol officer parked in front of the house."

Dan started to object. Elba held up his hand. "Formality, Mr. Ramsay." He paused. "If Mrs. Ramsay isn't back by dawn, we'll start a search. I asked your sister-in-law to give us some clothing that Mrs. Ramsay wore recently. She brought us a red sweater and some Ugg boots. Does that sound right?"

Dan's stomach lurched again. Jill's clothes? Were they going to put dogs on her trail?

"You mean for…dogs?"

Elba nodded. "In case we need them."

"Yes, Jill loves that red sweater and her Uggs. Don't lose them. She'll kill me."

Dan couldn't believe he just said that. Great. Tell the cops his wife would kill him.

"Good night, Mr. Ramsay. I'll see myself out."

Dan closed the door behind him, slid down the back of the door, and cried himself to sleep.

# CHAPTER

# THIRTY-THREE

Dan woke with a start. His body was being pummeled. Earthquake. There'd been a 3.5 on the Richter Scale a year or so ago. Buildings in the county had collapsed. He needed to make sure everyone was safe. He needed to get up, but he was disoriented.

Someone was pounding on the front door. He realized he'd slept against the door all night or until whatever time it was now.

He rubbed his eyes and opened the front door. Two patrol officers stood there. The female officer spoke.

"Mr. Ramsay, it's six-fifteen. The sun's up. Mrs. Ramsay is officially missing and the search is starting. We're changing shifts." She introduced the officers.

Dan's mind was as gritty as his eyes felt. "Okay." He couldn't think of anything else to say. "Wait…Should I send my daughter to school?"

"It's up to you. Mrs. Ramsay's name and photo will be aired in the media. If her school administration thinks they can contain gossip and speculation, then she probably should go. We can always collect her if there's a change in circumstances."

Dan mumbled his thanks and closed the door. He dragged himself upstairs, peeled off the clothes he'd worn home from the health club, showered, shaved, and put on a clean polo and khaki slacks. He put on socks and shoes. He had to maintain a sense of normalcy for Katie.

"Katie," he knocked on her door. "Time to get up. Get dressed. Meet me downstairs."

Dan made breakfast while he called the headmistress—a formidable woman with whom he interacted little. He normally left her to Jill. The woman was understanding and promised to alert the staff and teachers to contain media to the extent possible. She'd enforce the No Cell Phone on Campus rule today. She hung up after saying she'd pray for Jill's safe return.

"Dad, it's too early. I could've slept fifteen more minutes." Katie stood in the kitchen in her school uniform looking like a miniature of her mother. Another piece of his heart broke off.

"I want to talk to you before you go."

Katie sat at the breakfast bar and started to eat the yogurt with strawberries and granola he set out. She looked at him expectantly.

"Katie, your mom didn't come home last night. I think she's coming home in time to get ready for work, but the police consider her missing."

"Why?" Katie seemed genuinely curious.

"She left her car parked illegally in a state park. I told them your mom wouldn't do that. She's strict about rules. They're taking the precaution of looking for her. They're saying she's missing and told the newspapers and TV stations."

"Oh, no, I'm going to be hammered at school."

Dan almost smiled. "I feel the same, but she parked illegally and the police proceed according to their regulations. They have to do this."

Katie finished her cereal. "You don't think anything's happened to Mom, do you?"

"No, of course not, Katie. I think maybe she got separated from her team at the trial and didn't get back to her car in time before the park closed. I think she'll be back in time for work."

"Me, too, Dad."

"Go brush your teeth, and I'll drive you to school."

The landline rang as soon as Katie went back upstairs. Dan jumped at it.

"Jill?"

He exhaled. It was Jill's father. No, Jill wasn't back yet. He was taking Katie to school. The police were going to start a search. He was certain it wasn't necessary. He expected Jill to be back in time to dress for work. Nine-thirty. Jill had to be at work at nine-thirty. There was still plenty of time.

# CHAPTER
# THIRTY-FOUR

Detective Elba and Lieutenant Winston arrived at ten fifteen. They asked Dan to sit down. He was back in the scratchy wing chair in the living room.

Both investigators sat on the sofa, but Elba did the talking.

"Mr. Ramsay, a body of a woman was found by a park employee this morning. She matches the description of your wife, Jill Ramsay. She was found lying fully clothed in what you described her as wearing when she left Saturday morning, hands folded over her chest, a navy fleece blanket covering her. She was found in a small flower garden near the lake. I'm sorry, Mr. Ramsay."

*No. No. No. No. No.*

"NOOOOOOOOOOOOOOOOOOOOOOOOO," he screamed and put his head in his hands.

Jill couldn't be dead. She was playing a prank. Testing him. Not dead. She was thirty-eight. It couldn't be true.

"How can you be sure?" he asked as tears ran down his face.

"We have photographs if you'd take a look."

"No," Dan shook his head. "I don't want to see any pictures. I want to see her. It's a mistake. It can't be true. It can't."

"Then, we'd like you to come with us, Mr. Ramsay."

"Katie. Katie's at school."

"Trooper Sanders will pick her up and bring her home. She'll ask your sister-in-law to meet them here."

"Oh, dear God, please don't tell her until we're certain. Please."

"We won't. We'll wait for the official identification, but it's best if Kaitlyn is out of school and away from any media. We'll block off this street for as long as we can."

Dan wasn't listening. Images of Jill—laughing on their first date, beaming as she walked down the stone pathway of Ginter Botanical Gardens at their wedding, announcing her pregnancy to him—played in his head. She was joyful, happy, and funny. Her brightness attracted him and kept his dark side at bay. No one could be sad around her for long. She couldn't be gone. He couldn't lose her.

"Mr. Ramsay, I said your brother will meet us downtown. He's leaving his office now."

He didn't respond. He couldn't move. He couldn't speak.

"Mr. Ramsay, come with us." Detective Elba held his arm and Lieutenant Winston walked behind them. Together, they got him down the steps and into the waiting sedan. He sat in the back with Winston.

He was unaware of movement and surprised when the car stopped in an underground garage and Winston opened the car door for him. The two investigators led him through two steel doors and into a small white room that smelled of industrial cleaning solutions. It was completely silent. Dan heard himself breathing.

"Mr. Ramsay," said Lieutenant Winston, "we're at the morgue. Just let us know when you're ready to look through the window. The woman we believe to be Mrs. Ramsay will be lying on a table with a sheet over her face. The technician will lift it so you can see her face. Let us know if it's your wife."

"It's not."

"Mr. Ramsay, we can have you view through a monitor into the room," said Winston. "Would that be easier?"

"No, no, no." Dan shook his head. "It'd be like watching TV. I want to see for myself."

"Just let us know when you're ready."

Dan stood there. Numb. He wanted to prove it was a mistake, but he didn't want to see someone else's dead wife, sister, daughter, mother. He knew it wouldn't be Jill. It couldn't.

He nodded his head yes.

Winston tapped on the window, the blinds were raised, a body lay under a sheet. A young woman in scrubs lifted the sheet from over the face.

Jill's face, eyes closed, rested peacefully under the sheet.

"Yes," rasped Dan. "Yes, oh my God, it's Jill. It's

my wife."

He ran and banged on the glass. "Jill, Jill, wake up. Wake up. I'm sorry, Jill. Please wake up."

Detective Elba pulled him away from the glass. The technician lowered the sheet and closed the blinds.

"I want to see her."

"I'm sorry, Mr. Ramsay, you can't."

Dan sobbed uncontrollably. "I want to hold her. She's my wife. I want to hold her."

"You can. You will. After the autopsy."

"Autopsy?" Dan was wild-eyed. "You can't cut her up. She's my wife. No. No one has permission to cut her up."

Elba led him to a vinyl sofa and sat him down. Winston put a paper cup of water in his hand.

"Mr. Ramsay, we need to determine the cause of death. Her body is evidence. Let her body tell us what she can't."

"I don't care what killed her. She's dead. Nothing else matters."

"It matters to the law. The state is going to find who did this and punish them."

"I don't care. I don't care. I don't care."

Winston turned away and spoke into his cell phone. Seconds later, a middle-aged woman came in the room from an inner door.

"I'm a coroner. You," she pointed at Elba, "know better than to put me in this position."

She looked at Dan.

"Shock," she pronounced. "I'll give you a wheelchair and call the ED. Take him up; they'll give him some fluids and oxygen. Maybe a sedative. Wait."

A tech returned with a wheelchair and a blanket. Elba lifted Dan into it, flung the blanket around him, and pushed through the doors to the elevator that would take them straight to the Emergency Department.

# CHAPTER

# THIRTY-FIVE

Dan was ushered into a room with a steel table and four chairs at police headquarters. Rob was seated with Winston. When he saw Rob, Dan started crying. Rob hugged him tightly, then held out a chair for him.

"Is this an interrogation room?" asked Dan.

"It's an interview room right now," said Winston calmly. "It's whatever you want to call it. A private place to sit and talk."

Elba entered with four bottled waters and a notepad. He sat. Winston continued.

"As I explained to your brother, your wife's death is being treated as a homicide."

"Why?" Dan whispered through his tears. He couldn't stop crying. He didn't try.

"She was found in Lake Anna Park in a flower garden. She had a blanket over her. Someone took time and care to cover her face and body. There were no obvious signs of struggle or anything that would suggest a cause of death."

Winston leaned forward, "Mr. Ramsay, if your wife hadn't been staged as she was, we'd probably think it was an accident. Heart attack. Embolism. Something natural. An autopsy would still be performed, but homicide is the only choice. Even suicide couldn't have been staged."

"Suicide?" These guys were nuts.

"I'm speaking hypothetically. What you need to keep in mind is that this is a homicide investigation. Anything you can tell us might be helpful. We have to move fast."

"I don't care who killed her," Dan repeated.

Rob gasped audibly.

"I understand that you mean that right now, but you may change your mind. In any case, we're going to investigate. We don't need your permission." Winston sat back.

Dan nodded. There was nothing to say.

"We'll be interviewing cycling club members," continued Elba. "They probably had the last contact with her."

"You brother has given us some background information on Mrs. Ramsay. Her employer, her sponsorship of a sports club at St. Margaret's, and her enthusiasm about competing in an upcoming one hundred mile cycling event. He said she had no religious affiliation."

Dan nodded.

"Earlier, you said you and Mrs. Ramsay were experiencing marital difficulties. Could you be more specific?"

"Rob said I shouldn't talk to you about Jill

because on TV the cops always suspect the spouse."

"Mr. Ramsay," said Winston, "we're not in a TV show. God knows, I wish we were. Statistically, it's true. Women are most often killed by someone they know, usually a male—boyfriend, husband, brother, son. You said marital problems. That's a broad topic. Abuse, divorce, separation. Gambling, drugs, alcohol. Mrs. Ramsay may have had a boyfriend or girlfriend, for that matter. We don't know the situation. You do. The faster we can get a handle on this, the more likely we are to find the killer."

"I don't…"

"Mr. Ramsay, we're investigating the murder of your wife. Now, Detective Elba and I have notified more people of their spouse's death than we care to count. We know people react differently. However, refusal to co-operate with us at the basic level might be considered unusual."

Rob put his arm around Dan. "Talk to them."

"It's not that I don't want to co-operate. I just don't care."

"Then co-operate so they can get on with their jobs and you can get home to Kaitlyn."

The mention of Katie stirred Dan to talk. He told them as much as he was able. His tongue felt heavy and he felt like cotton was in his head. He spoke to Elba. "Jill discovered I'd been having an affair for about a year around Christmas. She and Katie went to Charleston to spend two weeks during the Christmas holiday with her parents without me. I stayed behind with a fake case of the mumps. When they returned, Jill asked me to move to the guest bedroom. We told Katie I had sleep apnea and needed to be in a room where the noise of the machine wouldn't disturb Jill."

"Did you see a marriage counselor or therapist?"

"No. Jill was too angry to go."

"Mr. Ramsay, did your wife ever indicate that she was afraid of someone? Found them too attentive? Creepy?"

Dan shook his head.

"Could you please answer yes or no?"

"No. No one."

"Did you notice anyone who paid unusual attention to her?"

"No," Dan spoke in the monotone of someone who was disassociated from the facts.

"Did she like her colleagues? Her boss?"

"She loved her job. I didn't know any of her colleagues. Some of them came to parties at the house, but I don't remember anyone in particular. She did say she had a new client she was sharing with Chloe. I don't know Chloe's last name. I don't think there was any real animosity between the two of them, but Jill thought Chloe was a pain in the ass."

"You said you didn't know anyone from the cycling club, correct?"

"Correct. I knew some names. Monika Traymore lives in the neighborhood, but we don't socialize."

"Did she mention anyone from the club as being offensive or upsetting to her?"

Dan shook his head. "No."

"How did she seem when she left Saturday morning?"

"What do you mean?" Dan didn't understand

179

how any of this mattered.

"Excited? Nervous? Your brother said she'd been planning to do the one hundred mile race for two years and this was her first practice of the season. Was she eager to go?"

"A little nervous. Worried," said Dan. "About the expense of the trip. I lost my job. She was worried about spending money for the trip. I told her to go. She'd already paid her fee. She'd packed lunch and snacks. Her only expense was gas."

"Why did she drive alone?"

"What?"

"If she was concerned about money, why didn't she ride with someone else from the cycling club? Split the cost?"

That had never occurred to Dan. "I don't know. I never questioned her about her team activities. Maybe she wanted to be mobile should something happen to Katie. She always wanted to be available for Katie."

He stopped speaking.

"Katie, how am I going to tell Katie her mother is dead? How can I do that?" He looked at Winston and Elba for help. How did he tell Katie her mother wasn't coming home?

Rob reached out and rubbed his brother's back. Dan couldn't stop crying.

"Had you and your wife made any progress toward reconciliation?"

Couldn't they stay on one topic at a time? "Maybe. We have reservations to spend a few days skiing in Colorado next month. Just the two of us. No promises from her. I also thought this cycling trip would clear her head and get her thinking about something other than our marriage. Maybe she'd be ready to work things through after the weekend."

"Was she seeing anyone else?"

He knew he should be offended, but he didn't know. He'd lost touch with any radar he'd had with Jill.

"I don't know," he whispered. "Her girlfriends might know."

"What about you? Were you seeing anyone?"

"Absolutely not. I promised her I'd never see or talk to Bella again and I haven't."

"Bella?" asked Winston.

Dan gave them Bella's name and business address. It stuck in his mind because it was on Wall Street and sounded so serious and sophisticated and glamorous. He'd tossed the burner phone with her cell phone number programmed into it away months ago so he wouldn't be tempted to call.

"Mr. Ramsay, what did you do while your wife was away?"

"I went for a long run Saturday. I drove down to the beach and ran a long time. I drove back, and spent Saturday night at home. I went to bed early. I'd overdone the run. I took Tylenol pm to soothe my muscles. I slept late Sunday. My calves hurt so I booked a massage at my health club. I had the massage, played shuffleboard with a neighbor, and came home to find out when I was supposed to pick up Katie. You know the rest."

"Colonial Beach?"

"No, no. Virginia Beach. Along the oceanfront. North End."

"Do you know anyone there?"

"Not anymore. I had some college friends who lived there. My parents had friends there."

"So, you didn't go to see anyone in particular?"

"No, I just wanted to run. I wanted to be somewhere out of Henrico County and my problems." He was getting sleepy. "Can I go now?"

"Why did you book a massage?" Winston cut in.

"Because my calves hurt."

"If there were financial problems, a massage seems a bit luxurious."

"There weren't financial problems. I lost my job and will get another one, but we have investments and I can get a partial pension. I wasn't worried about money. Jill was."

"Excuse us."

Elba and Winston went outside.

Dan and Rob sat in silence. Dan felt like he wanted to put his head on the table and never get up.

The door opened. Elba stood there. "Mr. Ramsay, you and your brother may go now. I'll have further questions, but you've been helpful."

He held the door open for the two to pass.

"Again, I'm sorry for your loss."

# CHAPTER
# THIRTY-SIX

The distance from the landing in the foyer up the stairs to Katie's room felt like it was the length of a marathon. Just over twenty-six miles. He forced himself to climb. One foot, then the next. He stopped at the top of the landing and took one deep breath. He didn't want to go through that door. He didn't want to break his daughter's heart. Maybe he could just stand here until the nightmare passed. He made the final few steps to Katie's room on leaden feet. He knocked on the door and went in.

"Dad," she went to him and hugged him. "Why did I get out of school at lunch period? Why did Trooper Sanders pick me up?"

Dan sat on her bed on a quilt made by Jill with a dust ruffle and pillow shams in blue. Periwinkle blue, Jill always corrected.

Katie's lip was quivering as she stood in front of him. "Dad, my stomach hurts."

She clearly knew something was very wrong. He

took her small soft hands in his.

"Katie, your mom isn't coming home. The police said someone killed her in the park where she'd gone for the cycling trials."

The dam that Katie must have been holding burst and tears flooded from her. "No, Dad, tell the police they're wrong."

He held her close. "I did, Katie, I did. I told them they were wrong. They took me downtown and I saw your mom for myself. She's dead. She's not coming back."

Katie sat on his lap and cried until she couldn't. He didn't know how much time had passed. It could have been twenty minutes or two hours. He held her and cried with her.

Finally, Katie lifted her head and asked, "Who would kill Mom? Why?"

Dan shook his head. "I don't know, Katie. The police are investigating. They have to ask a lot of questions and look at the scene where she was found."

She seemed to absorb this silently.

"Will they ask me questions?" she hiccupped.

"Maybe one or two, but I'll be with you." He hoped he sounded reassuring.

She started crying hard again. "Dad, the last time I talked to Mom I yelled at her. I was mad she called me at Sophia's. I told her she embarrassed me and not to call me again. I didn't mean to be mad. Do you think the police will think I hurt her?"

"Oh, no, Katie. Don't worry about the police. Your mom knew how much you loved her. She understood that you're getting to be more independent. She wouldn't have been upset that you asked her not to call."

"You think so?"

"Yes, Katie, I do. Your mom loved you, and she liked that you were sassy sometimes."

"Dad, are we going to have to put her in the ground, too? Like granddad?"

"Yes, sweetheart."

"I don't want her to be there. She likes to be outside, just like granddad."

Dan couldn't answer.

"Kaitlyn, that's just your mom's body. Her spirit is free and soaring and living right inside you and your dad. The service will just be an earthly show of respect." Dan saw his mother in the doorframe.

"Gran," Katie ran to her and held tight. "Gran, I don't want mom to be dead."

"Of course you don't. None of us do. Something terrible happened. I don't know why it had to happen to her. She was the best mom a girl could have, wasn't she?"

Katie nodded her head and still hung onto her grandmother's waist.

His mother opened her left arm for him. "Dan," she whispered as she hugged him, "I'm so sorry. I'm just so sorry."

The three of them hugged each other for a long time.

# CHAPTER

# THIRTY-SEVEN

When they broke apart, Dan asked his mom how she knew.

"Rob called me last night. I booked a flight for this morning. I wanted to be with you and Kaitlyn until Jill came home. I never dreamed this would happen."

"I can't believe it, Mom. It's too painful."

"Dan, I know. It's too soon. Your dad and I had a long life together, and it broke my heart. I can't imagine how you must feel."

Dan was limp. "Mom, could you stay up here with Katie for a while? I have to call Jill's parents. They don't know, yet."

"Of course, Dan. Anything." She hugged him again. "I wish you didn't have to tell them."

He went into the office, closed the door, and used his cell to call his in-laws' home number. No answer. They didn't have an answering machine. He called Jill's older sister, Jane, at work and gave her the news. She was shocked and started to cry. She said her parents had left Charleston to fly to Richmond around noon. They wanted to be there if Jill were truly missing. She said their plane would land about five o'clock. They'd made reservations to stay at the nearby Hyatt House.

Great, just what he needed. Jill's parents. Today.

Jane said she'd tell her younger sister Emily.

When Jane asked about funeral plans, Dan cried. "I don't know. She was murdered, Jane. Some monster killed her. An autopsy is being performed. I can't stop them. I don't know when they'll release…" he couldn't say the word *body*. "Jill. When they'll release Jill to the funeral home."

Jane said all the right things. She said it must be terrible for him, to give Kaitlyn her love, and that she'd wait to hear from him before she and Emily and their husbands came up.

"Thank you, Jane. I just can't process all this. I want to ask Jill to help. I want her to just be waiting downstairs. I'll call."

He ended the call. There was no one else he wanted to speak to.

Suzanne knocked lightly and let herself in. She went over and hugged his neck while he was still seated at the desk.

"I'm so sorry, Dan. I wish I could say more."

Dan motioned that he didn't care.

"Dan, people are starting to stop by. Some of them with food. I can take care of it for now, but I think we need to talk to a funeral home. They'll give you a guest book and handle the obituary. Rob said your family has used Smythe's in the past. Should I call them? They'll send someone to the house so you don't have to go to them."

Dan nodded. "Thanks, Suzanne. I don't know what to do. I don't want to see anyone. I just spoke to Jill's sister Jane. The Carters are landing in Richmond about five. I don't want to see them, but I'll have to. Katie will want to see them."

"Oh, Dan," she sighed, "I wish you had another day before they arrived. Do they know?"

"I don't know. Jane might call them once they land."

"I know you don't want to hear this, but there are media crews at the entrance to the community. Some reporters have snuck through on foot. There's a patrol car outside. There's another shift change soon."

"Screw the media. They're not going to get photos of a grieving Katie. We have to protect her, Suzanne. Please, can you help do that?"

"Of course, Dan, I'll do anything. I'll draw all the drapes. Why don't you lie down until the people from Smythe's get here?"

He nodded.

He started towards the guest room and realized now he could go back to the master bedroom. Still alone. Maybe it would make him feel a little bit normal. Suzanne had already drawn the drapes. Not normal. Never.

# CHAPTER
# THIRTY-EIGHT

Dan couldn't have slept more than two hours. He unplugged the landline, threw his clothes in a heap on the floor, and dived under the covers. He hoped a trace of Jill would be there. It wasn't. She'd changed the sheets before she'd left. All he could smell was fabric softener.

Even without her scent, Dan felt better being in the room he and Jill had shared for their entire marriage. On her bedside table, he noticed gym socks, Katie's school picture, and a stack of pamphlets on nutrition for tri-athletes. A crystal frame held their wedding picture in plain view. She would have seen it every night before falling asleep.

Dan hoped she hadn't lain awake alone and hurting. What a fool he'd been. How could he have thought she wouldn't be dumbstruck by learning of his affair? Hearing his plans to divorce her to marry Bella? Trade her in for a woman he loved more?

Looking at the wedding picture reminded him of

how drawn he'd been to Jill. He hadn't dated much until he was in his thirties and was almost forty when he'd met Jill at a birthday bowling party for one of his colleagues. She was happy and funny and pretty. His co-worker encouraged him to ask her out.

*On their third date, she'd asked him to marry her. They'd gone skiing at Wintergreen with two other couples. At the top of the chairlift, she'd looked at him and said, "I like you a lot, Dan Ramsay. I think you should marry me." She'd whooshed down the slopes ahead of him. When he'd met her at the bottom of the slope, she'd asked for his answer. Yes. They hadn't even had sex yet, but it felt right. Marrying her in a garden setting on a beautiful sunny day seemed to be an omen that Mørk and all bad things were behind him.*

"Dan?" his mother called from the hall.

"Come in, Mom." He sat up and rubbed his eyes.

"Did you get any sleep?" She brought him a glass of iced tea.

"Some, yes."

"Dan, the man from Smythe's is here. Where do you want to speak to him?" *Nowhere*. He didn't want to talk to anyone about how to best formalize Jill's death. "Are there people downstairs?" He couldn't be with people. He didn't want to be an object of curiosity. He didn't want the depth of his grief to be judged by Jill's friends. He'd reached his limit and the Carters hadn't arrived yet.

"Some neighbors, friends of Jill. Suzanne and

Rob. There's a patrol officer outside."

"Could you ask the Smythe's man to come to the office in about ten minutes?"

"Of course, Dan."

"Katie?"

"She's in her room with her friend Sophia. Mrs. Cruz thought Kaitlyn would like to have a friend with her."

Dan nodded.

"Thanks for moving the clothes, Mom." He'd noticed all his clothes had been returned to the master bedroom closet and dresser from the guest bedroom.

"Anything."

\*\*\*

Rob joined the man from Smythe's in the office. Dan appreciated the support. These were decisions he didn't want to make. How could he pick out a casket for Jill? He should be helping her pick out a new bike.

He broke down twice during the short conference, but Rob kept him steady. He sobbed uncontrollably at the mention of burial clothes. His mind was empty when asked how to dress Jill for eternity. Rob reminded him that Jill had looked nice in the black sleeveless sheath she'd worn to their father's funeral. Jill had liked that dress, too. She wore it on special occasions.

Dan wanted the obituary published quickly to convey the message that the funeral would be private and graveside; Jill liked simple and outdoors. She hadn't set foot in a church except for someone's wedding, funeral, or christening since she had been seven and declared God to be Mother Nature.

Smythe's would coordinate with law enforcement about timing. A date for the service couldn't be selected until the coroner approved the release of Jill's body. How he hated that word. He wished he could believe as his mother did that it was just an earthly vessel and Jill's spirit lived on. He couldn't separate the two. He wanted a living Jill. Otherwise, she was gone forever.

# CHAPTER

# THIRTY-NINE

The day was endless. Had it only been this morning when he'd been told Jill was officially missing? Then dead? Then murdered?

Dan was back in the living room again with Detective Elba, Lieutenant Winston, and Rob. The doors at either end were closed to obstruct any curious listeners. Why didn't those people go home when the police obviously needed to speak to him? It must be late—after nine o'clock—far too late for social calls. The officers sat on the dusty rose velvet sofa. He sat in one of the scratchy wing chairs with Rob on the footstool next to it.

The autopsy had been completed an hour earlier. "We wanted you to know as quickly as possible before the results are made public," said Detective Elba.

Public. Strangers were going to know about Jill's most private self. He nodded. He still didn't care who'd killed Jill.

"Mr. Ramsay, there were no signs of any struggle or any injury. The toxicology reports won't be back for about five days. They should confirm the coroner's opinion. Mrs. Ramsay died of cardiac arrest. Most likely, from a substance injected into her neck. A tiny injection site was found there."

There was a low, long wailing in the room. Rob rubbed his back until it stopped. Dan realized it was coming from him. He stood and walked toward the door. "I don't want to hear anymore. I can't. I can't listen to this."

"Mr. Ramsay, it's important for you to understand what happened. You might know something about the killer from the way she died. You may not realize that you know something significant. "

"Can we just hit the important points, Detective?" asked Rob. Dan turned and sat next to Rob.

"The scenario seems to be that someone was in the back seat of the car Mrs. Ramsay was driving who stabbed her in the neck with a syringe. The estimated time of death is Saturday morning. She probably never got out of the car once it was parked."

Oh, good God, Jill had been in the car with a killer. She must have been terrified.

"Mrs. Ramsay died instantly. At most, she might have felt the slight sting of a needle. The killer or killers took her body into the park and down to the garden where they staged her to be found lying peacefully with her hands folded and her face and body covered. The fleece blanket used to cover her was navy blue.

"Does any of that resonate with you? The color navy? The garden?"

Dan shook his head. He was so tired.

Rob spoke. "Jill wasn't much of a gardener. I don't think she sought them out the way people who love flowers and landscaping do, did she Dan?"

"No." They'd married at Ginter Gardens because it was an available outdoor space, not because either one of them were drawn to its renowned landscaping. If anything, Jill didn't like nature to be forced. She liked wildflowers in meadows.

"What about the color navy?"

Dan shook his head. Rob answered for him again. "Navy is the color of St. Margaret's uniform blazers. Jill wore one when she attended and now Kaitlyn does." He thought for moment. "It's one of the University of Virginia's colors. That seems to be a stretch, but Dan and I both went there."

"Where did Mrs. Ramsay go to college?"

"Virginia Commonwealth University. She majored in business. Its colors are black and gold."

Dan couldn't believe he was listening to Rob talking about school colors. Blue, black, gold. He didn't care about the blanket found with Jill except he hoped it had been warm.

"Did Mrs. Ramsay take any medication?"

Dan again shook his head. "Vitamins, that's it. She didn't like to take medication. She would occasionally take an over the counter pain reliever if she'd been training hard."

"Do you know if anyone she knew had access to drugs? Legal or illegal?"

Jill didn't want to be near drugs of any kind. She wouldn't go looking for them.

Rob answered, "I'm a dentist. I have some medications, but nothing lethal. Jill had an unplanned hysterectomy at the end of August and was prescribed pain medication. I don't know what. I looked over the cycling team list and noticed that two of the members are physicians. One is a nurse practitioner. No one else is a medical professional that I recognized. I doubt anyone on the team would use illegal drugs unless they considered them to be performance enhancements."

"Mrs. Ramsay didn't take any performance enhancements, correct?"

"Not that I know of," said Dan. "She took vitamins. That's it."

"May we look at her vitamins?"

Rob started to object. Dan felt like his entire life had been sliced open to scrutiny. "They're in the kitchen in the top left cabinet next to the back door. You can check the medicine cabinets, too. I don't care."

The detectives exchanged a glance. Elba left with Rob for the kitchen.

Dan heard sounds of women being hurried out the front door. Detective Elba must have told them he was on police business and they needed to leave.

"The vitamins will be sufficient," replied Winston. "Then we'll leave you alone for tonight. I'm sorry. It's been a difficult day for you."

*Understatement.*

"How's your daughter?"

"Devastated, but her grandmother is staying

here. My mother is comforting."

"Good. We're keeping the lane blocked off, but by tomorrow night we'll have to let traffic flow freely."

Dan nodded. He was so tired, but there was something he should ask. Not for himself, but for Jill's parents. What was it?

"Leads. Do you have any leads?" asked Dan. His voice was devoid of any interest.

"We're checking the whereabouts of people known to frequent the parks along I-95. People who've come to our attention in the past. None are violent, but they might have seen something.

"The park has a small campsite. We're interviewing anyone who is still there and we'll follow-up with campsite check-ins for the weekend."

"Do you think someone from the campsite might have killed her?" asked Dan.

"We don't know. We're comparing reservations against actual check-ins."

Detective Elba returned holding what looked like a transparent food storage bag. Presumably, Jill's vitamin bottles were in it.

"We'll leave you now. Call us if you need anything. There's a patrol officer right outside."

***

"That's the last of them," said Suzanne as she sat on the sofa in the den next to Rob. "I told everyone they had to leave while the police brought you up to speed. I could tell some of the women wanted to

197

listen at the door. Detective Elba showing up in the kitchen got rid of them."

"It's after eleven o'clock. No one should visit that late," said Dan's mom. She slipped into the room after checking on a sleeping Kaitlyn. "Dan, let me get you something to eat."

"Not yet," he said. "Where are the Carters, Mom?" He was relieved he hadn't seen his in-laws.

"Elizabeth called to say they were at their hotel. Jane told them the news. They were distraught, especially George. They decided to rest at the hotel tonight and see Kaitlyn tomorrow."

"That's the best news we've had all day," said Rob. "I don't think we needed anyone else in the circus this afternoon and evening."

"Rob, she's their child," said his mother. "They've lost their daughter far too soon. Kaitlyn is the closest they can get to her."

"I want to see Katie," said Dan. "Was she okay after seeing Sophia?"

"I think it helped. It's hard to say," said his mom.

Dan stood. "Thank you all. I think I would've died today myself if it hadn't been for the three of you."

"Dan, you don't have any....urges, do you?" asked his mother.

He had no reason to lie to his mother. Of course, he wanted to kill himself. To stop the pain. The people. The questions. He couldn't imagine a day without Jill.

"Yes, I do Mom, but I'd never put Katie through that. She's already lost one parent. She needs me."

"I need you, Dan. I need you and Rob and

Suzanne. Please don't do anything to harm yourself."

He kissed his mother.

Dan dragged himself up the stairs and looked in on Katie. She was asleep on the bed, wearing the skirt and blouse of her school uniform and hugging a faded and frayed Mr. Rabbit. He'd last been seen in the back of Katie's closet, but he'd been needed tonight.

Dan wished he had a Mr. Rabbit.

# CHAPTER FORTY

Dan was awakened by voices in the hall outside his bedroom. Muffled, at first.

As soon as he opened his eyes, he remembered that Jill was dead. Dead. He couldn't believe it. Maybe if he went back to sleep he'd wake up to a different world. One where he and Jill and Katie and Abbie were a contented family.

"How can he be asleep? It's past noon. His wife is dead and he's sleeping like a baby." Mrs. Carter. Jill's mother. His mother-in-law.

"Let's go downstairs, Elizabeth," said his mother. "Dan was in the emergency room yesterday and was given a sedative. The police were here until midnight last night."

Mom the cavalry.

He should get up. Who knows what had happened while he slept? He showered, shaved, and dressed. At least he looked presentable.

He went straight to Katie's room. "Dad," she cried. "Grandmother and Grandfather Carter took me out to breakfast. I had pancakes with cherries on top. And a scrambled egg white. I knew Mom wanted me to eat something healthy." She wrapped her arms around him and he lifted her. "Dad, I miss Mom." She buried her face in his shoulder.

"I do, too, Katie." Tears trickled down his cheeks.

***

"Well, look who's up," chided Elizabeth. Dan reminded himself her daughter was dead. He had to cut her some slack.

He walked to the velvet sofa in the living room where she sat next to George and kissed her on the cheek. "Hello, Elizabeth."

George stood and hugged him. He'd never done that. Not even on their wedding day or when Katie was born. George held him close before letting him go. Dan saw tears in the older man's eyes. "George," was all he could say for a few minutes. After taking a breath, he said, "Thanks for taking Kaitlyn to breakfast. It's good for her to be with you and out of this house."

"No need to thank us. We know how upsetting this is for her. She needs to be with her grandparents."

Dan nodded. His mother brought him a cup of black coffee and placed a coaster on the mahogany end table next to his chair. "Dan, I'm making you breakfast. It'll be ready in about fifteen minutes."

He held her wrist lightly. "It can wait, Mom. Catch me up, please."

She perched on the arm of his chair. "The patrol

officer is still here. He's stopping visitors at the curb. I asked him to do that. There's too much confusion and curiosity to have a house full of people. I gave him a list of people to admit today. Elizabeth and George, of course, Rob, Suzanne, and Kaitlyn's friends. I unplugged the landline this morning. Reporters have been calling. Rob knows to call my cell or yours."

"Thanks, Mom."

"Exactly when will we be receiving?" asked Elizabeth.

"It's up to Dan when he wants people to visit his home, Elizabeth," said his mother gently. "If you have friends you want to see you can make arrangements at the hotel. Dan and Kaitlyn need privacy."

George patted Elizabeth's hand. "We'll get a suite or schedule some hours in a private room at the hotel. I'll call the concierge now." He went into the kitchen to make the call.

Elizabeth honed in on Dan. "The obituary was printed without consulting us."

"Was there something missing?"

"Her ancestry was light, but I realize the Richmond paper doesn't have as much sensibility to such things as *The Post and Courier* in Charleston does. I didn't understand about a private funeral. Graveside." She emphasized the last word. "What church will hold the service? I'd like to meet the priest."

"There's no church. Graveside is what Jill wanted. She loved the outdoors. We all know she didn't attend church."

"You mean my daughter is going to be buried like a heathen?" her dark eyes widened in disbelief and she leaned back into the sofa.

"Certainly not," said his mother. "She'll have a dignified service outdoors in the presence of those closest to her. Dan's not going to give an opportunity to curiosity seekers and the press."

"The press?" Elizabeth sounded as shocked as if she'd been told snake charmers would attend.

Mom intercepted more of Elizabeth's disapproval. "Elizabeth, none of us have experienced a murder in the family. Jill didn't die from an illness or accident or natural causes. Some savage killed her. There's no etiquette for that." Mom was a tiger. A polite tiger, but ferocious none the less. He was glad she was willing to take on Elizabeth. He didn't have the strength.

"No date was mentioned for the service. Is that to keep the press away, too?" Elizabeth said scornfully. She was getting defensive. That always made her even more imperious than normal. She didn't understand that the Virginia Bureau of Criminal Investigation and local cops didn't know or care about her pristine southern lineage. Her vaunted position in Charleston society didn't do anything to protect her from a murder investigation in Virginia.

Dan didn't want to be cruel, but he had to be forthright. "Elizabeth, we don't know the date. The autopsy was performed late yesterday evening and some results won't be in until Friday at the earliest. The coroner will determine when she can be released."

"Autopsy? Coroner?" These sounded foreign coming from her. Probably as foreign as they felt to him. Both referred to Jill. He couldn't grasp that.

"This is indecent." She dabbed at her eyes with a lace-trimmed white cotton handkerchief that carried a light touch of soothing lavender. She shifted her seat on the sofa and changed course. "What time will the detectives be here?"

"I don't know. They come and go," said Dan.

"Without an appointment?" Elizabeth was incredulous. "Is decency just tossed aside?" Dan's mother left the room.

Elizabeth was out of her depth. She was a master of fund raisers, cotillions, and polo matches. She was incapable of understanding what a murder investigation entailed. Frankly, he couldn't either. They had that in common.

"Elizabeth, this has devastated us all. I feel like I'm sleepwalking. The police. The morgue. The press. I'm doing the best I can. I loved Jill. I can't believe she's gone, but she is. The best thing for all of us is to throw protocol to the winds and protect Kaitlyn." He made an effort not to refer to her as Katie in front of Jill's parents. "I appreciate your taking her to breakfast. She needs to be with you and George. She was glad to see you.

"I know Jill is your daughter, but she's Kaitlyn's mother. She was murdered. As sickening as it is, that makes news. The press want pictures of a grieving child or Jill's grieving parents. Please be careful."

Elizabeth cried softly. He knew she hated herself for doing that in front of him. It wasn't proper. She

204

didn't realize only she cared about what was proper. He didn't.

"Dan, I had no idea people could be so cruel."

"I didn't, either, Elizabeth, until yesterday." He paused to collect himself. "The press will go away as soon as there's another news story. The most frightening people are those who take pictures with a cell phone. People right in this neighborhood. Right in this house. People who were Jill's neighbors and some who said they were her friends."

"No," she insisted. "They wouldn't."

"Yes. Anyone who comes must leave their cell in the basket in the foyer. They can pick them up on their way out."

"Oh, Dan, just a few years ago no one had cell phones. No one took pictures of absolutely everything they did. No one spied on their friends."

"I know, Elizabeth, but we have to deal with what is. People want pictures of Kaitlyn. She's a sweet grieving child. People will post her picture on Facebook or Instagram or Tumblr. They can make up a caption. It doesn't have to be true. That's worse than anything the media would do.

"No one knows the truth. The police have just started their investigation and won't make any comments. I'm not going to say anything. We don't owe anyone an explanation, especially when we don't have one."

She dabbed at her eyes again. "I don't even know what Facebook is."

He couldn't explain social media to this elegant, clueless woman. She'd never understand the need for some people to have hundreds of imaginary friends and followers with whom to share true or imagined stories. Her daughters and other grandchildren could try. He couldn't.

"Why don't you and George go to your hotel and rest for a while. Please come back for dinner this evening. Kaitlyn and I both want you here."

# CHAPTER

# FORTY-ONE

After dinner, George asked to speak to Dan in private. Normally, Dan would have suggested taking a walk around the neighborhood. Tonight he suggested sitting outside in the back yard that flowed into a wooded area behind the fence. It was quiet, peaceful, and the trees showed signs of spring.

He and George sat in Adirondack chairs Jill had painted periwinkle blue. George had brought a scotch with him; Dan had a beer. The older man looked haggard. In the two days since Jill had gone missing and found murdered, George had aged. He and Elizabeth were in their sixties, but George now looked eighty.

"Dan, Elizabeth and I were interviewed by the police at our hotel this afternoon."

Dan nodded. He expected the police to talk to anyone who'd ever met Jill.

"A Detective Elba and Lieutenant Winston."

"They're the lead investigators."

"Elizabeth was put off that they hadn't called first, but I think they wanted to surprise us. Throw us off balance so we wouldn't have prepared responses."

"Probably. I've talked to them whenever they show up. I told them they can search anything in the house. I don't understand how anything in the house could help find the monster that killed her, but I let them do their job."

"They seemed to think Jill might have known the person."

Dan was surprised. He poured out his beer. It had no taste whatsoever.

"Why would they think that? Why would anyone who knew Jill want to kill her?"

"They wouldn't answer me when I asked."

Dan didn't respond.

"Dan," said George. "They asked us about Christmas. How Jill seemed at Christmas without you. They asked if she seemed worried or angry."

Now he understood. The police wanted to know Jill's reaction to his confession of the affair and anything she'd told them since. As if that could help.

"George, I didn't have the mumps at Christmas. I stayed here because Jill found out I'd been having an affair for the last year the day before we were supposed to leave for Charleston."

He put his hand up for George not to interrupt. He had to get this out all at once or he'd never be able to do it at all.

"It was wrong. It was stupid. I hurt Jill terribly.

Terribly. I wish I could take it back, but I can't. I promised Jill I'd never see or speak to the woman again and I haven't. I've been sleeping in the guest room. We told Kaitlyn I have sleep apnea and occasionally use a machine while I sleep that is quite noisy and would disturb Jill's sleep. We bought a used machine on eBay to give the story credibility. She seems to believe it.

"It's the worst thing I've done in my life. I begged Jill to let me stay. To at least let me try to be a good husband. For Kaitlyn's sake, she let me stay. She wanted to forgive me, but I don't know if she could. I love her, George. I was cruel and selfish and stupid, but I love Jill."

George sat for a while before he spoke.

"Did Jill know the woman? Was it one of her friends?"

"No, no, nothing like that. She's my age. She was my college girlfriend. The girl who broke my heart and damn near my mind. I've never been unfaithful to Jill. No one except this woman would have tempted me.

"I ran into her at a meeting. She's a widow who lives in New York. As soon as I saw her, it was like I was possessed. I couldn't stay away from her. Not literally. Much of the affair was by phone. We'd talk for hours when I was at work."

"Did this have anything to do with losing your job?"

"No. It had always been a possibility once the new system was operational. It made me and three of my colleagues redundant. There was a statewide reduction in force. I was the oldest and most senior.

Someone less expensive took my position. "

"Did you tell Jill about the affair?"

"No. The woman sent Jill an email the day before we were to leave for Charleston."

"Why?"

Dan let out a long sigh. "My dad knew about the affair. He guessed as soon as I'd told everyone that I'd run into the woman. He was on me the entire year about risking my marriage for a woman who'd dumped me—who'd made me try to kill myself and sent me to a psychiatrist for three years. He said I was bewitched by her.

"When he died, Jill was wonderful to me. I realized how stupid I'd been. I'd been chasing a dream. Jill was real. She was my wife. I loved her.

"I never called the woman again. I was ashamed of myself and wanted to pretend it had never happened. I realize now I should have at least told her it was over. She wasn't a mind-reader. She called me every day until I finally answered.

"We had a nasty argument. I'm sure everyone in my office heard me yelling at her. She wasn't that upset about ending the affair. She was angry that I hadn't done her the courtesy of telling her it was over. I threatened to get a restraining order if she didn't stop calling me. That was the second stupidest thing I've ever done.

"The woman is a lawyer. She sent Jill an email at work saying that she didn't take threats lightly. She essentially told Jill to get me under control or all hell would break loose. If I followed through on my threat and went to court, she said that would make the affair public. That everyone would know. My employer would find out how I was spending my time at work. That Kaitlyn would find out. That I wouldn't be successful in getting a restraining order and I would put Jill and Kaitlyn through a public spectacle for no reason.

"Of course, Jill showed me the email. She was more hurt than angry. She said I was disinvited to Christmas vacation because she needed time away from me to think. When she came back, she asked me to move to the guest room, but she didn't ask for a divorce. She was giving me a chance."

Dan threw out his hands as if to say that's the whole story.

George had sipped his scotch while listening. He didn't respond immediately. Dan wondered if he was ever going to say anything.

"Thank you for telling me the truth, Dan. I suspected you didn't have the mumps, but I didn't pry. Jill did seem to think a lot while she was in Charleston. She let Elizabeth take over Kaitlyn, which she normally wouldn't have allowed. It kept both Elizabeth and Kaitlyn distracted."

"I'm sorry, George. I was selfish not to think she'd be terribly hurt."

"I know you're sorry. I think Jill was wise enough to see that one mistake shouldn't ruin a good marriage. I think you two would have been all right."

"You do?"

George nodded. Of course, George's opinion about the prospects of his marriage meant nothing, but it somehow made him feel less awful.

"Dan, how did this woman know Jill's email

address?"

"I don't know. We agreed at the beginning to never mention our spouses—not her late husband, not Jill. She didn't want to know Jill's name or anything about her. She wanted our time to be just us. No one else."

"Hmmm," he said. "That's certainly the way to conduct an affair. When it ended badly, she had the advantage of being a lawyer. Finding your marriage record and learning Jill's name wouldn't have taken more than a second. She could easily find employment history after she had the name. After that, getting email was a snap."

"I was stupid, George. I was angry when I threatened her. I didn't think about court proceedings being public. I wasn't going to actually do anything, but it gave her an in. She was protecting herself. She didn't want her professional reputation sullied by some stupid married man in Virginia even though she'd win the hearing. She knows me well. She knows I can be stubborn, so she basically put Jill on the case to rein me in."

George finished his scotch. "The woman was smart. She might have been fine with ending the affair, but she didn't want to jeopardize her career. You went too far. It's not smart to threaten lawyers."

"Now, I know."

"Dan, do you think Jill and this woman ever met?"

"No," Dan scoffed.

"Why are you so sure?"

"She was adamant about not knowing anything

about Jill. She basically sicced Jill on me and went away. I can't imagine Jill would want to meet her. Why, do you think it's possible?"

"Women do strange things when they're hurting."

The two men sat silently.

"George, it's going to be public that I had an affair. It's part of the investigation. Did the police tell you and Elizabeth?"

"No, they wanted our answer about Christmas then changed the subject. I'll tell Elizabeth tonight. This is the sort of thing that won't be kept quiet. Gossip spreads quickly." George hauled himself out of the chair. "Damn, those things are uncomfortable. Why do women like them?"

"Don't know, George. I'm horrible at women."

# CHAPTER
# FORTY-TWO

Dan wished he had said yes to water. He was tired, nervous, and now felt faint in this airless room. His mother had been trying to get him to eat, but he hadn't been hungry. He hadn't been nauseated. He just hadn't thought he could choke down food. She'd resorted to giving him soups.

"Excuse me, Detective Elba, may I have some water? Or soda? I feel light-headed."

"Sure. Lieutenant Winston, do you want anything while I'm taking orders?"

"Coke," said Winston.

Dan sat across from Winston. He was beginning to think of Elba and Winston as friends of the family. He'd spent more time with them in the last five days than he had with anyone who wasn't family.

Winston looked like a recruitment model for law enforcement. Tall, lean and muscled, and hands that looked like they never got dirty. Light tan. No mustache. Winston didn't wear a ring. He acted married, though. Just didn't wear a ring. Only an inexpensive watch.

Elba was back with sodas. Dan drank a third of his in a few gulps. He burped and felt better.

"Okay, now?"

Dan nodded.

Elba sat with a folder open in front of him and resumed questioning.

"As I said, the toxicology reports on Mrs. Ramsay are back. She died of an overdose of liquid morphine. There was a tiny injection site on the right side of her neck. A trace amount of blood was found on the headrest of the 2012 Kia Sorento. Do you know anyone with access to morphine?"

"No." He was a civil servant. He didn't know about pharmaceuticals or drug dealers. Which one were they pursuing?

"Sure?" Elba was giving him a chance to reconsider his answer. He didn't need it.

"No, I don't know anyone with access to morphine."

"What about Mrs. Ramsay?"

"My mother doesn't take morphine." There was another screwy question.

"Did your wife, Jill Ramsay, have access to morphine?"

"No."

"Mrs. Ramsey was prescribed 10 mg of morphine every four hours for ten days on August 23 of last year. The prescription was refilled twice. Once on August 31 and again on September 9."

Right. Her pain medication. "That was for pain

after her hysterectomy."

"Mr. Ramsay, the hospital records indicate that Mrs. Ramsay expressed concern about opiates. Could you explain that?"

"She thought they were a gateway drug. She led a healthy lifestyle. She didn't want drugs to be a part of that. She was afraid of them. I filled the prescription in case she needed pain relief once she came home. She had a long recovery period with some pretty bad days."

"Did she take morphine over that period?"

"Occasionally. For the first two weeks, she couldn't climb stairs. She kept the pills in the kitchen cabinet with her vitamins."

"Was there morphine left over?"

"I don't know. After the first week, she was mobile. She managed her medication."

"There wasn't any in the medicine cabinets in your home."

Was that a question? "Then I guess she took it all or threw it out. She was diligent about not keeping anything past its expiration date."

"How did you get the bruises on your right thigh?"

He ought to know by now that they switched subjects to keep him off balance.

"I fell out of my single bed in the guestroom the week before Jill…went on the cycling trip. I banged my right leg on the corner of the bedside table and broke the lamp. Katie heard the crash. I told her to go back to bed. I was fine, but embarrassed. I'm used to sleeping in a king bed and rolled off the single."

"What happened to the lamp?"

"The lamp?" These questions were so bizarre.

"The broken lamp. Did the bulb break? Did you sweep up the glass? Take the lamp to be repaired? Buy a new shade?"

"I don't know. I mentioned it to Jill. She decorated the guest room with pieces she'd collected. I don't know what she did."

"You don't know if there's a lamp on your bedside table?" Elba sounded skeptical.

"There's a lamp, but I couldn't tell you what it looks like if my life depended on it."

Another great answer. My life could depend on whether I broke a lamp or carried my wife's body through the park.

"And this incident woke your daughter?"

"Yes. She used to sleep with Abbie, our dog, and doesn't sleep as well without her."

"Tell us about the woman with whom you had an affair."

"Why? I don't want to drag her into this nightmare, too."

"Why not?"

"It's bad enough everyone, including Katie and my in-laws, know about it. I don't want to rub their faces in it."

"Commendable," said Winston.

Elba gave Winston a look. "Well, you two may be fine Virginia gentleman, but I'm from New Jersey. I want her name and contact information."

Dan provided Bella's name and business address again. "That's all I have. We used burner phones to communicate. I never went to her apartment. Hell,

I've never been to New York."

Elba passed the file to Winston who ignored it. Elba crossed his arms over his chest and didn't speak. Without taking notes or looking at the file, Winston spoke to Dan in an easy style and conversational tones.

"Mr. Ramsay, we're refining our timeline and trying to narrow the number of people who might have been in contact with Mrs. Ramsay. You said earlier Ms. Davis didn't take the break-up well. What did you mean?"

For what felt like the tenth time, Dan relayed the story of how he'd stonewalled Bella after his father died, lost his temper and threatened her the one time they spoke, and her response in the form of an email to Jill. "You haven't heard from Ms. Davis since December?"

"No." She made her point.

"Did Mrs. Ramsay communicate with her after December?"

"No. Of course not, why would she?" First George and now Winston. Maybe they knew a lot more about women than he did, but he couldn't envision a lover and a wife having a chat about the man they had in common.

"Do you know everyone Mrs. Ramsay communicated with?"

"No, but I can't imagine why she'd talk to Bella. She was terribly hurt. We were trying to keep our marriage together and maintain a sense of normalcy for Katie. I don't think her talking to Bella would help."

"You said talking. Could they have met?"

Dan shifted in his seat. "That's preposterous! Jill never went to New York."

Elba jumped back in. "People travel between New York and Richmond every day. You said you were reunited with Ms. Davis when she made a day trip for a speaking engagement. She could easily have come to Richmond," Elba suggested reasonably.

"I guess. I don't know. I don't see why Jill and Bella would have talked or met."

"Women size up the competition, Mr. Ramsay."

Dan threw up his hands in frustration. "I don't know for certain, but I don't think Jill would have talked to or met Bella."

"Ms. Davis hasn't contacted you since Mrs. Ramsay's death?"

"No."

"Seems convenient. With Mrs. Ramsay gone, you said Ms. Davis is a widow….."

"That's disgusting. I haven't seen or spoken to or communicated with or however you want to phrase it with Bella since that horrible conversation in December. Could we take a break? This is all too much."

"You have to pee?" asked Elba.

"Sure, if that will get me a break."

The two investigators conferred and apparently decided to continue without a break. Elba continued.

"You've isolated yourself. How do you know who's called or visited?"

"I don't. The funeral home provided a guest book for condolence callers to sign. I haven't looked at it.

The landline's been unplugged. I haven't talked to anyone directly except family."

"Did Mrs. Ramsay show any signs of having become addicted to morphine?"

"I don't know what the signs are." Dan couldn't believe how this investigation worked.

"Other drugs?"

"No way. Jill was health conscious." He almost pleaded for them to understand.

"Would you recognize signs of addiction?"

"I've been in psychiatric hospitals. I've seen people with terrible addictions. I know what that looks like."

"Once they've gotten treatment. What about signs before that? Did Mrs. Ramsay have changes in her appearance? Sleep habits? Mood swings?"

Dan was mystified. He couldn't think of Jill as an addict.

"I can't…"

"Mr. Ramsay," said Winston, "you told us your wife believed morphine was a gateway drug. She expressed concern about addiction while in the hospital for a hysterectomy. She managed her medication so you don't know what she had.

"You said she'd shaved her head, she seemed to stall about going on a cycling trial, she was more concerned about cash flow than you. Her colleagues said she'd lost weight and had circles under her eyes." All laid out nicely to make a case that his wife was a drug addict and he didn't know it.

"Jill wasn't an addict. She'd never be impaired around Katie. I can't tell you about her sleep habits because I was in the guest room. Her gynecologist warned us that until synthetic hormones replaced her own she'd have mood swings. I attributed any change in her moods to hormones or my affair."

"We're pursuing every angle," said Elba. "If she had become an addict, she might have come into contact with unsavory and dangerous people. If she seemed concerned about cash rather than investments, that would suggest an immediate need for money to buy drugs. It would explain why your job loss was a significant concern."

Dan shook his head in disbelief. "I don't know what to say."

"Have any of her doctors offered condolences?"

"I don't know. It would be in the book from Smythe's."

"What about William Bowles, III?"

"The lawyer?"

"Your lawyer, Mr. Ramsay."

"He's our tax attorney. His father handled everything. When he retired, Will took over his father's clients. Rob's spoken to him. Rob is the executor of my father's will and trustee of most of his trusts."

"Has Mr. Bowles passed on his sympathies?"

"I've no idea. You just said I was isolated. All I know is that Rob handed me a check from Dad's estate. I haven't had any discussions with Bowles."

"What about Mrs. Ramsay? Did she say anything about her meeting with Mr. Bowles?"

Dan's stomach lurched again. They were making stuff up to confuse him. "What meeting? Jill didn't meet with him. Why would she?"

"Mrs. Ramsay's appointment calendar indicated

a meeting with him March 11. His secretary confirmed the appointment was kept. Did you attend that meeting or did Mrs. Ramsay go alone?"

He felt faint. Nauseated. Had Jill gone to see him about a divorce?

"I thought you hadn't found Jill's cell."

"We didn't, Mr. Ramsay, but her cell was synched to her computer at work. We were able to re-create most of her data."

"I don't know. I don't know. I don't know," he shouted. He stood and angrily swept his empty can on the table to the floor.

Elba and Winston stood. Ready to subdue him.

"I'm not answering any more questions. I want a lawyer. Am I free to go?"

Elba walked to the door, opened it, and let Dan pass.

# CHAPTER
# FORTY-THREE

Jill's funeral was neither more nor less traumatic than he'd expected. It was held early Saturday morning in an attempt to keep the media and onlookers away. The family had been driven away from the house at eight o'clock. No reporters were in sight.

Dan was unaware of the funeral. He sat silently at the end of the front row holding Katie's hand as tears ran down his face. Elizabeth had recruited an Episcopal priest, a St. Margaret's alumna, to officiate. It didn't matter. He didn't hear a word that was said. The woman could have been reciting basketball scores for all he knew.

Jill. Pretty, happy, sunny Jill was dead. He'd never nuzzle that spot on her neck under her ear, taste her mouth, or feel her skin on his again. Never. He howled inside. All he saw was vibrant Jill. *Let's dance* when he'd never tried. *Let's have a picnic in the snow. Let's have a baby girl.*

Elizabeth had made one request and Dan had agreed whole-heartedly. "I want a priest to conduct a traditional service. This new format when anyone and everyone stands up and says something about the departed is undignified. I want it to be respectful and peaceful."

"That's all I want, too, Elizabeth."

She'd seem pathetically grateful to have claimed this small victory in planning her daughter's last earthly observance.

Katie cried softly and held his hand tightly. At a loss for what she should wear, he'd asked Elizabeth to handle it. She'd done a splendid job and seemed pleased to have been asked. Katie looked pretty in a navy dress and matching navy and white cardigan. She wore navy ballet slippers. Her shoulder length brown black hair was glossy in the sun. Through his tears, Dan saw a miniature Jill.

Only family and a few exceptional people had been invited. His mother, Rob and Suzanne, and their two sons. The Carters, Jane and her husband, Emily and her husband. Jill's boss, her two best friends from childhood, her team leader from the cycling club, and the leader of her quilting group. Katie had invited Jada, Sophia, and Josie without their parents. They sat next to her and each had placed a rose on the casket. Elizabeth and George completed the row.

"Dad, don't let them," shrieked Katie. He realized the service was over and they were being directed to leave. "Don't let them put her in the ground. It's dark. She'll hate it. I want her to come home with us."

He held Katie in his arms and let her sob. Everyone filed out and went to the waiting cars.

Dan squatted in the late spring grass to be eye level with his daughter. "Katie," he said, "your mom loved you more than anyone else in the world. She didn't want to leave you. She wouldn't have if she could've prevented it. You have lots of memories of your mom. We'll remember her together. She'll always have a place at home. She'll always live in your heart. And my heart. I love you."

Katie stopped crying and looked at him solemnly.

"You hurt her, too, before she died. Just like I did."

"Yes, I did. I'm sorry. I wish I could take it back, but I can't."

"You said Mom would forgive me. Did she forgive you?"

"I think so, Katie. I think she did. She was a loving woman. She wouldn't let anything bad stay in her heart."

"I love you, Dad." She took his hand and started forward. "We have to go to the cars or Grandmother Elizabeth will be mad."

# CHAPTER
# FORTY-FOUR

The funeral guests were invited to the house for brunch. Dan's mother had it catered from Jill's favorite natural foods restaurant, taken floral arrangements sent to the house out of their containers and mixed and regrouped them in Jill's vases to look more natural and less funereal, and closed all the window coverings in the house for privacy. Dan felt like he was in a cocoon. Only safe people were around him.

Katie and her friends filled plates and took them upstairs to her room. The girls could help Katie more than he could right now.

He sat in the goddamned wing chair and sipped black coffee. Suzanne brought him a plate with fruit and what looked like banana bread. He held her hand when she presented the plate. "Thanks, Suzanne, for all of it."

His two nephews stood around him. He asked them questions. Jobs. Apartments. Cars. Chicago

Cubs. Houston traffic. Anything to not talk about Jill. He sensed they were protective of him and appreciated it.

Eventually, he got up and went to Jill's sisters. Both remarked on how much Kaitlyn looked like her mother at that age. Jane seemed calm. Too calm. Sedated so much he was surprised she could keep her eyes open. Emily cried openly despite the occasional disapproving glare from her mother. Their husbands were nice enough guys. Gamecocks to the core, Jill called them referring to their graduation from the University of South Carolina. Dan couldn't remember what Jane's husband did. Emily's was so rich he didn't have to work. They owned a horse farm in Aiken. Emily was in her final year of professional equestrian competition.

"Dan, is there any news on who might have done this?" asked Emily.

He shook his head. "It's been six days since she was declared missing and from the questions they asked me, I don't think they have a good lead. They suggested that Jill might have known him. I can't believe that."

"No way. No one who knew Jill would have killed her."

"The police questioned us yesterday," said Jane. "Sounds like the same thing. Enemies, clients she had lost, competitive colleagues."

"Lovers," said Emily quietly.

Both husbands immediately excused themselves to freshen drinks.

"I'm sorry. Jill and I were trying to work it out. I think she was trying to forgive me. I hope so. I loved her."

"She never told us," said Jane. "She would have told us if she planned to leave you. She would have wanted to talk about Kaitlyn with us. She wouldn't have talked to girlfriends here. She considered most of them to be back stabbers."

"She did?" He was learning how little he knew about his wife.

As stoned as she appeared to be, Jane was coherent. "Oh, Jill was outgoing and friendly, but she thought some of her neighbors were envious of her seeming to have it all. Jill said some of their husbands had made passes and the wives probably knew it. She liked the people in the cycling club, but there was an element of competition. And, of course, Jill loved to win.

"She felt most at home, though, with the quilters. There's something about women sitting in a circle working on a project together that builds bonds. I know I'm more at ease with my quilting circle than even my sorority sisters."

"Me, too," said Emily. Her tears kept coming. "Will Kaitlyn go back to school Monday?"

"What do you two think? You went to St. Margaret's."

They nodded their heads simultaneously. Jane spoke. "She should get back to a schedule. St. Margaret's isn't truly a Mean Girls school. It has its share of them, especially the boarding students. I don't know that they've ever had a murder in the school family, though. I'll call one of my friends on the board. Make sure they're sensitive to Kaitlyn's privacy. She'll get the headmistress in line."

Dan laughed—an unfamiliar cracking noise. He hadn't laughed since before Jill left on the cycling trip. Neither of the women seemed to notice. "I used to be intimidated by her. Now, I don't think I'll be afraid of anyone or anything again. The worst has happened."

He leaned down to kiss them both. "I appreciate everything you do."

\*\*\*

"Dan, you do know the police were at the funeral. That's unacceptable. So intrusive."

"Elizabeth, that's what they do in cases like this. I think they also kept any gawkers and press away."

"Well, that's something," she sniffed.

Dan walked Elizabeth and George to the door. George hugged him hard and left without saying a word. His shoulders slumped as Dan watched him go down the steps to the car. His suit coat seemed to be one size too large. He clearly couldn't bear the loss of his daughter.

Elizabeth was standing in the doorway talking to him.

"I'm sorry, Elizabeth. I didn't hear you."

With exaggerated patience, Elizabeth repeated herself. "The movers will be here at eight-thirty tomorrow morning. I wish I could be here to oversee things, but George wants to get back to Charleston. I ordered the white glove service and I hope it's as good as I've been told."

"Why are you sending movers?" asked Dan. Everything in his life was odd these days, but some things were more odd than others.

"For Grandmother Charlotte's furniture, of course. It's Kaitlyn's now and we'll see that it's properly stored in Charleston until she's ready to use it. No need to risk damaging it here."

He processed what she was saying. She was talking about the hideous living room furniture. What did she mean it was Kaitlyn's?

"I don't understand," he said.

"Dan, really, Kaitlyn is next in line for Grandmother Charlotte's furniture and I want to make certain it's properly preserved for her."

What he wanted to say was that everything that had belonged to Jill was now his. Their wills left everything to each other. Katie hadn't inherited anything. She was the beneficiary of Jill's life insurance policy as she was of his. Who was Elizabeth to dictate what was and wasn't Katie's? She was talking about that furniture, though. He didn't want it. Why not let her take it? Let her have something of her daughter. Even if it wasn't technically correct that she should have it.

"Fine, Elizabeth."

"Someone will be up to greet them, won't they? It's Sunday."

"I'll be sure of it, Elizabeth. Have a good flight."

He closed the door on her heels.

# CHAPTER
# FORTY-FIVE

Early Saturday evening, Dan poured himself a scotch and sat in his favorite chair in the den. Suzanne had gone to drive his nephews to the airport. Katie was asleep or at least lying on her bed with the door closed. It was just Dan, Rob, and his mom.

"Is that it? Is it over now?" He inhaled the smoky scent and took a long slow swallow.

"I hope so, Dan, but I think people will still want to make condolence calls."

"I just won't answer the door or the phone."

"What about Kaitlyn?" asked Rob.

"I asked her aunts whether they thought she should go back to school Monday. Jane said she'd call someone on the board to pave the way. They both seemed to think it's a good idea. I don't know what good keeping her at home would do."

"I think they're right, and if they know someone on the board to keep an eye on things, all the better," said his mother gently.

Dan sighed long and loud.

"I have to find an attorney. I'm pissed I let those guys get to me, but I was sick of their questions and half questions and insinuations. I don't think they have any leads at all if they think Jill was an addict looking to score and was killed by her dealer. If they want to track down Bella, they're desperate."

"Bella?" asked his mother. She sat up straighter.

"They seem to think she and Jill might have been in contact. It sounds crazy to me. Why would either one want that?"

"No, that makes no sense at all. It would be humiliating for Jill." His mother put her hands in her lap and nervously picked at imaginary loose threads on her skirt. Dan and his mother had never discussed his affair. She was probably pained by Dan's actions, the damage he'd done to his family, and the distress he'd caused his father.

"Mom's right," said Rob. "If she didn't feel bad enough, Bella would do a real number on Jill."

"Jill wouldn't know that. She'd be no match for Bella," he said.

"What's this about drug addiction?" asked his mom. She seemed eager to move on to another theory. "Jill was devoted to healthy living."

Dan sipped his scotch. He shouldn't drink alcohol at all given the level of psych meds he was taking, but he craved the taste, the smell, the comforting liquid sliding down his throat.

"They think if she used morphine, then she might have become addicted. It would explain her shaved head, weight loss, and concern about cash.

She might have made a drug deal that went wrong."

"That's just preposterous, Dan. Is that what the investigators believe?"

"Mom, that's one of two logical scenarios if Jill knew her killer. The other would be that Jill got involved with a guy who didn't want her to reconcile with me. He might've been one of those 'if I can't have her no one can' type of guys."

"You can't consider that to be a possibility, surely."

"Mom, I don't think it's plausible at all.

"I think someone from the campsite killed her. There's something like twenty-two campsites. I don't know how many were being used or how many people used each one. The police haven't said. Could be someone watched the comings and goings in the parking lot and took a chance. Beyond that, there's a maniac killing people off I-95."

Dan looked at his mother. He wondered how she functioned. Her husband had died, he had disappointed her, and now her daughter-in-law had been murdered. She'd lost weight on her already trim frame. He noticed wrinkles that hadn't been on her forehead before. Yet, here she was doing all she could to take care of Katie and her youngest son at an age when she should have been relaxing.

"Mom, you must be exhausted. Have you seen any of your Richmond friends? Have you rested?"

"Yes. I've spoken to Irene. She's the most discrete. She helps behind the scenes. I do need some rest. I'm going to make a cup of tea and go to bed. I'll leave you boys alone." She kissed each of them on the cheek and left.

"There's another alternative," said Rob after his mother was out of the room. "Bella. Bella could've killed Jill."

Dan looked shocked. "Why would she do that?"

"To get back at you. You stopped calling. You threatened her. You made her angry. She could've killed Jill to keep you from having her."

"That's the most ridiculous theory yet." Dan got up and put more ice in his drink. "Want any?" he asked holding the tongs over the ice bucket. Rob shook his head no.

"After killing her, Bella picked Jill up, carried her a mile into the park, and positioned her with a blanket over her? Come on, Rob. Bella isn't that strong.

"Besides, Bella is many things, but not a killer. For one, she's a big time New York lawyer. She sicced Jill on me just for threatening to initiate proceedings for a temporary restraining order. She's fiercely protective of her reputation. She wouldn't risk her livelihood, much less her freedom, by killing Jill."

"No, you're not worth it." Rob agreed. "To her, I mean."

"Exactly. She said she wasn't upset about breaking up. It was not telling her. Leaving her hanging. That pissed her off. She probably has a new man by now."

"How do you know she didn't have one during the affair?"

"What?" This conversation. This event. This situation was surreal to Dan.

"You're married. She's single. She could've been

seeing other men while you were having an affair. You didn't have any claim on her."

"She said she didn't want another man."

Rob shrugged his shoulders. "Whatever. I'm just saying we know you didn't kill Jill. We're pretty sure she wasn't doing a drug deal. We don't know if Jill had a boyfriend who might have wanted her all to himself. So, that leaves Bella."

Dan stood and paced. "Or that nasty piece of work Monika Traymore might have killed her because her husband made a pass at Jill. Or a cycling club member did it because Jill had better time trials. There are all kinds of crazy scenarios if the police believe it was someone she knew."

"I don't think it has to be someone she knew," countered Rob. "The police could've gotten how she died wrong; she wasn't necessarily killed in the car."

"Rob, I don't know. I don't care who killed her. Jill's gone. I have to live without her and I don't know how to do that." He sat and started crying. "What am I going to do about finding a lawyer?"

"I made some calls. Brian, my college roommate, is a criminal court judge. He said there's only one person who could handle a case like this if it becomes something big. Nina Lombardi. She's in Alexandria and she's expensive, but he said if he needed a criminal lawyer, that's who he'd call."

"So, let's do it."

# CHAPTER
# FORTY-SIX

"What's the story? Make it short," barked Nina Lombardi. "I'm expensive and impatient with clients."

Another one who was going to beat him up. It was eleven o'clock Sunday morning—the day after Jill's funeral—and he and Rob were sitting in her office in Alexandria. No condolences from her. Her office wasn't plush. Spare. Angular. White. They'd left Richmond two hours earlier to allow for traffic. I-95 was always dicey. Parking near DC was impossible. Other than a bottleneck in Fredericksburg, they made good time and the office building had a parking garage. Rob drove. Dan stared at blurred scenery.

Now, he wanted coffee.

"You want coffee, too? A latte, maybe? Pastries? Bagels? I'm not a barista. You're not here for brunch."

Nevertheless, she spoke into an intercom, "Three

black coffees, Seth."

"Which of you is Judge Meacham's friend?" When Rob said he was, she nodded. "Good judge. Fair. Pro-Defense. Smart. Puts him three steps ahead of most of the judges in Virginia."

Seth, dressed in a shirt and tie even on a Sunday, walked in with a tray, served three black coffees, and left. He didn't say anything.

"Let's go," she directed Dan.

Dan spit out the story as fast as he could.

"So, they pushed you until you lost your temper to see just how short your fuse is and now you need me," she summarized. "Twenty minutes? Fifteen?"

"Less. Plus the five days before," he added.

"Elba and Winston. Good cops. Winston's the lead. Virginia Bureau of Criminal Investigation covers the park. Also keeps city of Fredericksburg and Spotsylvania County out of it. Doesn't act like it. Lets Elba be the front man."

That surprised him.

"So, you think they've got nothing. Probably not. They've got you, your lover, and the victim's hypothetical lover or drug dealer.

"You've got access to the murder weapon morphine, no alibi, and three of the top ten stressors—parent's death, job loss, and marital problems. All circumstantial, but you look good to them. You inherit?"

"Everything's already joint. My daughter is the beneficiary of Jill's life insurance."

"Pour over trust, no doubt. With you as trustee. Access to the money."

Dumbstruck. She was lightning fast. Dan nodded

yes, he'd control Katie's money until she turned eighteen.

"You're the prime suspect. Your lover is a close second. They're going to poke around your lover's movements and the victim's love life. Follow up on gossip. Talk to some known dealers. If they come up short, they'll arrest you."

"What? They can't do that. I didn't kill my wife. I loved her."

She looked at him sharply. "Why are you here, then?"

"I need someone to answer the questions that keep coming. I need interference."

"I'm not a football player, Mr. Ramsay. The cops aren't playing indefinite word games with you. You're their prime suspect. Get on board."

Dan was so stunned, he started to cry.

Lombardi whipped out two tissues from a box on her desk and handed them to him.

"Settle down. Listen to my fees. I'll leave you two alone for a few minutes afterward and then you can retain me. Or not."

*** 

"I can't believe what just happened," Dan said to Rob after they'd headed south on the highway. "She's a nightmare."

"But she's your nightmare now."

"A lien on the house, guardianship for Katie, $10,000 money transfer tomorrow. I feel like she took the last of what I had left."

"She made sense. I remember OJ signed over his

house to Shapiro."

Dan gave Rob a hard stare. "I'm not OJ Simpson," he snapped.

"The point is, I don't think it's that unusual for defense lawyers to have collateral to make sure they get paid. You're unemployed. How else would she get paid?"

"Okay." Unemployed. Zero chance of employment now.

"It also makes sense for Kaitlyn. Jill's will stipulates that in the event you and she were to die simultaneously, Suzanne and I would become her legal guardians. If you're arrested, she'd have the motion ready to go so Kaitlyn wouldn't have to go through some custody hearing unless things go downhill. She said Jill's parents or sisters would want custody. You know they would."

"And the cash?"

"Money to open a case file, do a little research, and speak to the cops for you."

"This is a nightmare. I keep saying that, but I can't think of another word. I feel like I'm under water or on an acid trip. I want to wake up and this to all have been a bad dream."

"I'm sorry, Dan. You're going to have to deal with the facts. I think you should ask Mom if she can stay with you for a while. If they arrest you, we don't want a last minute scramble. Kaitlyn needs continuity."

Dan couldn't put arrest and himself in the same sentence. Yes, he'd broken his marriage vows with Bella, but that's the worst thing he'd ever done. Now, Katie might face a custodial hearing because her mother was dead and her father was in jail.

"Do you think she'll stay?"

"Of course, she will. Mom loves you and Kaitlyn. She's got no reason to rush back to Florida with Dad gone."

"Why does Lombardi want my medical records?"

"To see if there's anything she can use. You have chronic depression. You attempted suicide. You've been hospitalized for it. She might be interested in that."

"Great. She'll think I'm a murderer and crazy."

"Dan, it doesn't matter what she thinks. If you're arrested, it's what twelve jurors think. For now, see your doctor tomorrow. Don't talk to the press. Don't talk to the cops. They have to go through Lombardi, now. Lay low. Don't piss anybody off."

# CHAPTER
# FORTY-SEVEN

Elizabeth was back in less than a week. Her excuse was Grandparents' Day at St. Margaret's School. She was an alumna herself, along with her three daughters, and the third generation, Kaitlyn, was a current student. By making her presence known as only she could, Elizabeth might be helpful to Katie with the faculty and staff. He didn't know how it would affect the behavior of other girls near Katie's age. Mean Girls existed everywhere.

Elizabeth arrived at six o'clock Thursday to pick up Katie for dinner. "You haven't cleaned the living room yet?" were the first words out of her mouth.

"No, I haven't thought about it." They walked through the empty living room, past the dining room, and into the den.

"Well, what are you waiting for? Kaitlyn needs a home. A place where she can bring friends. She can't have a bare living room with patches on the wall where Grandmother Charlotte's artwork hung."

She harangued him until she sat on the edge of the sofa cushion, back straight, legs to the side, ankles crossed.

Dan shrugged. He had no excuse. He had no interest. He didn't care.

"Do you want me to hire a decorator?"

Dan sat in his comfortable club chair. "No, thanks, Elizabeth. That's very generous, but I'll do something. My mother can help."

"How can she help from Florida?"

"She's living here now."

"Your mother lives in this house with you and Kaitlyn?" Her eyes got wider with every question she asked.

"Yes, for now. She can drive Kaitlyn to and from school without attracting attention. I'm lying low."

"The press is still interested in you?"

"Unfortunately, yes. Nothing has come along that's more sensational."

"You sound as though you want someone else to be murdered."

Dan ignored her and stood. "Would you like a gin and tonic?"

"Yes, please. With a slice of lime."

He went to the kitchen just off the den and mixed her drink. He poured himself a glass of orange juice. After seeing Dr. Spellman, he was more serious about staying away from alcohol while on antidepressants. He also didn't want to drink before his nightly run.

Every weeknight at nine o'clock, Rob picked him up and drove him to a high school in neighboring Hanover County where he ran three to four miles.

242

Rob wore binoculars around his neck and sat in the bleachers. Rob had emerged not only as his champion, but the family patriarch. Dan was lucky to have him.

"Is that why the drapes are closed?" she asked when he handed her a drink with a cocktail napkin. He wasn't the complete barbarian Elizabeth assumed he was. Jill probably had a supply or his mother had bought some.

"Yes," he said as he sat. "There are still photographers who slip into the community with their long lenses."

"Are Kaitlyn's curtains drawn, too?"

"Yes, to be safe. My mother had the car windows tinted so no one can see inside. She drives Kaitlyn directly to St. Margaret's gate. As you know, St. Margaret's has had children of public figures enrolled over the years, so they're equipped to keep photographers away."

She sighed just a bit and shook her head.

He knew she was thinking she'd never expected anyone from her family to be considered a public figure and newsworthy.

"I'll drive Kaitlyn to school tomorrow. Surely, no one will be looking at my rental car departing from the Hyatt House. In fact, why doesn't Kaitlyn spend the night with me? I have two queen beds. It would be a treat for both of us."

"I think Kaitlyn would like that. Why don't you ask her and help her pack an overnight bag along with her school supplies?"

Before she left the room, he said "Elizabeth, there's a small Japanese restaurant near your hotel.

Jill and Kaitlyn both like it. You might want to have dinner there."

"Japanese?" She asked as though she'd never heard of a restaurant that served such food.

"Only if it works for you. I just thought I'd mention it."

She left, careful to go along the inner hallway to avoid the empty living room. "Kaitlyn, it's Grandmother Elizabeth."

"Grandmother," he heard Kaitlyn's delighted cry from the top of the staircase.

\*\*\*

In the four days she'd been back at school, Katie said it was fine. She did her homework, which Dan checked every night, and hadn't come home in tears. He could only guess that she was as good as she could be. She played on the softball team. Her art teacher seemed to have given her attention and a special project. At least one of her trio of friends— Jada, Sophia, Josie—came by after school each day. His mother drove Katie to and from school so his presence wouldn't attract attention or reflect badly on Katie. She slept with Mr. Rabbit every night and said she wanted Abbie to come home.

Abbie wasn't coming home, but Dan still called the animal shelter every day. A physical exam showed he was physically sound. His blood pressure was a little high and his weight was down. The doctor asked about the large bruise on his thigh and he told him about falling out of the single bed. At least there was confidentiality there. Not like when Orlo had asked that day at the health club in the era before he knew Jill was dead.

Dr. Spellman might be as bored as he was in their sessions. They went through the same checklists, discussion of medications, and his insatiable craving for sleep every week. Spellman quizzed him on where he was on the suicide scale and didn't like the response. Dan claimed he was a ten. He'd kill himself in a heartbeat if he didn't consider what that would do to Katie. On his worst days, he wondered if Katie wouldn't be better off without him. It was the thought of what surely would be a nasty custody battle between Elizabeth and Rob that kept him earthbound.

When asked how he felt, the responses never varied—his brain felt like cotton, he couldn't follow conversations, and. every day became more surreal. He didn't tell Spellman he believed this was a nightmare from which he eventually had to wake.

# CHAPTER
# FORTY-EIGHT

"The jewelry's gone," announced Lombardi as she stood behind her desk.

She'd called the night before and asked Dan to be at her office at noon. Once again, Rob drove. He didn't know what Rob was doing about his patients and didn't ask.

"That's impossible," said Dan. He'd been jittery on the drive. Now he was on the verge of panic.

"Search warrant on the safe deposit box inventory." She handed a photocopy of the VBCI form listing everything found in the safe deposit box rented by Mr. and Mrs. Daniel Ramsay.

Dan scanned the document—Batman figurines, Redskin game ticket, infant photograph, 45 rpm record, certificates, trading cards, and small filigree ring. He handed it to Rob who blanched.

"The gold," said Rob. "There were seventy-five gold coins in the box. They're not listed."

"Then jewelry and gold are missing. You left out

some information during our meeting."

Dan didn't know what she was talking about. He wished she would sit.

"Bank visits. Records show you went to the safe deposit vault in September, November, and December of year before last and December last year. Mrs. Ramsay went once in February. Tell me."

He couldn't speak. He couldn't keep up. Mørk seemed determined to put him behind bars because he couldn't defend himself. He couldn't understand the questions. "Speak." She rapped the knuckles of her right hand on her desk.

He stammered through an explanation. "I went in September a year ago after I cleaned out my childhood bedroom at my parents' house. It was being sold and I had some things I wanted to keep. That November was right after I'd seen Bella and I sent her a pair of my grandmother's earrings. Rubies."

Rob made some sort of guttural noise.

"She sent them back. She had a no gift policy because I was married. I returned them to the vault as soon as I received them in early December. I went December last year after Jill found out about Bella to make sure I hadn't kept anything from Bella."

"You didn't know?"

"I was confused. I was stressed. I wanted to be sure."

"And Mrs. Ramsay?"

"I didn't know she went."

"Anything else missing? Weapons? Drugs? No

lies. I don't care about possession. I can't help you if you lie."

"No drugs. I stopped doing coke when I met Jill."

Another noise from Rob.

"Limited access to the box. You and the victim, right? Where'd you keep the key? The safe deposit box key?"

"In a magnetic box in the garage."

"Good. That's good. Open access."

He'd thought it was clever.

"Which one of you took the jewelry and coins?"

"I didn't."

Jill wouldn't take anything that belonged to his family. Not his great-grandmother's jewelry and not his father's gold coins.

"Do we know this jewelry existed? Coins?"

"Yes," said Rob. "I have pictures of the jewelry my father took for insurance purposes. Everything has a Russian mark for gold. When we each graduated high school, my father gave us seventy-five gold coins for a rainy day. I passed mine on to my sons when they graduated, but I knew Dan still had his."

"Get me those pictures to circulate."

Where? Where was Lombardi going to circulate pictures? Why? Lombardi was talking to him again. "Winston likes you for the murder."

"What does that mean?"

"You're suspect number one."

"Is he going to arrest me?"

"Not yet. No rush. When he's satisfied, he'll call me and I'll take you in."

Dan felt sick. He thought he might vomit on her desk. He started gagging.

"Will I have to spend the night in jail?"

"Lamb, the question is whether I can get you out on bail. This is a capital case. You're facing the death penalty."

He vomited.

# CHAPTER
# FORTY-NINE

"Come," she said and walked briskly out of her office into Seth's. "Call maintenance, Seth. I need your office. Amelia's out taking a deposition. Use hers." She closed the door, but Dan could still smell the contents of his stomach on the floor of Lombardi's office.

"Your brother shouldn't be here. If he is, anything we say today isn't confidential. Are you waiving privilege?

He needed Rob. "Yes, I waive privilege."

Once he and Rob were re-seated, she continued as she paced the room.

"What've you got, asset wise?"

"House, car."

"Cash, Lamb, cash. Can you do $500,000?"

"Yes, it might take a few days."

"Get it together now. That'll be good for up to $5 million. More than that, no bail. I'll do a speedy trial motion. That's probably 90 to 120 days before trial."

His stomach retched, but it was empty.

She crossed her arms in front of her while she walked.

"Your alibi. It's got to be better."

How he wished she'd sit. She was whippet thin. In a black suit with a black asymmetrical haircut, she looked like the hand of a clock ticking. Back and forth. Back and forth.

"I can't make it better. I told the truth about how I spent my day."

"Tell me again." A command not a request.

"I intended to spend the day working on my résumé and looking at online job sites, but the weather was so nice I didn't want to be inside. Jill was away; Katie was away. I was on my own. I felt pretty beat up after four months of sleeping in the guest room, begging to stay married, and keeping all of it from Katie. Bella had been really tough on me, too."

"In one phone call?"

"That, and the email to Jill."

"Go on."

"I got out of town. I drove to Virginia Beach."

"How?"

"Directly. I-64."

"Stops? Speeding tickets?"

"None."

"GPS?"

"No." He hadn't thought that was a necessary option when buying a car. "I parked on Eight-first or Eighty-second Street near where Shore Drive and Atlantic Avenue intersect. It's residential. Free parking. I parked at the end of the street under a tree. There's no sidewalk. Just grass, gravel, and sand. I walked on the decking to the beach and ran to about Thirty-Eight Street or Fortieth Street where the tourist area starts. It's three miles. It took about forty-five minutes. Running in sand is hard. I sat on the beach and rested for about fifteen minutes. Drank from my Thermos. Watched a couple of guys in wet suits trying to surf. Ran back to the car."

"Bathroom?"

"I relieved myself in the sea grass above the dunes before I got to the car."

"See anyone?"

"No. It was early April. A few people sat in beach chairs by the dunes, but not many. The water was still cold."

"No one asked the time, no runners coming from the other direction, no kids digging in the sand?"

"No."

"Hotels?"

"I passed the Windjammer if that's what it's still called around Fifty-Seventh Street. I don't know if it's open year-round."

"People might have seen you if we looked for them?"

"It's possible. I was only in that three mile area."

"What about your clothes?"

He looked blank.

"Sand, Lamb?"

"I brushed off my running shorts before I got in the car. Kicked my running shoes against the car until most of the sand was gone. I changed my tee shirt before getting in the car. When I got home, I washed my clothes."

"Shoes?"

"I gave them another rinse in the kitchen sink and put them in the boot tray in the mud room. Jill's meticulous about tracking stuff through the house. I've been extra careful about little things since I moved into the guest room."

"How soon did you wash your car?"

"The next day, Sunday. I went to a self-service car wash, cleaned it inside and out, and rinsed the tires carefully. I didn't see any sand."

"Receipt for the car wash?"

He shook his head. "A couple of other guys were there. I didn't talk to them."

"Maintenance on the car?"

"My mom had the windows tinted. I don't know where. I think she saw an ad to have it done in a half day. She didn't want anyone trying to see Katie in the car."

"How does that work? Does someone have to get inside the car?"

"No," said Rob. "A serviceman opens the car door and rolls the window up and down, but doesn't have to sit. The front windshield was already tinted as much as allowed by law."

"Lamb, I haven't received your medical records."

"I didn't request them. Besides, I went for a physical last week. Nothing's wrong. I've lost a few pounds since Jill." He stopped himself. "Since the funeral."

"Dan," said Rob. "Tell her about the specialist."

No. He wasn't going to humiliate himself any further. What possible reason would she have to know he saw a psychiatrist and a therapist?

"You see a therapist." Indifferent. Matter-of-fact. She was a mind-reader. "Grief counseling, job loss, marriage counseling?"

"General counseling."

"He has chronic depression," said Rob. "It started when he was sixteen. He had a couple of episodes in college. He was fine until Bella broke up with him when he was in graduate school and he attempted suicide. After being hospitalized for ninety days, he lived with our parents for more than two years and tried a boatload of medications before he could live independently. He had two hospitalizations before he married Jill when he was almost forty. He still has mild episodes. He's been on anti-depressants since our father died, more when Jill found out about the affair, and even more when Jill was murdered. The psychiatrist sees him every two weeks and requires he see a therapist weekly."

"Thanks." She turned to Dan. "That wasn't so hard, was it?"

She stopped pacing.

"The bruising on your right thigh? Sticking with the fell out of bed story?"

"It's the truth. I thought you hadn't gotten my medical records."

"Health club masseur told Winston and Elba."

They'd talked to Orlo…Probably anybody at the club that Sunday. He'd never be able to go there again. Or Katie.

"Didn't Ms. Davis grow up at the Virginia Beach Oceanfront?"

"Yes.

"Go by the house? Take a peek for old time's sake?"

"Bella's parents moved to St. John after she graduated college."

"Didn't answer my question."

"No, I didn't go by Bella's old house. If anything, I'd avoid it. It's painful."

"I'm done. Questions?"

Yeah, maybe if he had some coffee and sat outside for about an hour, he'd come up with dozens of questions. His mind wasn't working right this minute.

# CHAPTER FIFTY

"Why is this a capital case?" asked Rob.

"Their theory includes kidnapping. Two felonies."

"You said all the evidence is circumstantial. What's the evidence?"

"Repeating myself," she glared at Rob. "Motive. He had an affair. Might be nice to have the wife out of the picture. Access to the murder weapon morphine, keys to the car, kid's out for the weekend, no alibi. Throw in missing gold and jewels, temper, and psychiatric history, and he's toast."

"That's circumstantial. Can't you counter all those things? None of it is beyond a reasonable doubt."

"At trial, yes. Doesn't stop the police from making an arrest of their most viable suspect."

"What about Bella? His…"

"I know who she is. She's unavailable right now."

"What does that mean?" asked Rob. Dan was suddenly alert.

Lombardi shrugged. "Out of town. Moved. Who knows? Cops can't find her. She may have sold great-grandmom's jewelry and is waiting for Dan to meet her in Monte Carlo. Dan admitted sending the jewelry to her."

"A pair of earrings. Not all of it."

"So he said."

Dan felt like he was watching a black and white movie. Lombardi, in her black suit, talking to Rob in his white shirt. He heard what they said, but it made no sense. It was a foreign film. Taking place in Monte Carlo. He wanted the credits to roll.

"Anything else?"

"How much notice will he have if they decide to make an arrest?" asked Rob.

"I'll know the night before and arrange to take him in the next morning before ten or so. Anything else?" Silence. "Good." She motioned for them to leave.

They stood. Before she walked away, Rob said "You know his last name is Ramsay, right?"

"Certainly."

"Why do you call him Lamb?"

"He's a dear naïf creature who doesn't have a clue what's about to happen to him."

# CHAPTER

# FIFTY-ONE

The drive home from Lombardi's that afternoon was tense. They rode in almost complete silence. Rob didn't ask any questions about revelations of drug use Dan had made and Dan didn't ask Rob why he felt it necessary to disclose his mental health history to Lombardi. Worse, the coins and jewelry were gone.

Late Friday afternoon, Elizabeth called. Grandparents' Day had been a tremendous success and she wanted to extend it a bit by taking Kaitlyn to the home of one of her classmates. Another classmate and her granddaughter would be joining them. The granddaughters were two years older than Kaitlyn and lovely girls, Taylor and Amy. Dan asked to speak to Katie.

"I know Grandmother Elizabeth is there listening to you, but do you want to go with her after school?"

"I think so."

"Are Taylor and Amy Mean Girls?"

Katie laughed. "Yes."

"Are you acting in front of your grandmother?"

"Of course, Dad. Don't be silly."

"Don't let those Mean Girls get away with anything. "

"Yes, Grandmother Elizabeth will be right there."

"Okay. Put her back on."

"Yes, Elizabeth, but please have her home by nine. Be careful the older girls don't pry."

"Of course, Dan, they're lovely girls."

\*\*\*

Katie seemed fine after Elizabeth's visit. She'd enjoyed having dinner and spending the night in a hotel with her grandmother. The activities at school were fun. She and Elizabeth had won a prize.

Katie seemed not to have been upset by the older girls. She was eager to take a bath, put on her pajamas, and go to bed.

"I missed Mr. Rabbit," she explained in her room.

"You didn't take him with you?"

"No, Grandmother Elizabeth would've thought I was being a baby."

Dan sat on her bed and patted a spot next to him for her to sit. "Katie, you're a sensitive girl. Don't let anyone, Grandmother Elizabeth included, tell you how to feel. Your mom just died. That's about the worst thing that can happen. You feel whatever you want to feel as long as you want."

She nodded. "I do, Dad. Grandmother Elizabeth is different. I don't feel like defending myself over things that aren't important. If I wouldn't have been able to sleep without Mr. Rabbit, I would have taken him no matter what she thought. I don't need him. I like him." She paused as though she wanted to get the next words exactly right. "Dad, did Mom have a boyfriend who killed her?"

"Is that what Taylor and Amy said?"

She looked down at her lap. "Yes, when Grandmother Elizabeth was in the garden with the other grandmothers."

He lifted her chin to look at her face. "The police don't know who killed your mom. If Taylor and Amy think they know something about it, tell them to talk to the police."

"Dad, I don't want them to think Mom had a boyfriend. She loved you. She didn't need a boyfriend."

"Katie, you can't control what other people think. I don't think your mom had a boyfriend. I think she was trying hard to forgive me for hurting her. She loved our family. Your mother loved us too much to have a boyfriend."

"I love you, Dad."

"I love you very much, Katie."

He watched her hop in bed with Mr. Rabbit. He pulled Jill's handmade quilt over her. He hurt so much, tears fell on a few patches of the quilt.

# CHAPTER
# FIFTY-TWO

Dan planned to nap Saturday afternoon. It was exactly one week since Jill had been lowered into the ground. It seemed like seconds and felt like years. He hadn't had a chance to mourn.

So far, he'd seen and pissed off the cops, retained Lombardi, seen two doctors and a therapist, started more meds that so far did nothing, and relied completely on his mother to keep the household running. She said she'd stay as long as he wanted. She wasn't missing anything in Florida. It was about time for the snowbirds, including some of her friends, to return up north.

Jill had always found that expression hilarious. "If Robert E. Lee knew Floridians referred to Virginia and North Carolina as Up North, he'd have to rise up and fight again. This time against barbarians in Florida. They were barely a state during the Civil War."

Dan was grateful for his mother. He didn't want

to think what would be going on if his father were alive.

He'd just laid down fully dressed except for his shoes on top of the sheets. He'd rolled back the duvet and was trying to make his mind blank.

The door swung open. Elizabeth. "Dan. What are you doing in here?"

He sat up. "It's my bedroom, Elizabeth. What do you want?"

"I'm going to go through Jill's clothes to take back a few things. I'd like to have something and I'd like to get things for Jane and Emily. They're her size."

"Back off, Elizabeth. Don't touch a single thing that belonged to Jill. They belong here in her closet until Katie and I are ready to put them away, if ever."

"Why, she's my daughter and she'd want me to have things. And her sisters."

"No, she wouldn't."

"Dan, that's a terrible thing to say."

"Elizabeth, nothing in this house belongs to you. Please leave my bedroom. Don't ever come in here again."

\*\*\*

At dinner Saturday evening, after Elizabeth had left for Charleston without saying goodbye to Dan, Katie elaborated on their time together. "We went to the Japanese Garden for dinner. Grandmother Elizabeth had never eaten sushi. She didn't want to eat raw fish so I helped her pick out a California roll, a cucumber roll, and an avocado roll. She liked the cucumber roll a lot. She said it was almost like a tea sandwich."

Dan smiled at that. It probably did seem like a tea sandwich to Elizabeth.

"Grandmother Elizabeth didn't know how to use chopsticks and asked for silverware. They didn't have any. She was so funny. She couldn't pick up anything without dropping it. None of it spilled on her dress, though. That would've been bad. She's meticulous."

"Like your mom," said Dan.

"Mom wasn't that bad. Grandmother Elizabeth is much worse."

"Did you like staying at the hotel?" asked his mom.

"It was fun. Our room overlooked the pool, but it wasn't open yet. I brought home soap and shampoo samples. Grandmother Elizabeth said it was okay. We didn't watch TV. She said it jangled her nerves. We listened to the classical music radio station. Why would TV jangle her nerves?"

"Some people find TV distracting. They don't like it as background noise. I think Elizabeth believes it's impolite to have the TV on while trying to have a conversation."

*Good catch, Mom.*

"Why?" persisted Katie.

"When she wants to watch a program on TV, she pays attention. If she's not watching a particular program, it's unnecessary noise when she's having a conversation with you."

And Elizabeth also prevented Katie from hearing

263

any news about her mother's case. Good for her.

"She said we need living room furniture, Dad."

"She told me that, too. What kind do you want?"

"I don't know. What kinds are there?

"There's antique, like Great Grandmother Charlotte's," he said. "There's formal, contemporary, and casual. I think that's it."

"I'm glad the antique stuff is gone. It was uncomfortable."

"I think we're all glad it's gone. Let's start with color. What color do you want to paint the walls?"

"Blue, of course, Dad." She looked to Selma as if to say what other color could there be?

"Blue it is. I think there are some furniture and home furnishings catalogues around here. We can look at them tonight and get some ideas. Tomorrow we'll go to the paint store and pick out a color blue. I can paint the room this week."

He hoped he could. He hoped he wasn't arrested this week. He couldn't believe he was going to be arrested, much less arrested for killing Jill. Surely, the police were smarter than that.

"I'm sorry, Katie. What did you say?"

"Dad," she gave him an exasperated look. "I said Grandmother Elizabeth asked me if I'd like to spend the summer in Charleston with my cousins. She said there was a day camp at the country club. Aunt Jane has a pool, and I could ride horses at Aunt Emily's."

Damn that woman. She was so manipulative. One good thing and then she'd do something sneaky.

"Katie, your mom and I already paid a deposit for you to go to camp at Summer Hill like last year.

Maybe you could visit your cousins in Charleston after that. I'll have to look at dates."

His mother took over. "Kaitlyn, do you want to go to Charleston?"

"Not really. I don't think I could live with Grandmother Elizabeth for a whole summer. I like Grandfather George, but she's too strict. I'm sure I couldn't play video games or watch TV or have any fun."

"What if you stayed with one of your aunts?"

"Aunt Jane has two teenage boys. They're noisy and smelly and tell the dumbest jokes over and over. I don't want to live with them. I think Aunt Jane drinks a lot or pops a lot of pills or something. She always seems out of it."

"What about Aunt Emily?"

"She's fun, but she has equestrian competitions this summer. I don't know if she'd be around much. Her daughters are okay, but all they talk about is horses. I don't really like horses."

"Have you been around horses much?" asked Dan.

"We went on that trail ride once on vacation, remember? Jada took us horseback riding for her birthday. It was okay, but kind of boring."

"We don't have to decide that now. Do you want dessert? Sorbet?"

"No, thanks. I want to look at those catalogues. Where are they, Dad?"

"In the wicker basket next to your mother's chair in the den."

"May I be excused?"

Dan nodded. He didn't want her to see the tears

in his eyes. The mention of Jill's chair in the den overwhelmed him. Grief hit him when he wasn't expecting it. Katie took her plate to the sink and dashed into the den. His mom suggested dessert for them.

"Dan, we'll have sorbet. I got orange cream."

His mother cleared the table and set a small glass bowl of orange cream in front of him.

"Eat it, Dan. You don't want to lose too much weight."

He took a bite to please her. Like he was eight years old.

"That woman," he started. "It's like she's trying to turn Katie into Jill. Jill ran away from that stifling house. Katie's a completely different kid. She's going to feel worse than Jill did. Jill hadn't had ten years of a different life."

"You don't have to decide anything now, Dan."

"Maybe I do."

His mother looked surprised.

He took the empty sorbet dishes to the sink. He went to the den where Katie was absorbed in the furniture catalogues.

"Katie, take those upstairs to your room. Try to narrow it to your three favorite pieces. I'm going to watch TV down here for a while with Gran."

When Katie had gone upstairs and the dishwasher had been loaded, Dan and his mother sat in the den. He had a large glass of water. His mother had coffee.

"Mom, the lawyer said I could be arrested any time."

She stared at him in disbelief. "Arrested? For

what?"

"For murder. For Jill."

"That's ridiculous. You didn't kill her. I thought that lawyer was supposed to be very good."

"She may be. It's not like I have any experience to compare. Lombardi said I'm the number one suspect. I don't have an alibi that can be proven, Jill had discovered my affair, and I was stressed after the loss of Dad and my job.

He lowered his voice. "Mom, Jill went to see Will Bowles.

"The lawyer?"

"Yes. I think she must have talked to him about divorce. He was cool to me when I called to change the names on our trust documents after Jill died. Mom, Jill went to our safe deposit box for the first time in our marriage. I don't know what she found. There was nothing there but some of your documents, Dad's gold coins, and your grandmother's jewelry. Oh, and I had put some stuff from my old bedroom there like my Beatles cards. Jill was suspicious of whether I'd told her the complete truth about Bella, I guess, or she could have added something to the deposit box. Maybe she put something about divorce in there."

Selma stared at him without speaking.

"The police think I had access to morphine. They don't believe me about what happened to Jill's prescriptions. Morphine is what killed her."

"But Dan, they can't prove anything. It's all circumstantial."

"Lombardi says most of her cases are circumstantial. She can argue everything at trial, but she can't prevent the police from arresting me. Mom, she said it's a capital case because they're including kidnapping with premeditated murder. I'd get the death penalty."

She covered her mouth to stifle a scream. "No, no, Dan. That's not possible. Nobody will believe it."

"Mom, I'm hiding. People already believe it."

She cried. "I'm sorry, I shouldn't cry in front of you, but…" She couldn't go on. She sat on the sofa and cried quietly for a while.

Her coffee had gotten cold. He picked up the mug and returned it to the kitchen just to have something to do. He gulped down his water. When he returned, his mom was somewhat composed.

"Dan, how do we stop this?"

"Lombardi is supposed to be the best."

"Before you're arrested, I mean. We don't want you to be arrested. Is there another lawyer? A better one?

"No lawyer can prevent the police from making an arrest. A judge issues an arrest warrant after reviewing police evidence. Their jobs are to get who they consider to be the killer off the streets and behind bars until a jury makes the ultimate decision. Lombardi thinks the evidence won't hold up beyond a reasonable doubt at trial, but she can't stop an arrest."

"Then we have to improve your side of the situation so the police have to focus on finding the real killer."

"Mom. I have no idea who killed Jill. I think it had to be random—except why would he take her to the garden, fold her hands, and cover her with a blanket?"

"Maybe that's part of his pattern or thrill or whatever killers have."

"That's TV, not real life. Katie said two girls from school said Jill had a boyfriend who killed her. I don't believe that, either."

"No, she wouldn't." His mother was firm.

"Mom, a year ago you would have said I wouldn't have had an affair, but I did."

"Only because it was Bella. You wouldn't have taken up with just anyone. Someone new. Jill was too practical and too sensitive to add a boyfriend to the mix. She must have wanted to keep your family together. She never asked you to move, she didn't tell her parents or her sisters at Christmas when she had the chance, and she never told Kaitlyn. She wanted to forgive you. I know she did."

"Did she say anything to you, Mom?"

"Never. She wouldn't talk about you to me or your father. She had boundaries. What was between the two of you stayed between the two of you."

They sat in silence.

Finally, his mother stood. She kissed him on the cheek. "Dan, I've had enough for one day. I'm going to bed. Don't stay up too late."

She rested her hand on his shoulder. He grabbed it and held it tight.

# CHAPTER
# FIFTY-THREE

Before going to bed, Dan took the landline phones from the foyer and master bedroom and threw them in the garbage. He and Rob would take all of it to the dump next week. Otherwise, reporters and curiosity-seekers would paw through trash left at the curb for regular pickup. He logged onto his computer and cancelled his landline account. At least that was one thing accomplished.

He'd looked at the cell phone carrier to see what he had to do to change his phone number and cancel Jill's account. It was easier to cancel the account and create a new one for his mother and himself. He still didn't want Katie to have a cell.

He'd just turned off the computer when his cell rang. He checked caller ID before answering.

"Lamb, new plans."

"I'm listening."

"Hired a PI. Best in the state. He'll get your car tomorrow morning by nine. Winston agreed it can be examined at a mutually acceptable garage. If we find sand, it doesn't prove anything. Just that sometime between the last time you had the car detailed and today, sand showed up. PI will get pictures before it's towed."

"Okay."

"Forensic photographer will call you tomorrow. Pictures of you in the running clothes you had on that Saturday. Face forward head shot. Profile each side. Full length running in both directions. Same everything. Headband, wristband. Thermos. Socks. Shoes. Sunglasses. Hair length. Whatever.

"Decided to blast the Oceanfront. You, the car, license plate. Save the Bay, right? Virginia Beach newspaper. Flyers. Door to door canvas. Maybe TV down there."

"Okay."

"Bad news, Lamb. The jewelry is circulating. Diamond Districts. New York, Antwerp, and Ramat Gan. Know anything about that?"

Dan's head was going to explode any minute. There wasn't enough room in his skull to hold, never mind process, the information that was bombarding him. "No," he croaked.

"You taking your meds, Lamb?"

"Yes."

"Goodnight, Lamb."

Dan simply couldn't grasp how jewelry from the safe deposit box was circulating internationally. Had Jill tried to stash money if they divorced? Could she have been an addict with a need for cash? Even if Jill had taken them, she wouldn't know how to sell them. He certainly wouldn't know where to begin. Rob was the one the family relied on to know things like that. Would she just give the jewelry to her dealer and let him cash out?

He called the car rental agency that delivered. A car with tinted windows would be here around eight-thirty tomorrow morning. They weren't sure what kind had tinted windows. Could be anything—sedan, SUV, hybrid.

With two things accomplished, he slept through the night.

# CHAPTER

# FIFTY-FOUR

"Dad, Dad," called Katie as she ran downstairs. "Why was Will Smith at our house?"

"He came over to get some acting advice from me," said Dan with a straight face as he closed the front door behind him.

"He did not. Why was he here?"

"It's a man who looks like Will Smith in a big black SUV. He came to get the car taken to a garage for analysis. I don't know when we'll get it back so I rented a car. The guy just dropped off the rental."

She looked out the window where a white sedan parked in the driveway was visible.

"When are we going to get Mom's car back?" She asked as they walked towards the kitchen.

"Probably never. The police took it apart looking for evidence."

"But my basketball is in there." A frown crossed her face. "And Abbie's blanket."

"They'll give us back anything that was in the

273

car. Just not the car itself."

He knew someone would get it back after trial if there was one, but he didn't want it. He hoped the police kept it forever.

"Breakfast first, and then show me your top three choices for furniture."

Dan poured cereal for both of them, added blueberries, and soy milk and put them on the breakfast bar. He put out juice for Katie and refilled his coffee cup.

"I'll get the catalogues." She ran back upstairs.

The photographer called. He wanted to meet at noon at a park in Chesterfield County. Dan agreed. They were going in that direction to the paint and furniture stores. Anything to stay out of his neighborhood.

"Here, Dad. I chose three, but this one is the best. She pointed to a living room with four white upholstered armchairs with thick cushions positioned in a wide circle in front of a fireplace. The walls in the photograph were blue.

"I like that a lot," he said.

"We could paint the fireplace white like in the picture. Then we can hang one of mom's quilts above the mantel."

"Katie, that's a wonderful idea. I think it'll look great. Do you like the round coffee table?"

"Round, yes, but not that one. I think one with a glass top would be better."

"You're right. We'll have to get a rug and end tables, too. And maybe a matching love seat to go under the front window in the living room."

"I like the rug in the picture. It's a circle rug. The

wood floors are bare."

"I see," Dan winked at Katie. "I'm going to have to take a look at the living room floor. It may need a cleaning or refinishing."

"I'm going to go get dressed."

"Be ready by eleven," he called after her.

His mother had been sitting in the den drinking coffee. She came into the kitchen and sat next to Dan at the bar.

"New plans, I gather."

"Lombardi called last night. She's going to have the car ripped apart to try to find some sand."

She hugged him. "Oh Dan, that's wonderful news."

"Not really. The car's been washed. Even if sand is found, it doesn't prove anything. It doesn't mean the sand was from that Saturday. Just sometime between the last wash before Jill left until today. They might be able to analyze the sand to determine if it came from Virginia Beach."

"They can do that?"

"I guess. Scientists can do all kinds of things. Lombardi hired a private investigator and a photographer. She wants pictures of me dressed exactly how I was that Saturday right down to my haircut. She's going to blitz the three mile area I ran at the Oceanfront. She said flyers, the newspaper, and a door to door canvas. Maybe TV. The photographer is meeting me in Chesterfield County at a park."

"Dan, I'm so happy. Someone must have seen you. They'll come forward. The police will have to believe your alibi."

"I hope so. There weren't many people out, but maybe someone will recognize me. It's a long shot. The photographer wants to meet at noon to be in the same general timeframe as when I was running. Light. Shadows. I don't know.

"I haven't had my hair cut since before Jill went missing. Do you think it's grown much? Could you trim it a little in the back?"

She leaned back in her chair and fingered his hair. "No, your hair wasn't in your collar then like it is now. I can trim a little bit. It won't be pretty, but it will be a better length. That lawyer is thorough, isn't she?"

"They say she's the best." He paused. "Mom, I'm sorry to tell you, but Lombardi said your grandmother's jewelry is circulating in international diamond districts."

All her Florida tan faded. She looked pale and shocked. She put her hand to her throat as if to adjust a necklace that wasn't there.

"Mom, I'm sorry. Lombardi says Jill was the last one to access the safety box. I thought she might have put something in there from Bowles. Maybe a draft separation agreement. I can't believe she'd take anything out. Certainly not the jewelry. Even if she did—and that's a big if—I don't think she'd call someone in Antwerp to sell them for her."

"No, no. Of course not," his mother agreed. "This is all so strange."

"Unless the addiction theory is true and she gave her dealer the jewels to fence. That just isn't Jill."

His mom sighed. "I know addicts are secretive and do things they normally wouldn't, but I just don't see Jill being addicted to drugs. If she was addicted to anything, it was cycling."

Dan put his arms around her. "Mom, please rest while we're out. Jill, the police, all of it on top of Dad dying. I know I've been relying on you too much. Please take a break."

"I will, Dan. I must."

\*\*\*

He now knew why supermodels got paid $10,000 a day. It was hard work. The photographer had found a sandy ring around a small pond in the park—enough that he'd be running in light sand at a slow pace similar to that at the beach. He ran around the pond three times in each direction. He'd stood for face and profile shots before and after he worked up a sweat. The man knew exactly what he wanted. He took close-ups of the Thermos and his watch. Dan didn't wear wrist or head bands. He never wore a hat. He hadn't worn sunglasses that Saturday.

Katie seemed mesmerized by the photographer. She stood silently away from him while he worked, but watched everything he did. When the photographer was finished and Dan stood trying to catch his breath, Katie told him what he did was cool and asked what kinds of photos he took. When he replied fashion and cars for magazines, she looked rapturous. He told her he also did occasional forensic work. Forensic meaning criminal. Scene of the crime stuff.

"I'd love to do that when I grow up."

277

"Miss Ramsay, you can start right now. I started taking pictures when I was eight. There's lots to learn about light, shadow, and movement. That's just to get the shot. Then there are all kinds of technical enhancements and editing."

"Where would I learn that?"

"Start taking pictures. Do you have an art teacher at school?"

"Yes, Ms. Vacarro. Art's my favorite class."

"Julie Vacarro? She's excellent. Just tell her you're interested and she'll get you started. And please don't take selfies. They're killing photography as an art."

"I can't. My parents won't let me have a cell phone."

"Good for them."

Dan walked up in time to hear that someone agreed with at least one of his decisions.

# CHAPTER
# FIFTY-FIVE

Dan asked the photographer to stay with Katie for a few minutes so he could change in the park's men's room. He ran water over himself to cool down. He'd just changed and was getting ready to comb his hair when the photographer called him.

"Mr. Ramsay, your daughter's run after some family with a dog."

Dan ran out of the wooden structure and in the direction the photographer pointed. He saw Katie talking to a redhead, a girl, and a boy with a black Schnauzer mix. Abbie. The dog was Abbie.

He caught up to them. The woman looked startled and stood between him and her children. Abbie was licking Katie.

"What's going on?" he asked.

"Dad, it's Abbie."

"I can see that." He turned to the woman for an explanation.

"Oh, dear. This is our dog Maggie. We lost her

about three years ago. A careless house sitter let her get away. We thought she was gone for good until one day, about six weeks ago, a woman called me and said she had Maggie. She said her husband had found Maggie at the animal shelter and adopted her. She somehow found us and returned her."

"Did this woman tell you her name?"

"Mrs. Ramsay. Jill Ramsay. I offered her a reward, but she said no. She said her family wouldn't feel right keeping Maggie if they knew another family missed her. My kids were ecstatic."

Dan's stomach muscles clenched and unclenched. Everything. Everything he did or saw brought new information about Jill and just how little he knew about her. She'd given Abbie away?

"I'm Dan Ramsay. This is my daughter Kaitlyn. We thought Abbie was missing. We put up posters and I've been checking the animal shelter every day."

"And your wife didn't tell you?"

"Mom died," said Katie.

The woman looked at Dan, who nodded. "Yes, my wife was killed recently."

"Oh, I'm sorry. She didn't have a chance to tell you. Oh, I'm sorry. So sorry."

Jill died three weeks after Abbie went missing. She'd had plenty of time to tell him what she'd done. Why would she put Katie through that? Him, maybe, but not Katie.

"Do you mind if I say hello?"

"Please."

Dan buried his face in Abbie's coat. He inhaled her special scent. It wasn't there. This family must use a different shampoo. "I missed you," he said into her fur. "I never thought I'd see you again. I'm glad you're not hurt." He hugged Abbie as hard as he could. She licked his face.

When he stood, Katie had assessed the situation and made the awful conclusion. "Dad, we're not going to get Abbie back, are we?"

"No, Katie. We can't. She belonged to this family first. We kept her safe for them."

He and the woman exchanged contact information.

"If you ever need to find a new home for Maggie, please call us. We'd be happy to have her."

"Of course, Mr. Ramsay. I'm sorry, Kaitlyn. She clearly loves you both."

Katie gave Abbie once last big hug and ran to their parked car.

"You still feel like shopping for furniture?" he asked Katie who couldn't hold back tears.

"No, but we have to. Not going isn't going to make them give us Abbie."

\*\*\*

"Mom, I'm going to lie down for a couple of hours. Katie's going to read. Suzanne and Rob aren't coming until six or six-thirty. The steaks are marinated. I won't have much to do."

He'd filled her in on the details of Abbie and furniture shopping. He'd persuaded the store to let him buy floor models even from other locations so they'd be delivered all at once. They'd bought a round coffee table, two end tables, and two lamps.

The matching love seat would be delivered in two weeks.

He thought Katie would be overwhelmed by the number of shades of blue at the paint store, but she walked right up to the one she wanted and handed the chip to the clerk. Dan bought all the stuff to use for painting. All he had was a ladder. He got some wood floor cleaner, too. He hoped he'd have a busy week.

Before he went to the bedroom, he called Bowles at home. Will pushed back, but Dan insisted that a file to probate Jill's will be opened tomorrow. He didn't tell him why. Just to do it. He was getting to be as bossy as Lombardi.

# CHAPTER FIFTY-SIX

## May

"Mr. Ramsay, we'd like you to walk us through events again, if you don't mind."

He felt like he was never going to get out of a windowless room with Elba and Winston. Ha! Last week he'd considered them friends of the family working towards a common goal. Now, he realized they considered him a suspect. Their best suspect. At least, he had Lombardi sitting in one of the rock hard metal chairs next to his. No beverages had been offered. With Lombardi there as his protector, the investigators had no need to try to soften him up or lull him into tripping over his answers. He probably should have been nervous, but Lombardi's bulldog personality comforted him at least enough to answer coherently. "Anything, if it will find the villain who did this to Jill."

"Let's start with before Mrs. Ramsay left

Saturday morning."

"I'd loaded her bike on the car the night before because I knew she wanted to get an early start. When I got up to see her off, she was having second thoughts. She said we couldn't afford it. Everything except gas was already paid so I told her to go. She did."

"Earlier you said she was worried and nervous. Why did you think she was nervous?"

Lombardi nodded for him to answer the question. She'd told him beforehand to wait for her to object before answering. If she didn't, keep his answers short, remain polite, and pay attention to exactly what was being asked.

"I got the impression she was stalling. Almost as if she wanted me to agree so she didn't have to go."

"Why would she not want to go?"

"She'd mentioned a couple of times earlier in the week that she was rusty and not up to her usual level. Even on bad days, Jill was as good or better than most of her teammates." He had to admit the second possibility. "This was her first team outing since she found out I was having an affair. She said once she'd been humiliated enough. She was embarrassed."

"Why would she be embarrassed? You were the cheater."

"Nice try, Detective Elba. Move along," said Lombardi.

"Any other reason she mentioned?"

"She didn't. I did. I thought it was too much to train and drive roundtrip. She said she'd stay with a teammate in Fredericksburg if she was too tired to drive. Even before we had problems, she never listened to me about cycling."

"Did you discuss your marital problems with anyone?"

"Only my psychiatrist. No one else. "

"Which is privileged," interjected Lombardi. "Keep moving, Detective."

"So if anyone knew about the affair and your marital problems it was because Mrs. Ramsay told them and they told someone else and so on."

"Yes."

"This was about six o'clock Saturday morning?"

"Yes."

"What happened next?"

"I went back to bed for a couple of hours. When I got up, I saw that it was a beautiful day. I didn't want to stay inside and work on my résumé and look for jobs online. I wanted to get out of town. I drove to Virginia Beach, had a long run, and got home about seven. I made dinner, watched TV, and went to bed."

"We're checking that out. Trying to see if your story can be confirmed."

"It's not a story, Detective. It's what I did."

"So, you went to bed before midnight."

"Yes. I got up about three o'clock because it was raining hard and I wanted to make sure the windows were closed in the office. I noticed Jill wasn't back and assumed she'd spent the night with her teammates.

"I went back to bed and slept until eleven o'clock. I was pretty sore from my run so I went to my health club and stopped to wash the car on the way. I had a massage, took some steam, and played shuffleboard with my neighbor."

"That checks out."

"The neighbor mentioned that I was late picking up Katie from a sleepover, so I came home to make sure someone else hadn't brought her home. You know the rest."

"And you were sleeping in the guest room because you were having marital difficulties."

"That's established, Detective Elba," interrupted Lombardi.

"The woman with whom you had the affair was Bella Davis, your girlfriend during the time you were at UVA."

"Yes."

"You haven't been in touch with her since the affair ended."

"Correct."

"Mr. Ramsay, Bella Davis is dead."

Stinging, searing, slashing pain ripped through Dan's heart. He stumbled out of his chair to the metal waste basket where he puked his guts out. He was sobbing and puking. He wanted to die. Bella. Beautiful, brilliant, passionate Bella couldn't be dead. Not now.

"My client needs a break. Find him an escort to a men's room."

\*\*\*

Dan sat frozen in his chair next to Lombardi and across from Elba in a different, larger room. Winston stood silently by the door. A can of ginger ale was next to him. He didn't know why it was there. He wrapped his right hand around the chilled wet can. The cold was comforting.

"How? How did she die?"

"Suicide. She hanged herself."

"Oh dear God," he sobbed. He put his head down on the metal table and wept uncontrollably.

Lombardi and Elba sat without speaking until Dan started rambling.

"It's all my fault. I didn't mean to hurt her. I didn't think she'd be that upset." He'd killed the best part of himself.

Winston waited until his sobs quieted. "Mr. Ramsay, Ms. Davis hung herself three days after 9/11. She had clients and friends in the WTC. Her husband died the previous year. She was overcome with loss."

*Was he being punk'd?* "That's impossible. I had an affair with her last year."

"Perhaps you can explain that."

Lombardi stood. "We're done. Anything further would be speculation on my client's part."

She pulled Dan up by his left arm and hustled him out the door. Dan, still sobbing, leaned against a wall. Lombardi went to Winston when he came out of the interrogation room. She stood within hearing distance of Dan.

"Nice. Could've just shot him." She held out her hand. "What've you got."

Winston handed her a folder. "Autopsy report. Death certificate. Obit. Press clippings. Probate. Everything, at least $25 million plus proceeds from the sale of the East Hampton house, Central Park

West co-op, and a villa in St. John, went to a wildlife charity."

"Thanks." She took the folder, pulled Dan away from the wall, and headed towards the elevator bank. "Lamb, out."

# CHAPTER
# FIFTY-SEVEN

Lombardi hustled Dan into her car in the police parking garage. They sat. She made no move to start the car. "Explain."

"I can't. They're wrong. I spoke to her in December. She couldn't have died almost fifteen years ago." Dan cried harder.

"Try again."

"You think I made her up?"

"She makes a good suspect."

"Why would I say I had an affair if I didn't?" He inched away from Lombardi toward the window.

"Impersonator?"

"No, it was Bella. I know her. Her voice, her body, how her mind works," he couldn't stop crying. "Maybe she faked her death after 9/11."

"Positive ID and autopsy." She turned sideways to face him. "Who's picking you up?"

"My mother. When I call. She's doing some shopping."

"Call her."

She drummed her fingers on the steering wheel while Dan called his mother. "Not good, Lamb."

He was incapable of following her train of thought. What wasn't good? She had an uncanny ability to read his mind.

"One less suspect." She started the car. "Out. I'll call."

She backed out of the parking space almost before he could get out of her way.

\*\*\*

"Better?"

Dan threw up his hands. He didn't know if he was better. What he knew was his mother had taken one look at him, driven him to his psychiatrist's office, and Dr. Spellman had given him Klonopin. That was half an hour ago. Dr. Spellman saw his last patient before lunch and now sat across from him expecting answers.

"What's bothering you most?"

"That they're saying Bella died years ago when I had an affair with her last year that ended in December."

"I've looked at the file your attorney faxed me. Why don't you take a look?"

Dan shuffled through the file. His tears fell on the obituary. The date of death was wrong.

The autopsy report indicated her fingerprints matched those the SEC had on file when she received clearance. She'd been positively identified by one of her law partners. Death by hanging herself from a silk scarf tied to a doorknob in her apartment overlooking Central Park. His hands shook so much he dropped the folder.

Pictures. Bella's wedding announcement, speaking engagements, professional headshot. All Bella. All gorgeous. Exactly as he had last seen her. And then they stopped.

"They're wrong."

"What other explanation is there?" Dr. Spellman asked reasonably when he picked them up.

"She faked her death. Things must have been chaotic in the Medical Examiner's office in New York after 9/11. They could've made a mistake. Someone could've provided the wrong files from the SEC."

"Might someone have taken advantage of you by impersonating her?"

"No," he shouted. "I know Bella," he shouted louder and stood. "I know every inch of her body. I know how her mind works." By now, he was shouting as loud as he could and waving his arms wildly. "I don't love an impersonator." He headed for the door.

"Mr. Ramsay. You're not leaving. I'm putting you on a 72-hour hold."

Wild-eyed, Dan opened the door and ran down three flights of steps to the lobby where he was subdued by two security guards. He kicked and screamed while he was loaded into an ambulance headed to Richmond Memorial Hospital for suicidal ideation and stabilization. Suicide watch.

# CHAPTER
# FIFTY-EIGHT

He walked the perimeter of the hospital floor five times in the morning and five times after dinner. He had no idea how to measure his mileage. He couldn't remember how to run. He was grateful for being able to walk. Walking cleared his mind so he could think of nothing. Nothingness. Not anything. Naught.

Dan had been told he spent his first five days sleeping. He'd been sedated upon arrival because he was agitated and lashing out. He'd started receiving a different antidepressant along with an antipsychotic. By the fifth day, Dan woke up on his own and stayed alert through lunch. An afternoon nap got him through dinner and visiting hours.

Rob must have come early in his stay. Dan found two pairs of sweats pants without drawstrings, five tee shirts that must have come from his running clothes drawer, and a pair of old running shoes without laces. He wasn't going to be able to kill himself with either shoe laces or drawstrings. He spent at least an hour upon finding the items wondering how he would kill himself with either. Not because he planned to kill himself. It was an intellectual exercise. He came up with nothing.

This afternoon he had a session with a therapist. He couldn't remember any of their names, but they all seemed benign. They asked him repetitive questions and then moved on to other topics.

This afternoon, he wore his sweatpants and a Grateful Dead tee shirt. He sat in a room on a sofa across from a young man in an armchair. "What would you like to have happen?" asked the young man.

"I want to wake up from this nightmare and go on with my life."

"Are you sleepwalking?"

"No. I'm awake. I feel like I fell off the world and need to get back to my life with my wife and daughter."

"And their names? I don't see them in my notes."

"My wife is Jill. My daughter is Kaitlyn with a K. I still call her Katie."

"Where do the three of you live?"

He gave his address and described the house. He mentioned that Jill's great-grandmother's ugly furniture was gone. Jill's mother had sent it back to Charleston.

"How's your marriage?"

"We're working it out. I had an affair that started Thanksgiving a year ago. Jill found out this past December. I was sleeping in the guest room, but I'm back in the master bedroom. Things are better."

"Did you have an affair with someone Jill knew?"

"No. I'd never do that. It was with my college girlfriend, Bella. She's a widow who lives out of town. When my father died, I felt so guilty because Jill took such good care of me. The last words my father said to me were that he was embarrassed I was his son because I'd been having an affair with Bella. I couldn't leave Jill. I promised her I'd never communicate with Bella again and I haven't."

"Do you think your wife will visit you here?"

"I don't know. She'd have to find a babysitter for Katie. My brother comes, though. He brought me clothes. I haven't actually seen him, yet."

"Dan, your brother is in the waiting room now. Would you like to see him?"

"Sure."

The young man held the door open and pointed to the waiting room. Dan shook his hand and said, "Nice meeting you."

\*\*\*

The best part of the hospitalization was pet therapy. Even during his earliest days, he woke to find a German shepherd resting his head on Dan's bed or a Pomeranian sleeping at the foot of his bed.

He asked if he could have a dog to take on his walks around the floor. Every morning at ten o'clock, a woman wearing an orange vest that read Pet Therapist would bring a dog who also wore a vest to him. The dog's vest read *I am a Therapy Dog* and had a medical patch like a boy scout gets sewn on it. She'd introduce them, tell him if there was anything unusual about the dog such as if he or she was deaf, and hand him a leash. She'd join them on the first half of his first circuit and then drop away.

He looked forward to it. He liked all the dogs, but his favorite was a black standard poodle who made him walk a little faster and nuzzled him. He usually got a small dog to nap with him. He had a brown and white Chihuahua with a vest that looked like it had been made for a doll. He smelled them all. He'd bury his face in their fur and feel like everything was right with the world for those few seconds. Most of them licked him. He loved the feel of their wet tongues on his face and hands. He didn't wash his hands before lunch so he could smell the morning dog.

He missed Abbie.

# CHAPTER

# FIFTY-NINE

Dan's memory gradually returned. One morning he woke to the familiar stomach wrench that reminded him Jill was dead. He still couldn't imagine why anyone would kill her. Maybe those two investigators got it wrong and it wasn't someone she knew. Dan thought it must have been a camper who knew women from the cycling club met in that parking lot. Jill must have been late arriving and the others left without her.

This morning's session was with an older woman with long curly grey hair parted in the middle. She gave off a hippie vibe. Her office smelled of patchouli. He thought she would understand him even if he was wearing a Lacrosse tee shirt. LAX to the MAX.

"I feel like I'm swimming and a wave will wash over me and then another and another until I feel I can't get out of the water because of so much grief. I remember my father is dead. I remember Abbie is gone. I remember Jill is dead."

"People often refer to being overcome with waves of grief. It's natural."

"Even when I'm in the water and the waves have already knocked me around, I feel like the biggest one hasn't come yet."

"Does that make you anxious?" she asked.

"Very." He couldn't imagine what could be worse. Katie. Katie could make it worse.

"You've experienced a great deal of loss in a short time," she said sympathetically. "There were these three horrible family losses, but I see in your file that you also lost your job."

"Yes, and it'll be hard to find another one because I'm over fifty in a young person's field."

"You lost your lover, too."

Bella. Gorgeous, brilliant Bella who was the best part of him was dead. He tried hard not to remember.

"Yes, I still can't believe she hanged herself. I didn't think out breakup would affect her so deeply. I've lost both the women I love."

"And your lover died when?"

"Late December, I think. After Jill found out about the affair and I told Bella I was trying to hold my marriage together."

"I'm sorry for all your losses. You're carrying a great weight of grief, Mr. Ramsay." She stood. "I'm going to make a change in your medication to relieve some of your anxiety. Now is not the time to be anxious about finding a job or anything, really."

Finally, someone understood.

# CHAPTER SIXTY

Rob came for dinner three nights later. He hugged Dan and stood back to look at him.

"You've lost weight. Do the sweats still fit?" he asked.

"Yeah." He walked down the hall to a small solarium. "We can eat in here." They sat in wicker chairs with a small plastic table between them.

Rob unpacked the bags of cheeseburgers, fries, and sodas. "No utensils, they said."

"The rules are so weird. How would I kill myself with a plastic spoon?"

A look of alarm crossed Rob's face.

"No, I don't mean that I want to. I just wonder how someone would do it. Someone must have been successful or we'd be allowed to have them."

"We can eat with our hands. I got extra ketchup for you. No onions on the burger."

"Thanks." Dan was startled by the way Rob looked at him. "Do I look bad?"

"I'm not used to seeing you so thin with long white hair. I didn't do the best job with tee shirt

298

selection. World's Greatest Dad is probably seven years old. You alert?" asked Rob as he bit into his burger.

"Pretty much. I know where I am, who everybody is even if I don't remember their names, and that I'm taking medications and seeing doctors and therapists. I remember Jill is dead. Did they find her killer yet?"

Rob shook his head. "The police haven't kept in touch, but no arrest has been made."

"How's Katie?"

"She misses you. She's happy that Mom is there. I think she's eager for school to be over. She said you promised you'd get a dog from the shelter the day after school ended."

Dan nodded. "I remember."

"Elizabeth's not too happy she found out from Kaitlyn that you're in the hospital."

Dan just nodded. "Elizabeth. She took the ugly furniture."

Rob finished his burger and wiped his greasy fingers on coarse brown napkins the size of paper towels. "Dan, I think that's not all she wants to take. I think she wants custody of Kaitlyn."

That was the next wave.

"She can't. I'm her father," he stated emphatically.

"Dan, I'm just telling you so you can discuss it here with the doctors. Elizabeth's willing to go to court and say you're an unfit father because of your mental health problems. Kaitlyn's mother is dead and her father is in a psych hospital. That doesn't look good."

Dan didn't feel angry. He kept eating. He felt like someone had thrown another punch and he was used to it. He didn't hit back. He'd be a terrible boxer.

"I won't be here forever. I'll be out once my medications are fully effective."

"She'll argue about not having a job, either."

"Even if I don't get a job, I have enough savings to live off and I can take my pension early. Katie's education is paid. We don't have financial problems."

Rob threw up his hands in surrender. "I'm not here to argue. I just want you to know what Elizabeth is planning."

Dan filled Rob in on the therapy dogs he saw twice a day. He spoke with enthusiasm. "I can't believe they're called therapy dogs. All they do is visit. It's great. I wish one could stay all the time. The Pet Therapist said all the dogs have to pass a test that they won't bite or startle easily to become certified. Maybe when Katie and I get our new dog, we can get him or her to be a therapy dog. Katie would like that."

"Yeah," said Rob. He picked up the paper plates, cups, and bag and balled them up for the trash. As they were walking out of the solarium, Rob asked "Do they ask you about Bella?"

"Sometimes."

"What kind of things do they ask?"

"I have to cop to the affair for the millionth time and tell them the last time I spoke to her was that wretched day in December before she killed herself."

300

"That's what you tell them?" Rob asked looking wide eyed at Dan.

"Sure, what else would I say?" Dan wondered if he should say something different.

"Nothing. I guess they need to keep making sure you're telling the truth. See 'ya."

\*\*\*

"High Life, what's with the pacing?"

Dan was on the fourth of his five nightly circuits around the floor. A young woman was sitting at the door to her room handcuffed to a chair. Dan kept walking. Keeping the same pace was good for him. He felt better. The meds were kicking in.

On his final round, the young woman repeated herself. He stopped and looked at her. Thin, stringy blonde hair, tattoos all over the body. He was old enough to be her father. He hoped Katie didn't want tattoos yet. Or piercings. He was pretty sure St. Margaret's didn't allow such body adornments.

"I'm Lou," she said.

"Why do you call me High Life?" He didn't want to engage her, but she was strangely attractive. Familiar. Not sexy. Interesting.

"Your shirt." She pointed one long forefinger with chipped blue polish at his chest.

He looked down. Miller High Life beer.

"My brother brought me a bunch of tee shirts. I've never paid attention to the slogans."

"Your brother dresses you? Guy like you must have a wife."

"Dead," he said. He'd become good at

301

monosyllabic answers.

"Girlfriend?"

"Dead," he repeated.

"Man, you're going to be on the market for a long time. You're a jinx." She licked her lips with her pierced tongue. "What's a nice cubicle farmer like you doing in a place like this?"

"Grief." There wasn't another word for what he felt. "You?" He tried to practice conversational skills.

"Schizo. I went off my meds. Did some crazy stuff. Have to go back to Petersburg until my meds kick in so I can have a trial."

"You mean Commonwealth Psychiatric?"

"Where else?" she said defiantly.

"Have you been there before?" He didn't want to be nosy, but he was curious.

"This will be my third time. It's okay. It's like this only dirtier with less supervision. I mean like one nurse per unit. I met some cool people there."

"You mean patients?"

She gave him the same exasperated look Katie did. "Sure, the smokers go outside more. We hang. We BS. There's nothing else to do. It's not like they actually treat you. I just chill until the meds kick in. Why, you thinking of going?"

"No. Just wondered." He wanted to seem off handed. "Were you ever afraid? There was a murder there not too long ago."

"The one where the girl said a ghost killed her nurse? She was cool," she said in tone of admiration. "It's no scarier than jail. The building's like five hundred years old. It's creepy in a good way."

He didn't know what to say. Jail wasn't a comparison for him. Creepy didn't seem like a positive.

"Don't you think the patient was hallucinating about the ghost?"

She tried to move her hands, but one was handcuffed. "Doubt it. A girl did die that way there."

So this Lou person believed in ghosts. Probably a good idea for her to go to Petersburg.

"My bus leaves tomorrow so don't look for me."

"You're taking the bus?" Everything people did seemed screwy to him. Would she be alone? Would she be handcuffed to the bus somehow?

She cackled until it dissolved into a fit of coughing. "Ambulance, man. Or cop car. Either one's cool." She started coughing again, and then gave him a piece of advice. "Chill man, the blues leave slow."

# CHAPTER

# SIXTY-ONE

He wasn't at all what Dan expected—not that he had specific expectations.

His mother had dropped him off at a storefront in a half-empty strip shopping center that housed a used book store, a lamp repair shop, and a weight loss center situated at an angle to a vacant grocery store and pharmacy along US Route 1 northeast of Henrico. The abandoned grocery store parking area had weeds and dandelions growing between cracks in the pavement. In the angled strip center, white parking lines had faded to grey or disappeared entirely.

"This doesn't look like a psychologist's office," his mom had said.

"It's the address I have. I'll call if there's a problem."

Ten minutes later, he had been seated in a serviceable office with a grey metal desk, two blue sofas, and a variety of plants. The walls were

304

painted pale green. Ambient lighting completed the soothing effect. Dan didn't smell any incense. No trickling water soundtrack played. No candles burned. It seemed normal enough.

The young man, dressed in a grey business suit, white shirt and no tie with a well-maintained five o'clock shadow, sat serenely on one of the blue sofas.

"Is what we discuss confidential?" Dan was cautious. Everything he did now could be used against him in court.

"No, but I don't keep records of any sessions that are outside my LMFC practice, including names. I don't know your name. I'm not charging you for this session. It's part of how the paranormal community works." He went on to provide credentials. "I'm a Sensitive, which means I'm unusually receptive to multiple layers of energies in the world. As a child, it set me apart after the age of having imaginary friends passed. I learned to manage my sensitivity and studied psychology and the paranormal."

Dan didn't know if that meant he was an expert, but he seemed reassuring and willing to help him.

"I don't think your story should be dismissed," he said after Dan recounted everything about his relationship with Bella. "You've had a long and highly emotionally charged connection with Bella since your teens. There's no reason that would end should one of you die."

At least this guy wasn't telling Dan he was crazy. The guy might be crazy, but he was also a Licensed Marriage and Family Counselor who had experience with the paranormal. Dan had found him through an internet search that meandered through ghost hunters, psychic mediums, and religious cults. Dan was desperate to reconcile his knowledge of Bella with the police insistence that she was dead and refusal to entertain alternatives. They were satisfied. Period. End of story.

He got right to the point.

"Is Bella dead?"

"I don't know. I'm not a medium. I can only comment on what I feel in my surroundings. If Bella were here, I would be able to tell you."

Great. He couldn't conjure Bella on demand. This wasn't helping.

"Have you tried to reach Bella?" he asked reasonably.

"No. I promised my wife I wouldn't after she found out about the affair."

"That hardly seems relevant now." Again, reasonable psych speak.

"As I said, things ended badly."

The guy closed his eyes and seemed to be in a trance as though he were trying to formulate a response. When he opened his eyes he looked at Dan intensely. "I can feel that you and Bella have a strong, if not impenetrable, bond. The energy around you when you speak of Bella whether you're loving or angry is the most powerful I've encountered. I've used all my abilities to retain control of myself in the face of this force. It fills the room. It consumes you."

"You feel that?"

"Absolutely. It's an amicable force. It's not threatening, but it's potent. The two of you together

306

are formidable. You had a high life. You would've given new meaning to the term power couple had you remained together.

"I suspect your father was a Sensitive, but unaware of it. Your description of his reactions to you and Bella and yours to him are much stronger than what is considered to be a normal father-son bond. He mistook his awareness of your bond with Bella as a warning rather than mere information. "

"You believe me, then?"

"Yes. It's exceptional that you and Bella made love. How did it feel?" The question didn't sound prurient. It sounded like a request for additional information.

"Fantastic. Like we were seventeen again." No one made him feel the way she did.

"Did anything seem unusual or especially remarkable?"

Images of the two of them flashed through his mind. Bella was so sensuous. She had soft, womanly curves with a beautiful mouth and hands. She wasn't a hard-bodied athlete. Sensuous. Loving. Generous.

"Weightless. Bella seemed almost weightless at times." She'd felt like air.

He nodded. "Truly remarkable."

"So, what do you think? "

"Based on what you've told me and the conclusions investigators have drawn from physical evidence such as fingerprints, I would say Bella is no longer living in human form. You may call her a ghost if that's the most comfortable term for you. Everything that happened between you was real."

"She's not a hallucination?"

"That's the term psychiatrists apply. It's their training and experience. It's a label."

"A label that could put me in prison." He threw out his arms.

"Correct. The legal system doesn't welcome anything other than evidence-based science. My observations are considered anecdotes not evidence.

"When you and Bella reunited, did she mention how the physical separation affected her? You were unable to fulfill your career expectations. What about Bella?"

A ridiculous question. Dan started to laugh and stopped to think. She was accomplished, but the Bella he knew wouldn't have settled for being a lawyer, even if she did write books, make speeches, and advise corporations and governments. Analyzing The Securities Act of 1934 and The Dodd-Frank Act must have been painfully boring. She had loads of opportunities after the *Sorbonne* and could've done something about which she was passionate. Maybe life with her husband satisfied her need to live loud.

"Maybe not." He wasn't here to talk about Bella's needs. He needed perspective. "What's your advice?"

"I can only validate that your encounters occurred. You experienced them, but you hurt Bella deeply. You dismissed her. You threatened her. You were cruel. My advice is to apologize to her."

"I don't want to ever see her again."

"Is that true? Your wife is dead. There's no impediment for you and Bella continuing your relationship unconventional as that may be. Even if you don't feel you can resume a romantic relationship, you owe her an apology. If you want to restore good will, you must woo her."

"I can't." He stood. He'd gotten what he came for. He wasn't crazy. One person on the planet believed his story.

"Sir, Bella could help you."

Intrigued, he sat. "Help me how?"

"Bella in her current form—let's call her a ghost—can see and do things humans can't. She could do things that might help the police identify Jill's killer and prove your innocence. Assuming you are innocent, of course."

Dan knew he belonged in a psych hospital. Or a research lab as a test subject. He sat in a seedy shopping center with a legitimate licensed therapist calmly discussing the advisability of adding a ghost to his defense team. His head was going to explode any second. What could it hurt to play along?

"What things might she be able to see or do to help?"

The therapist leaned forward. "I'm not an expert on ghost behavior, but their primary advantages to living in human form are invisibility and fluidity. Bella would be able access places—locked places— as well as eavesdrop under her cloak of invisibility. She could find answers for at least some of your questions."

"Bella can eavesdrop? She's invisible? She could sit invisibly in my den and listen to every conversation I have? She could invade my privacy?" He wasn't safe in his own home.

The therapist re-adjusted his position on the sofa and closed his eyes. When he opened them, he spoke as though he were summoning all his patience to speak to a deliberately slow learner

"Yes, Bella could do that among any number of more helpful activities. I doubt Bella has been in your house if she was as adamant as you say about not entering the space you occupied with your wife and child. I doubt she's interested in you at all. You angered and hurt her. You haven't asked for forgiveness much less help. No doubt, she's doing something she enjoys in a place she likes with people who are much kinder to her than you."

*Ouch.* Starting with Dr. Spellman, everyone with whom he'd discussed Bella in the psych community had taken Bella's side. They pointed out his unjustifiably bad behavior. Not one of them sympathized with him.

"Sir," the LMFC looked at him with a neutral expression. "Think about whether you want to leave things this badly between you and Bella. Her emotions are human. She can hurt you as easily as help you. You know whether you're innocent in the death of your wife. I don't.

"Don't reconcile because you want her help or to avoid recriminations. She won't accept that. Do it because you have this rare bond. It's exceptional. It's a gift very few have in this or any other life."

No friggin' way.

# CHAPTER
# SIXTY-TWO

The clock read one forty-five AM. Dan was awake and sprawled in the middle of the king sized bed with three pillows around him and tangled sheets. The room was black. The drawn drapes didn't allow even a sliver of light into the room. He might as well have been in a coal mine.

He untangled himself from the sheets, got up, and opened the drapes. Moonlight flooded the room. If anyone was out there ready to catch him lying awake after his wife's murder, let them. He hadn't been granted the sleep of the just. He padded into the bathroom. One look in the mirror reflected the battery of losses he'd suffered in the past few months. His face bordered on gaunt. His cheekbones were not quite prominent but close. His hair had turned completely white during his most recent hospitalization. He didn't recognize the man staring back at him. He splashed water on his face and put a cold wet towel around his neck.

311

Back in the bedroom, Dan slipped on sweatpants and the soft suede mocs he wore around the house. He went quietly down the stairs and headed into the den, opened the single locked door of the media cabinet, and felt blindly on the bottom shelf. His hands touched a fold of worn leather He pulled until he held his photo album from college in his hands. It was time to face some truths about himself.

Dan poured himself a Scotch, sat in his favorite chair, and turned on a dim light. He intended to go through what was essentially his memory book of life with Bella. He'd found it in his childhood bedroom when he cleaned it out before his parents' estate sale almost two years ago and stored in the cabinet with a false bottom. Jill wouldn't have cared, but he wanted to have one private thing. He was pretty sure she kept mementoes of life before she'd met him in a jewelry box or carton of things she was keeping for Katie.

The first page was a picture of a seventeen year-old Bella at the beach behind her parents' oceanfront home in Virginia Beach. She wore a blue sundress that complemented her tan, beautiful curves, and long blonde hair. Her blue eyes, the color of which was indescribable, shone with happiness. When they'd met, the empty part of his heart was filled. He was his best self with Bella. Tears rolled down his face as he looked at the dazzling girl who changed his life.

The first few pages of the book were of their early times at the University of Virginia. Him at lacrosse practice, Bella seated at an ebony concert grand piano, and the two of them slow-dancing at a party. The next pages were his first Christmas at her parents' villa in St. John which became his favorite place in the world.

He spread his palms across these pages. Calm radiated through him just by touching the photos that held such happiness. The flight there was his first. He'd gripped Bella's hand when the mountainous landing strip to St. Thomas came into view. She'd laughed and told him to finish his beer. The ferry between St. Thomas and St. John had felt like he was gliding on turquoise sea glass. The water had been so transparent he'd seen vibrant tropical fish just by looking over the side.

When they'd docked, Bella had hopped into the family jeep and skillfully driven them up, down, and around the hillsides, slowing only for hairpin turns, and stopping occasionally for goats and donkeys to cross the roads. Roads. That's what Bella had called them. They were dirt trails. Bella easily had driven on the wrong or left side of the road and had laughed with the wind in her flying blonde hair all the way to the villa.

A photo of the two of them in front of the villa. The family had called it modest, and he supposed it was. There was a great room with a tiny kitchen from which four latticed breezeways covered by blooming bougainvillea led to bedrooms. He'd taken pictures of the outdoor showers, salt water pool, and beach just down the hillside. He'd photographed the cistern. Water was a sacred commodity on the island. He'd learned to ration flushing toilets.

Dan closed his eyes and recalled everything he could of that first visit. Snorkeling, eating exotic fresh fruits and catches of the day, and sleeping in a hammock under the stars. That first trip had been the most magical experience of his life. On their last day, Dan had asked Bella to promise to have their ashes mixed and buried in the Caribbean.

He turned the page. More pictures of life at UVA. He was smart, but he recognized Bella's brilliance. She'd encouraged him without knowing it. He'd pushed for an extra edge. Not to compete with her, but to make himself better. He'd researched deeper because Bella read his papers aloud to hear how they flowed. She'd asked such piercing questions about game theory that he'd used the topic for his senior thesis.

A shot of their dorm room after a fight. Every pillow in the room was in a heap on his side of room. When their passionate natures had clashed, fireworks would ensue. Bella could and had cursed in three languages. She'd thrown pillows for emphasis. Why did they fight? Mørk. Depression made him feel insecure. He simply couldn't believe she loved him when she could have any guy on or off campus. Her answer had always been the same. Why would she want anyone else when she had him—her rare, precious gift of a soul mate?

Bella had had her own demons. Anxiety that she could lose him caused panic attacks. She'd said she couldn't imagine life without him. He'd said the same. Yet, they'd lost each other.

# CHAPTER
# SIXTY-THREE

"Dan?" His mother came in the den wearing a white velour bathrobe that flattered her short silver hair. "Are you all right? Do you need anything?"

Despite the tears running down his face, Dan shook his head. "I'm good."

Selma eyed the scotch. She looked like she was going to say something about him drinking alcohol while on psych meds, but didn't. Instead, she headed to the kitchen to make tea for herself.

Dan moved to the sofa. When she returned from the kitchen, his mother sat next to him. "Did your session with that new therapist today upset you?"

He shook his head. "Confused me. I woke up in a sweat and decided to come down and face some things." He held up the book in his lap. He'd never discussed his affair with his mother. He didn't want to now, but he wanted to look at his past.

"You do love photographs." She touched a corner of the leather photo album. "What have you got?" The book was open to a page of the party Bella had thrown for him before graduation. A big white outdoor tent. Friends, teammates, and even some faculty. A local band he'd enjoyed had played all afternoon.

"What fun. Bella certainly knew how to throw a party and keep it under control. It was a classic lawn party. That was for your All American award, wasn't it?" Division 1, Honorable mention for Lacrosse. "Your dad was so proud. Look, there's Rob and Suzanne. That was the day he introduced her as his fiancée." She examined all the pictures. "You had so many friends."

Yes, and Bella had invited all of them. "The party wasn't just for Lacrosse, Mom. It was for getting that internship. The one that led to a job offer once I'd gotten an MBA." With Bella's support, Dan had won a coveted summer internship with a major talent agency. Even though it meant he'd spend the summer away from her in the agency's offices in Los Angeles, Detroit, and Nashville, she'd been the one who read, edited, and re-read his application, helped him select the best professors to provide references, and prepped him for the interview. He'd thought his chances were zero. Bella had thought he could do anything. She'd made him see the best in himself.

The remaining photographs were of year-end parties, graduation, and the last time he and Bella had seen each other. He'd asked a stranger to take a picture of them at the airport when she'd left for her fellowship at the *Sorbonne* in Paris. They looked so happy. Bella looked especially radiant. If he'd known he'd never see her alive again, he would've disintegrated into nothingness right at the gate.

"Dan, what happened? You two were a perfect couple. Your dad and I thought you'd be together forever."

Dad certainly had changed his mind about that. "Mom, I was stupid and stubborn. It's that simple. Bella begged me to come to Paris with her. She believed I'd be accepted into MBA programs at prestigious places like Wharton, Yale, or London School of Economics. With my summer experience, references from some of the biggest names in entertainment and sports, and maybe some international experience if I studied or worked even a little in Paris. I'd start the following fall. In the meantime, we'd live in Paris and travel around Europe on her breaks."

"Bella always was ambitious. That sounds so exciting." She shifted to look at him directly. "Why didn't you do that?"

"I thought the agency might withdraw its job offer if I didn't get an MBA ASAP. I'd been accepted by University of Miami before I'd been offered the internship much less a job. I didn't want to wait a year before starting grad school. I couldn't count on being accepted at some more famous school. I didn't think there would be any difference in marketing or business law classes no matter what school I attended."

"Oh, Dan." Even his mother knew an Ivy degree made careers. "Did you discuss this with your father?"

"No. It was my life, my decision. I didn't want

his opinion."

She looked surprised. "Did Bella break it off when you didn't join her?" He shook his head. "No, she said a year was nothing and I'd visit her."

"Then why, Dan?"

"When I got to Miami, I realized I'd made a huge mistake. School wasn't interesting. Almost everyone was bi-lingual. I felt like an interloper. I didn't make friends or find a mentor. I missed Bella. I was lonely. She wrote almost every day. I couldn't bring myself to answer. I was embarrassed. Finally, she wrote that she'd received offers of work in Europe after the *Sorbonne* and she'd take them if I wasn't interested in her. I didn't answer. I assumed she'd met someone else and was letting me down easy."

She put her tea cup on the end table. "Why would you think that? Bella loved you. You loved her." He couldn't respond. "Dan, you and Bella were the best-matched couple I've ever seen. The two of you almost glowed. Can't you see it in these pictures? She'd never have left you for someone else."

"Mom, I didn't believe that. I always thought she was on the verge of leaving me. I didn't know what she saw in me even though she told me I was everything to her."

"You just let her go?"

He nodded. "After she was gone, I thought my life was over. Mørk arrived. I got so depressed I quit going to class, slept all day, and tried to commit suicide. You know the rest. I lived with you and Dad for the next three years because I was too sick to get out of bed."

By now, tears flowed freely down his face, onto the towel, and on his tee shirt. His mother put her arms around him and hugged him. She hadn't held him like that since he was about six. "Dan, I'm sorry. I'm sorry Mørk made your life so hard."

"Me, too, Mom. Bella's gone. Jill's dead. Dad's dead. Katie is who matters now. "

# CHAPTER

# SIXTY-FOUR

His improved health, the passage of time, and fresher news stories that turned media attention from Jill's stalled murder case allowed Dan to slowly emerge from hiding. Tomorrow would be Katie's last day of school. He thought both of them would be relieved not to be on St. Margaret's schedule. They'd have time to breathe away from academic requirements, sports schedules, and the still-prying eyes of the most die-heard Mean Girls and their mothers

Dan resumed running along his former route. He went early mornings just after Katie left for school. The weather was getting too hot to run later in the day. He found his zone where he heard only the rhythm of his feet and heartbeat. His mind was blank. He finished six miles, slowed to a jog/walk, and drank from his bottle of electrolyte charged water. He walked home and into the kitchen. The house was silent.

Dan showered, shaved, and dressed in the master bath. He felt right being in the bedroom he'd shared with Jill. He felt her sunshine there. Sometimes, he'd open her closet and just stand next to her hanging clothes. He'd cry. He'd talk about Katie. How she was doing in school, her newfound interest in photography, and her readiness to adopt another dog. He went downstairs to read in the den. His concentration was better after his hospital stay. He read non-taxing books such as celebrity autobiographies and found a surprising kinship with country music singers who had started with so little, endured a lot, and made a career. Not that they had become rich and famous so much as they made their lives and those of their families better by doing what they'd been born to do.

His schedule for the next few days was a happy one. His mother was coming home from Florida where she'd arranged a permanent move back to Richmond. He and Katie planned to go to the animal shelter to adopt a dog tomorrow. Rob and Suzanne were coming for dinner Sunday evening to celebrate his mom's return, Katie's completion of fifth grade, and the start of summer. He wondered what vegetables from Suzanne's garden might be ready to add to the menu. He'd text her. He'd become afraid of phones. They heralded panic and pain.

As if on cue, his cell rang. Lombardi. He hadn't seen her since that day in the police station parking garage.

"Lamb, update."

"I'm better, thanks, Nina," he replied. He wasn't

going to piss her off, but he wasn't going to meekly allow her to steamroll him.

"I don't visit clients in their homes, but today's an exception. I'm turning into the neighborhood. I'll be there in five."

Something awful had happened. His heartbeat increased. He felt like he was being pulled back into a wind tunnel from which he had just escaped.

Lombardi was at the front door in less than five minutes. His first thought was that Monika Traymore would spread the news that he'd received a late morning visit from a sleek woman driving a late model Jaguar. Before he could pursue that notion, Lombardi was barking orders. She led him into the kitchen, sat at the wooden table, and motioned for him to sit opposite.

"Winston's on the move. You're going to surrender to Winston and Elba Monday. I'll pick you up at Starbucks off Exit 73 at ten o'clock."

The worst case scenario had begun. His body reacted as it had throughout this ordeal. His stomach clenched, his muscles contracted, and tears flowed.

"You'll be booked and go straight to arraignment. You'll plead Not Guilty. I'll move that a psychiatric evaluation take place to determine your competency to stand trial. The Commonwealth Attorney won't oppose. You'll be evaluated as an outpatient at Richmond Memorial Hospital. The evaluation determination will be Not Competent to stand trial. You'll go to a psych facility under the jurisdiction of the Department of Behavioral Health Services AKA Commonwealth Psychiatric. There is no other forensic hospital under its jurisdiction."

The worst psychiatric hospital in the state, possibly the country. "I'm going to be in the state psych hospital for an undetermined amount of time? How is that a good thing?"

"Lamb, I'm telling you what's going to happen. Hold your questions. You go off to Petersburg to be treated until you become competent. The court will check in with you every three months. Once you're found to be competent, you'll be released to stand trial. In your case, once you become competent, the case will be dropped.

"Your lack of competency is what provides the motive in this case. Once you're determined to be competent, you'll have no motive and the CA will drop the charges. The case will be dismissed with prejudice meaning there's a snowball's chance in hell of the charges being raised again."

She stopped talking and looked quite pleased with herself.

As always, he felt like his head would explode during a conversation with Lombardi. He stood, drank a full glass of ice water from the refrigerator, refilled his glass and returned to the table.

Where to start? He wished Rob was here. He wasn't. Dan could have a conversation with his attorney without his big brother's assistance. He had to go slow. Lombardi would be irritated, but she seemed to be irritated with anyone who didn't speak Legalese.

"Monday, I'll meet Lieutenant Winston and Detective Elba. They'll arrest me, book me—that means fingerprints and mug shots like on TV, and then what's the word?

"Arraignment. You'll skip the night in jail waiting for arraignment.

"Arraignment is where I'm asked to enter a plea?"

"Your plea is Not Guilty. I'll immediately make a motion that you're Not Competent to stand trial. The CA won't object. The judge will order a hearing."

"How do you know? You sound certain."

"I am. That's the deal we made."

"You made a deal without consulting me?" Lawyers weren't supposed to do that.

Lombardi stood. She was back to her habit of pacing back and forth in front of him. Still in a black suit. Still reminding him of a ticking clock.

"Not technically. I have the agreement for you to sign. Is there another route you'd like to take? Maybe going to trial where twelve people who can't get out of jury duty decide whether you killed your wife or whether you killed your wife while you were insane? Any ideas how often NGRI pleas are successful? Less than one percent. Do you prefer those odds? Remember, Lamb, if the jury doesn't buy insanity, the sentence is death. The death penalty is popular in Virginia."

Dan pushed his chair back from the table so hard it fell on the ceramic tile floor. "Dammit, stop talking to me as though I'm stupid. I'm not. I don't understand anything about criminal law. I'm your client. I need you to explain things to me. This is my life."

Lombardi looked him up and down. "That,

Lamb, is exactly why you don't want to go to trial. You have a temper. You've been under psychiatric care since before I met you and you still vacillate between being dumbstruck or angry. Nice to see a show of spine, though."

# CHAPTER SIXTY-FIVE

Dan stepped outside to get some air. He was angry, but he'd learned techniques to control his temper and cooperate. Otherwise, he acted against his best interest. He stood outside for about fifteen minutes. He didn't want to think about what Lombardi was doing. Probably ranking him in order of stupidity of her client roster. So what? He wanted to know why being at Petersburg was the best strategy.

Dan checked his watch. Time for a couple of meds. He returned to the air-conditioned kitchen, took his meds, and poured himself an iced tea. He wondered if Lombardi ate or drank anything substantial. He'd never see her drink anything other than black coffee.

"Do you want anything?"

"No, Lamb."

Dan walked back to the table, picked up the chair, and sat. He noticed there was now a crack in two ceramic floor tiles. Easily fixed. He took three deep breaths before he felt ready to continue. "Please explain the difference between Competent, Not Competent, and NGRI." He liked using legal jargon. He felt like he was in the trenches now and had a glossary if not a guidebook.

"Pre-trial determination. Competency. The question is whether you're fit to stand trial. Competent means you're sane and ready to go to trial. Not Competent means you're not so sane, but there's a chance with some psychiatric treatment you'll become sane enough for trial. It's a low bar.

"Two part test. Understand the proceedings against you. Ability to assist with your defense.

"Solid on number one. You can identify courtroom, judge, and jury. Know what a prosecutor does. Charge is capital murder. I'm your lawyer. Ace.

"Epic fail on number two. Unable to assist in your defense. In fact, you created the case against you. With the dubious circumstantial evidence they have, I'd get the case dismissed. Hell, the CA would drop the charges. You, however, handed them a big fat motive with talk of an affair. Even that I could overcome.

"Problem? Your lover has been dead since 2001. Shrinks call her a delusion. Diagnosis—delusional disorder with psychotic AKA violent episodes. Whether your lover was alive or not, your mind believed she was alive. Killing your wife to be with your lover is a powerful motive.

"No one can overlook mental status. Your diagnosis is undisputed. No dueling shrinks. That, along with your persistent belief in this delusion, bring your competency into play. All the players want to win or at least not lose. No one wants a delusional defendant.

"I can't craft a defense. The CA doesn't want a conviction that can be overturned on appeal. The judge doesn't want to be overruled on appeal. Someone is going to raise the issue of competency, and I prefer that it be us. We're in control."

He wish he'd taken notes. He almost understood. Almost.

"How? How are we in control?"

"Our deal. Waiting for the CA to raise competency makes it look like you have even more to hide. Off to Petersburg. A judge who gets a whiff of a delusional defendant? Off to Petersburg."

"You're sending me there, too." Dan wanted to cry.

"Lamb, I'm going to climb all over everyone's asses every two or three months to force a hearing on your progress. I'm going to be on your shrinks to help you past your delusion. The CA is running for re-election and is going to be out glad-handing. The judge is going to forget you as soon as your case disappears from his docket. No one other than me is going to hustle things along at Petersburg. You're damned lucky you can afford me. No public defender would be all that interested in hand-holding in addition to an oversized case load. So, deal?"

The front doorbell rang.

Dan didn't move to answer the door.

"Still hiding, Lamb?"

"No. It's Monika Traymore, Jill's so-called friend and neighborhood gossip. Your car's been here long enough for her to make it her business to introduce herself."

"Damn. This is when I hate cell phones."

What? Had Lombardi suddenly lost her mind, too?

"Don't look so panicked, Lamb. In the pre-cell era, I would show a little skin and answer the door myself in an alluring pose while you were theoretically upstairs in the shower. No fun anymore. The probability that the Monika Traymores of the world have their cell phones ready to snap a pic or video to post to Instagram and Tumblr ruins it. My credibility in this case would be shot with the jury pool. Not that you'll need one."

"Wouldn't you be disbarred?" Dan wondered if Lombardi was joking.

"For what? Screwing a client? No."

He had to get the picture of a naked Lombardi out of his head. Monika could ring the doorbell all afternoon, but he was rooted to this spot.

# CHAPTER

# SIXTY-SIX

Helpless. Dan would be completely dependent on Lombardi to get him discharged from Commonwealth Psych. His family could lobby for him, but that might backfire. There were cases in the news where families of people who were obviously crazy like that movie shooter in Colorado or guilty like Scott Peterson petitioned for the release of their relative. Not that he was in that category.

Dan put his head in his hands. That girl with all the tattoos and handcuffed to a chair at Richmond Memorial Hospital. She was waiting for her bus to Petersburg. She'd said it was better than jail. She'd said it was a psych hospital that just wasn't as clean or well-staffed as where they were. She'd also said patients weren't treated. What if he didn't become competent? She had, though. She said she was going in order to become competent for a trial for crimes she'd committed when she went off her meds. She'd done it before. Schizophrenia. He was evaluating his options based on Lombardi's brashness and the opinion of a schizophrenic patient he'd met in a psych hospital. The nightmare was getting worse.

"Mr. Ramsay is not receiving." The front door slammed shut.

Lombardi's voice sounded far away. He looked up. Her chair was empty. She'd answered the door to Monika Traymore. Within what seemed like seconds, she was back in the kitchen with all her clothes on, reseated, and ready to continue.

"Lamb, she had to go. I was polite. Next time, it's trespass. She's been warned."

Dan didn't care about Monika Traymore. He'd stopped hearing what must have been the persistent doorbell. He was in a tunnel where he couldn't hear anything except the sound of Lombardi's voice. He was frightened. Going to Commonwealth Psych scared him more than anything else. He wanted to understand why he couldn't just plead NGRI and go to trial.

"What's the case against me?"

Lombardi raised one black eyebrow.

"CliffsNote version. No interruptions. I'm already repeating myself. Every single piece of evidence is circumstantial and can be shredded at trial in the unlikely event that you have one.

"Victim died of cardiac arrest from a liquid morphine injection. No proof the liquid morphine and morphine tablets prescribed for Jill were the same compound, no special chemical knowledge on your part, no mortar and pestle or equipment to turn tablets into liquid, and no syringe purchase. No evidence you purchased liquid morphine. Marks on your body. Home accident. Daughter can alibi.

"Weak alibi. Your vehicle had sand you didn't pick up driving around Richmond. Witnesses recall a lone man running on the beach. Couple making out on the beach remember lifting their heads enough to see a person run by. A seventy-one-year-old man who lives along the oceanfront saw a man run up the beach and back from his living room window on a Saturday. Golf was on TV, but he watches the Golf Chanel. Can't pinpoint a time, but it plants doubt.

"The prosecution only has a list of what was in the safe deposit box when the search warrant was issued. Jewelry that once belonged to your family circulating for sale. Irrelevant and inadmissible. Non-existent gold coins. Inadmissible."

That all sounded good. The prosecution had nothing Lombardi couldn't dismiss.

"Then why not go to trial? You just shot down every piece of evidence the prosecution has."

Lombardi didn't reply immediately. "I'll take that water you offered. Preferably bottled."

Dan got up, took a bottle of water from the refrigerator along with fresh squeezed orange juice, and put two glasses on the table. Lombardi could drink from the bottle or use the glass. He poured orange juice into his glass.

"Lamb, repeating myself. You couldn't even be arrested if that was the whole picture. I explained that no one in this case—not me, the CA, or the judge—can ignore the fact that you're officially delusional and occasionally psychotic. You aren't competent to stand trial."

Bella. Could the LMFC's opinion counter the psych diagnosis? Maybe, but he didn't keep records of patients and didn't know his name. He said the law didn't accept anything other than science. A marriage counselor with paranormal experience probably wouldn't trump a string of MDs.

"Couldn't I plead NGRI and avoid a stay at Petersburg?"

"Lamb, what do you think NGRI means?"

"I've been arrested for a crime I didn't commit and I have a mental illness so I couldn't have done it."

"No. 'Not Guilty by Reason of Insanity' means 'I did it, but I was insane when I did.' Off you go to Petersburg for the rest of your life if the jury believes you. If they don't, then death row awaits."

Dan pressed his hands against his temples.

"I'm not John Hinckley," he said finally.

"You're not Andrea Yates, either. Point?"

"They were obviously crazy. Insane."

Lombardi touched him for the first time. She reached across the table and put her bony hand on his forearm. "Lamb, to normal people, you sound just as obviously insane. Hinckley had Jodie Foster. Yates had God. You have Bella."

He felt like a gorilla had punched him in the stomach. Did his family think that, too?

Lombardi stood. "Lamb, enjoy your weekend with your daughter. Call me if you want to talk. Take your meds. Don't be stupid."

She saw herself out. Dan had no idea how long

he sat at the table. When he stood, he was drenched
in sweat and he'd wet himself.

# CHAPTER
# SIXTY-SEVEN

Sunday morning, Dan got up early, dressed, and went to the back yard. Both newly-adopted animals, Holly and Ivan, slept in Katie's room last night. He didn't see any reason to discourage it. He called Lombardi. Katie and the animals were still sleeping.

"Lamb," she sounded wide awake as if she'd been waiting for his call.

"I've got some questions."

"Shoot."

"If I'm found not competent to stand trial, how long will I stay at Petersburg?"

"Until you're competent. Indefinitely. Repeating. I'll insist on evaluations and hearings every three months. If for some reason after three to five years at Petersburg, you can't give up the idea that you and Bella had an affair, I can move to have you declared Unrestorably Incompetent. Options there. Release to private hospital, group home, or family

335

custody.

"Will the charges ever be dismissed?"

"Short answer: Not unless the real killer confesses."

"What if I say I was wrong about Bella?"

"Didn't hear that part about my suborning perjury."

"What if we could prove Bella is alive?"

"Anything else?"

"I left something out." He rushed to tell her before she had time to beat him up about withholding information. He recounted his session with the LMFC.

Lombardi yawned. "This is Virginia. There's not a judge in the state who would entertain the deposition, never mind the testimony, of a paranormal therapist who doesn't know your name or have records of a session. Law accepts proven science. A string of psychiatrists have diagnosed you with a severe mental illness. Lamb, there's no way around Bella." She yawned again. "Tomorrow at ten o'clock, Lamb. Bring your meds."

\*\*\*

Dinner was pleasant. Dan grilled tuna, made basmati rice, and served a salad with late spring vegetables Suzanne had brought from her garden. He set the picnic table outside with a cotton tablecloth and lots of citronella candles. He'd broken out a bottle of champagne to celebrate his mother's return to Richmond. Iced tea was served with the meal. Dessert was the oatmeal raisin cookies he and Katie had baked that afternoon.

Katie was eager to tell the story of Holly the cat and Ivan the dog. The woman who had lived with and loved them had moved to a nursing home that didn't allow pets. She'd tried to find a home for them together, but people could only take one or the other not both. She entrusted them to the realtor who sold her house to find them a good home or take them to a no-kill shelter. The realtor had dropped the grey tabby cat and boxer-chocolate lab mix off at the animal shelter the next day.

"I saw Ivan first. He looked so sad. He perked up a little when I put out my hand. Then the assistant manager said Ivan came as a pair with a cat. I took Ivan outside and the guy brought Holly out, they ran towards each other. Like in a movie. They were so happy together. I couldn't separate them. Besides, Mom was the one who didn't like cats."

"Allergic," said Dan. "You mom was allergic to cats."

"Whatever. Mom couldn't have cats, but Dad and I can. So, we got both. I want to get the name of the woman in the nursing home and write her about Holly and Ivan. I won't tell her we found them in the shelter, though."

"That would be very thoughtful," said his mom. "She must miss them terribly."

"Are you going to start looking for a condo here, Mom?" asked Rob while munching on a carrot.

"This week. My friend Irene's daughter is a real estate agent who has several communities in mind. "

"I'm sure Dan's not going to kick you out,"

laughed Suzanne.

Dan slapped his arm. "Ugh, I think mosquito season has started. Let's get back inside." Dan started to gather empty plates. Suzanne cleared the rest of the table and Rob cleaned the grill.

"Gran and I'll do dishes," offered Katie.

"No, go in the living room," Dan said. "I'll rinse them off and put them in the dishwasher. Suzanne, would you make a pot of coffee? Katie, take the cookies in on a platter. With napkins."

"Dad," she gave him an exasperated look. "I know we need napkins. Anyone want milk and sugar for coffee?" She received a collective no. "No spoons, then."

Dan finished the dishes and joined them in the living room.

"I'm stuffed," said Rob after three cookies. "Excellent meal. Excellent service. Nice surroundings. I have to say I really like this room now that the antiques are gone."

"Blue's very soothing," said his mom.

"Jill's quilt as the focal point of the room is spectacular," said Suzanne. "Kaitlyn, you've got an eye for color and design."

"I hope so. I'm going to take two art courses next year. One in photography. I'm going to practice this summer taking pictures of Holly and Ivan. Dad, I told Sophia I'd call her after dinner. Do you mind if I go upstairs and use your phone?"

"No," he handed her his cell. "Don't pick up if anyone calls. Let it go to voice mail. Just call Sophia."

When Katie had gone upstairs, followed by

Holly and Ivan, Dan spilled his story. "I'm surrendering to the police tomorrow morning. Lombardi is taking me in instead of having them come to the house to arrest me. She's making a motion for me to be found incompetent to stand trial. The Commonwealth Attorney agrees. I'll go as an outpatient to be examined by a court-appointed psychiatrist. He or she will find me incompetent, admit me to the hospital, and transfer me to Petersburg."

"Commonwealth Psychiatric?" his mother cried.

Dan nodded. "Lombardi said it's the best way."

Rob stood. He looked as shaken as Dan felt.

"Back up. I missed several steps along the way. I thought Lombardi said you had a good chance at being found not guilty at trial. Everything is circumstantial. Not one shred of hard evidence.

"After she hired the PI, Lombardi got results, right? People maybe saw you at the Oceanfront that Saturday. Sand was found in your car even though she can't prove when it got there. The murder weapon was morphine with a syringe. Jill was prescribed morphine in tablets and you picked up the refills, but there's no proof that the prescription morphine killed her or that you ever bought a syringe. The only thing that might be bad is that you had serious bruising on your thigh. Kaitlyn can confirm your story if it comes to that. So, why wouldn't you go to trial and just plead not guilty? Why can't the charges be dismissed?"

"I don't understand, either, Dan," said Suzanne.

"You're right. All of that would give a jury reasonable doubt. Lombardi said the CA would drop the charges and not even go to trial."

"So why this new plan?" asked Rob.

Dan let out a long sigh.

"Because I said I had an affair with a woman who has been proven to be dead since 2001. I have a diagnosis of delusional disorder with psychotic episodes. I had motive to kill Jill if I thought that would clear the way for Bella and me to be together. The cops have the diagnosis and record of my long psychiatric history. If Lombardi didn't raise it, the CA or even the judge would question my competence with that kind of mental health history. If they didn't, whatever verdict they got would be appealed. Their reputations would be damaged if the verdict was overturned on appeal. It has to be addressed now."

Rob sat and rubbed his forehead. He looked beaten down. Suzanne was on the verge of tears. Dan couldn't bear to look at his mother.

"Dan," it was his mother, "forgive me for asking you to go through this again, but why wouldn't you just plead Not Guilty by Reason of Insanity? Surely, if the evidence of mental illness is so strong, the jurors would see that you weren't in your right mind if you did such a horrible thing."

He reached out and held his mother's hand. "Right, and I'd be sent to Petersburg for the rest of my life. I wouldn't go free. NGRI offers the choice between Petersburg and death row. Mom, the insanity defense is successful in less than one percent of cases."

Silence as everyone seemed preoccupied in finding a solution. Finally, Suzanne spoke. "This is temporary Petersburg, right? You avoid a trial by raising your competency to even stand trial."

"Yes. Lombardi thinks the sooner I raise it, the sooner I'll be treated and cured of my delusion." He'd never believe he and Bella hadn't been together, but he wasn't going to say that. "Once I'm found competent, the charges will be dropped. Being competent means I've overcome my delusions about Bella. If I no longer believed I had an affair, I'd have no motive to kill Jill. As Lombardi says, no affair, no reason to kill my wife."

"What's the catch?" asked Rob.

"Everything depends upon how quickly I become competent. The CA who is currently assigned the case and has agreed to drop the charges when I'm released from Petersburg has political aspirations and might not be on the case. He could be running for Governor by the time I'm found competent to stand trial. His replacement might not be so agreeable, but the case is so weak without motive Lombardi doubts anyone wants it. She doesn't have a crystal ball. She's making the best recommendation based on bad circumstances."

"What about the judge? Wouldn't he still be held to the agreement?"

"Rob, the judge doesn't care. If Petersburg says I'm competent and the CA says that means I had no motive and drops the charges, he'll dismiss the case."

"Dan, I can't believe you have such terrible choices," said his mother.

"Mom, I've been in psych hospitals before. I

have to believe Petersburg is better than death row."

"How long will you have to stay in Petersburg this way?" asked Rob.

"Maybe a year." Dan talked over his mother's intake of breath. "I'll have evaluations and hearings every three months until they decide I'm competent or something called unrestorably incompetent that would probably get me released to a private hospital or even home with supervision. I met a young woman at Richmond Memorial Hospital who was headed to Petersburg for the third time. She said it wasn't too bad. She said there's just not much supervision."

Rob looked at him in disbelief. "You're trying to make Commonwealth Psychiatric Hospital sound not like a hell hole based on a conversation with a two-time former inmate heading for her third? Solid."

Dan ignored him. "Mom, will you stay in the house with Katie until custody is sorted out? Lombardi found an experienced custody lawyer to represent Katie. I can't imagine what the Carters will do. I hope they don't take Katie away from Richmond. Even if she boarded at St. Margaret's and went to Charleston for holidays would be something."

"Dan, anything at all, Dan," said his mom.

Rob was back on his feet pacing. "I still don't get it. Why don't you just say you were mistaken about Bella?"

"Because it's a lie. I would perjure myself and Lombardi won't suborn perjury. She'd get disbarred. She's not going to lose her livelihood for me."

"What if someone's impersonating Bella?" asked Rob and held up his hand for Dan to let him talk. "No one needs your permission to follow that angle. We know you didn't kill Jill. Someone, possibly this impersonator, did or knows who did. They ruled out a lover for Jill, right?"

"Yes," whispered Dan.

"Then why not consider an imposter?"

"They're satisfied Bella is dead and don't give the imposter theory any credibility."

Rob opened his mouth to speak and Dan cut him off. "Think about it. Who would impersonate Bella to kill Jill? Who even knows Bella except the four of us?"

"Lots of people knew after Jill told them about your affair." Rob was the one digging in his heels.

"I don't know if Jill told anyone her name. Even if she did, one Google search and people would know Bella is dead. I really doubt Jill would've mentioned her name. It wouldn't mean anything to any of her friends. Jill was hurt, but she tried to limit her humiliation. She probably said the woman wasn't important or she wasn't anyone they knew or she lived out of town."

"What about someone in Bella's life? An old lover?"

"Rob, that's a real stretch. Anyone who was close to Bella knows she's been dead since 2001. Who would impersonate a dead person? Much less kill Jill?"

They sat in a silent circle for a long time.

"I've got nothing," Rob said and threw up his hands, but their mother spoke.

"Rob, what about Brian? Does he have any advice?"

Rob shook his head vehemently. "Brian is my buddy and college roommate in the real world. In the courtroom, he's Judge Meacham. He won't discuss it with me. Like Lombardi, he's not going to risk removal from the bench for Dan."

"Mom," said Dan. "Elba and Winston have sized up their case and settled on me. A judge ordered a warrant for my arrest. I have to go with those facts."

Suzanne came over and hugged him close. "We love you, Dan. We'll take care of Kaitlyn and Holly and Ivan."

# CHAPTER
# SIXTY-EIGHT

Dan picked up the green recycled shopping bag lying on the console of Rob's Saab sedan. He looked inside, saw packs of money in rubber bands, and threw the bag on the floor.

"What's that?" he turned to Rob who kept his eyes straight ahead while he drove along East Parham Road toward Route 1. Rob had returned after dinner ostensibly to say goodbye to his brother before Dan surrendered to the police the next morning.

"Fifty thousand dollars in used bills of different denominations. Only $1,000 in hundreds."

The money felt like a poisonous snake about to strike. "Get it away from me." He kicked it further from his feet.

"It's not stolen, Dan."

"What is it? Why do you have it?" Dan felt the familiar pangs of anxiety.

"It's yours. Take it and run."

"That sounds like a bad movie line. What do you mean?" Dan was frantic. He wondered if he could jump out of the car at a light.

"Calm down," said Rob. "What's wrong with you?"

"Are you trying to frame me or what?" What if he couldn't trust Rob?

Rob's eyes never left the road. "Dan, I'm trying to help you. Think about it. You're going to spend the rest of your life on death row or in Petersburg. Those are your choices. There's a third. Get out of the country or at least out of Virginia until you find somewhere to go."

"I can't run away. I'd be a fugitive." Dan felt like his throat was closing.

"Right now, you're a murderer or a psycho or both."

"I can't abandon Katie."

Rob pulled into a nearly empty fast food restaurant. One that used to be part of a chain but was now a non-descript eatery. He parked in the back near the dumpster and turned in his seat to face Dan.

"You're not going to see Kaitlyn any time soon, Dan. You're going to be in one of the worst psych hospitals in the country or prison. How often do you think Elizabeth and George will bring her to see you?"

No, he'd see Katie. "Katie has a good lawyer."

"Maybe, but look at a judge's choices. The brother of her mother's killer or her mother's parents or sisters? Or maybe she could go to foster care while the court sorts it out." Rob's voice was harsh.

Never. Katie would never be put in foster care.

"Rob, you're over-reacting. Is this a joke?"

Rob looked like he wanted to slap Dan. "You're not getting it. The best—the best Lombardi is offering you is hope. Hope that you'll be found unrestorably incompetent five years, ten years, twenty years from now and maybe released to a private psych hospital or group home. You're not going to walk out totally free. You think you're going to do a year in Petersburg and then be allowed to come home?"

Yes. That's exactly what he thought.

"I can't run. It makes me look guilty."

"It makes you look like a middle class guy who's never had a parking ticket who's scared to death of prison or the death penalty or the horrors at Petersburg."

"You believe I'm guilty, don't you?" Dan questioned Rob for the first time.

"No, I don't. I don't think Winston and Elba have a clue. I think it must've been a camper who was an opportunist. I don't know why he had morphine and a syringe unless he was a junkie. I don't know why he chose Jill or why he carried her to a place where she obviously would be found. But I have zero confidence in the system. Zero.

"If you want to stay alive and maybe see Kaitlyn twenty years from now, then run. I can drive you to the outer banks right now. You can lose yourself in tourists. Get fat, keep your hair white, and add a buzz cut. Get a tan and a tattoo. Lose all your ID. Quit running for exercise. Change every habit."

He couldn't think. His brain was stuffed with

cotton again.

"Then what?"

"I don't know. Hop a freighter to China. Become a hermit. Become a monk. What do I know? I'm a suburban dentist with no imagination. You'll have to have some. Figure it out."

"What about you? The cops will question you."

"I saw you to say good-bye. You didn't say anything about running away. I don't know anything else. Suzanne knows nothing. Mom knows nothing. The money's not marked. Stay away from my kids. Don't go to Chicago or Houston."

Rob pulled out of the parking lot and continued south on Route 1. "Never call, email, or contact us. Ever."

No. He wouldn't run. "Turn around, Rob," he pleaded. "Please."

"Sure?" Rob waited for his answer before turning the wheel.

Dan nodded. "Mørk follows me. I need meds. Wherever I go, I'll need meds. If I don't have them, I'll just lie around, forget to be on guard, and make mistakes. Or I'll use street drugs. I'll get caught. It'll be worse for Katie. I can't, Rob. I can't."

"Your call," said Rob. He turned right at the next intersection and drove Dan home.

# CHAPTER
# SIXTY-NINE

The locked steel door to the Quiet Room closed behind him. Dan timidly surveyed his surroundings. The white windowless room had padded walls, a white carpet-covered floor, and no bedding. No doubt everything was arranged so he didn't kill himself.

This was the first time he'd been alert, albeit sedated, upon admission to a psych hospital. When the enormous decaying brick building had come into view, Dan had started crying. Except for this room, the place was filthy, reeked of urine, disinfectant and something he didn't want to identify, and echoed horrifying sounds. Screams, howls, and sobs were unrelenting. People sounded like they were being tortured. He saw guards but no one who looked like a doctor, nurse, or even an orderly. No one in admissions seemed interested in his medication schedule. His hands shook. He couldn't function without his meds.

This hospitalization was involuntary. He couldn't leave without a judge's order. He could only communicate with Lombardi. He'd forgotten to ask if Dr. Spellman could see him. He stood frozen unable to think or feel or move. Numb was good. Frozen and numb.

A key turned and the door opened. Her seductive scent preceded her.

Bella. She wore a red silk wrap dress that looked fabulous on her figure. Her long blonde hair curled seductively around her shoulders. She wore his great-grandmother's ruby earrings. Her heels must have been five inches high. Her brilliant blue eyes honed in on him.

"Bella." He felt a rush of relief. "Bella, they said you were dead."

"Let's just say not living as a human." She smiled the way only she could. It went straight to his heart.

"A ghost?"

"Some people would call me that."

"Am I dead?"

She glided seductively towards him. "Not yet."

"Why can I see you?"

She laughed with her full-throated voice. "You shouldn't have to ask that. You know what we have transcends everything." She whispered, "Everything."

He wanted to grab her and hold her forever. Never let go again. "I knew you'd come. You'll help me."

With a languid motion, she stretched out her hand to touch his hair. He leaned his head into her

350

hand. She laughed. A deep-throated, velvet purr.

"Help you? We were meant to have a high life together."

"That's what I mean. Together we can do anything. We'll make them understand."

She curled herself catlike around him without touching. "Daniel, you're in a psychiatric hospital. I don't think there's much chance of us being together."

"But you can explain. Tell them I'm not crazy."

"Oh, Daniel. How do you think you got here?"

She traced her index finger under his chin and along his neck. A scarlet fingernail.

"My lawyer said it was best."

She stretched behind him and spoke into his right ear.

"I told you not to mess with me, but you didn't listen. You stopped calling. You abandoned me."

"I was a wreck after my father died."

She circled until she stood in front of him, her hand sliding down her throat toward her décolletage.

"Pity. You made me suffer, Daniel. You promised you wouldn't. I couldn't let you get away with that."

"What do you mean?"

She flicked her tongue. "I returned Maggie, known to you as Abbie, to her rightful family. I fiddled with your credit card accounts, helped myself to some jewels, and had a chat with that condescending attorney of yours about estate planning. I stole morphine from a hospital."

She took a step closer. "I killed Jill." She leaned

in to whisper in his ear, "And I was very, very, very careful to make it look like you did it."

He looked at her in horror.

"Gotcha."

She raked his right cheek with the nails of her left hand and sauntered away. Blood oozed down his face.

He screamed and screamed and screamed. When he eventually heard the door open, Dan was alone in the room and curled into the fetal position with blood covering his face and hands. He screamed one word over and over.

"Bella."

# About the Author

Born in Venice, Italy, Adam Zorzi is the author of Blind Spot, Blind Trust, and Blind Rage that comprise the Blind Justice Trilogy. He lives in New York.

**Facebook:**
https://www.facebook.com/profile.php?id=1000122
63627516&fref=ts

**Blind Justice Trilogy Facebook Page:**
https://www.facebook.com/BlindJusticeTrilogyAda
mZorzi/?fref=ts

**Twitter:**
https://twitter.com/adamzorzi

**Website:**
http://www.adamzorzi.com/

www.ingramcontent.com/pod-product-compliance
Lightning Source LLC
Chambersburg PA
CBHW030515120726
47904CB00005B/1477